Historical fiction

THIS IS MOSTRIM

~ ~ ~

THE HOMECOMING

MARK CASSIDY

Copyright © Mark Cassidy, 2025
First Published in Ireland, in 2025, in co-operation with
Choice Publishing, Drogheda, County Louth, Republic of Ireland.
www.choicepublishing.ie

Paperback ISBN: 978-1-917242-42-4

The moral right of the author has been asserted.

All rights reserved. No part of this publication may be reproduced, stored in a retrieval system, transmitted in any form, or by any means, electronic, mechanical, photocopying, recording or otherwise, without the prior permission of the copyright holder.

TITLES IN THIS COLLECTION

This Is Mostrim – The Famine

This Is Mostrim – The Exile

This Is Mostrim – The Homecoming

To Petrina

Also

In remembrance of all those who never came home

Key

—— Sugrue's journey from Maynooth to Mostrim to Tunbridge Wells
10th August 1850 – 17th August 1850

—— Sugrue's Journey from Tunbridge Wells to Mostrim
21st February 1851 – 22nd February 1851

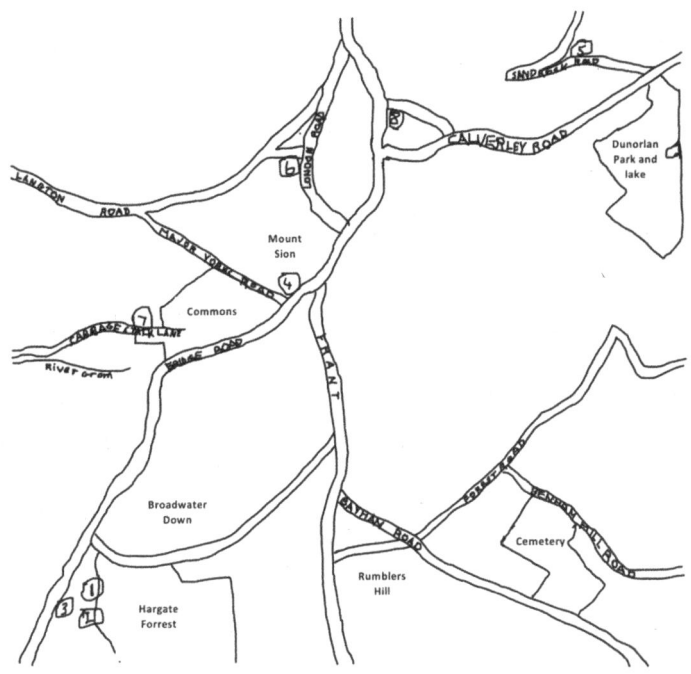

Key
1. Tunbridge House/Burke Residence
2. Finbar's Bivouac
3. Strawberry Hill Farm
4. The Queen's Arms Tavern
5. Loch Lomand Cottage
6. Holy Trinity Church
7. House on Cabbage Stalk Lane
8. Finbar Ryan's House

One – A Changing of the Guard

Acroflavin. That's what Missus Langan tells me. It's a watery-yellow solution. She presses it into my heel at least four times a day. I don't know whether it's the right way of saying it, because of the good lady's stroke. She's clear of it now, apart from the odd word – the telltale signs which will always betray her. But her movement is first class. She admits to having been completely paralysed on the left side of her body for about six months. You'd never know it now. She gallops about the house in a full-time hurry.

'She died in those sheets, Mister Sugrue, on the very spot where you're lying.'

I didn't know what to make of that. She eyed the letter again and I just knew she was dying to ask me to read it.

'Young Joseph had just gone out the door when she turned to face our Blessed Mother, rustled the beads in her fingers and nodded off for good. The strange thing was she had a lovely smile on her face for someone coughing up blood by the bucketload.'

'Where is she now?'

'Where do you think – the same place we'll all end up. She's on the top row in Aughafin, with the husband lying to her left.'

'No, I don't mean Missus Farrell. Where's our Blessed Mother gone?'

She laughed. It always takes me by surprise when older, more reserved, women like Missus Langan let their emotions go.

'She's below in Daverns. I took her to the wake and forgot to bring her back. I'll go down for her now, when it's in my head. You must have got an awful doing in England, Mister Sugrue, with how badly your system is run down? You had no business going to a place like that at your age.'

'What do you think of Jabber getting married,' I asked, while I had her in good humour.

'What's the world coming to,' she answered. 'And to a black woman? I remember the day young Joseph left here for the priesthood. I thought Milly was going to burst with pride. The whole parish went to the clachan to see him off.'

'Not much sign of a priest in him now,' I quipped, holding Jim Gorman's American letter in mid-air, 'four children – according to Father Murtagh on the day of the weddings – and him not three years married. He's not hanging about, Missus.'

'You're an awful villain, Mister Sugrue, you and that crew-cut of yours. It takes me back to my childhood – all the men had cropped hair when I was a girl. Oh it's true what my dear mother used to say, God rest her – a man doesn't know his own mind until he's beyond thirty years of age.'

I pointed to the postmark dated May 31, 1850, and then to the American stamps – the Franklin five-centers – in the corner of the envelope. It was nearly time to put her out of her misery.

'Would you whisht about thirty years of age. Jabber Farrell must be forty and the rest of it. I'll read you Jim's letter when you get back.'

'Great, I love a good letter from America. I could have gone out there too, if the cards had fallen different. By the way, Missus Ryan was here looking for you for the dancing. She was very disappointed when I told her that you were in no fit state to be spinning around the Auburn Hall. I'll put more acroflavin on your foot when I get back. The Auburn Hall you know. Wouldn't you think the straw loft in the clachan would do her, after all they've been through?'

'Don't be long,' I said, and Missus Langan threw her eyes skyward.

'So that's where you were hiding out and every peeler in Ireland after you – Maynooth,' she declared, reading the postal address on the front of the envelope and buttoning her coat at the same time.

'Yes. I was with a good friend named Jeb Turling. We know each other from the rebellion. Give my condolences to Anthony Davern,' I shouted after her as she made for the door.

It's always a relief when Missus Langan goes out. There's nothing wrong with her – she's kindhearted and companionable. But when she's absent I don't have to pretend that, apart from my heel, everything else is in order. Because everything is far from in order. My heel was badly cut up in England and nursing women the likes of Missus Langan will tell you that there's nothing as dangerous as a cut on the heel, especially if the cut is not tended to and dressed daily. But I know my heel won't kill me. My side is a different matter. I won't be so lucky with regard to it.

Scratching the nape of my neck reminds me of the scalping I gave myself. I think of Finbar as I run my fingers down my newly-blossomed moustache. I stick my feet and arms out from under the covers. The bed is too comfortable and I'm not used to it. Ella May once told me she prayed that I would die in my warm bed in Mostrim, far away from my enemies. This is a warm bed. It may not be mine, but it's so bloody warm. And this is Mostrim. So her prayer was answered more than adequately. But the strange thing is, right now I'd give anything to be facing the canons and bayonets of the British in the cold wet fields of Ballinamuck once more.

I scratch along the scar. Then I think of Roger Giles. It was only right to give back the powder flask. Although, having had it for almost fifty-three years, I miss it dearly. No doubt he would love to see me now – to know it was the business end of his knife, during the Battle of Tunbridge House, that has laid me so low. On my arrival home from Kent, I could have sought out a doctor. But I'd prefer to leave it to God. Time moves on and we must move with it. I have no choice now but to leave the fight for Ireland to younger men. That's the way of the world.

> *'Twas early early in the spring; the birds did whistle and sweetly sing; changing their notes from tree to tree; and the song they sang was old Ireland free.'*

The feeling has come over me again. Only this time it's much worse than before. This time there's no going back. I think Missus Langan will be reading Jim's letter for herself. I'll place it in her prayerbook on the mantel. As for you, stay awhile with a dying man. Let me tell you all about the last tour of duty – my final fling on the battlefield of this earth – while there's still a breath in this weary old body.

Two – The Road to Damascus (Part 1)

You see, it all started in earnest some four months before the arrival of Jim Gorman's letter from America – around about early March of 1850. While I was thriving like a fatted calf at Jeb's hideaway in Maynooth, Lady Jane Teale was sweating, or should I say perspiring – for a lady doesn't sweat – in the beautiful leather coach seat of her husband's brand-new burgundy Brougham. She clenched her hands and went through the lines once more. Her driver opened the door and her flow was disrupted.

'All ready to go, m'lady.'

Words which were not exactly music to her ears. What Lady Jane wanted to hear was that a telegram had just arrived saying the whole event had been postponed, if only for twenty-four short hours. That would have given her enough time to get it right. After all, it wasn't just a social commentary on *Castle Rackrent*, but the honour of regaling the distinguished guests – *her* distinguished guests – with the life-story of the one and only Maria Edgeworth. What an honour lay in store – and not just for Lady Teale but the fairer sex in general. In memory of the world-renowned novelist, Lord Colehill and the Edgeworthstown Foxhunters' Association had ruled in its wisdom that indeed a woman should and would present the celebration at the Edgeworth manor house. It was such a distinction that her husband, Lord Harold Teale – or Lord Lacken, as he would be addressed in this esteemed company – reckoned it only fit and proper to ride in a separate coach in order to leave the limelight of the grand arrival to the star of the show – his darling wife.

But the star of the show was now feeling the strain. What if she couldn't carry it off. What if she messed up the whole affair. Surely the critical male presence would guffaw and say: *that's what happens when you hire a woman to do a man's job.* She hadn't even departed the Lacken House forecourt and already she was forgetting her lines.

'M'lady? Are you okay? I'm ready if you are.'

'Carry on, Driver,' she replied against her will.

As the wheels began to take them towards the Longford Road and out of Lacken, the real reason for Lady Jane's anxiety returned to haunt her once more. When she would deliver her speech later that evening it was the good lady's intention to use Thady Quirk as an example in how to address a present political problem which had dogged Ireland for centuries. She would endeavour to show, through Thady's loyalty to Condy in spite of his own son, Jason, how Protestants and Catholics should put their personal feelings aside for the greater good of Ireland as a nation. If only both sides could pull together and stop tearing each other apart, then the country that Maria Edgeworth had cherished could emerge from the horrors of the famine a stronger and more independent force within the Union.

'Lord Colehill will throw me from the stage,' she said to herself, anticipating the angry reaction she would surely receive from landlords and gentry-men steeped in British traditions and deeply loyal to the Crown.

Lady Jane Teale was trapped by her own conscience. She could say all the things her audience wanted to hear. She could receive their applause, allowing Lord Harold the congratulatory pats on the back for training his wife with such diligence. But she believed in what she had to say and knew there would not be a stage of this magnitude again. The moment was almost upon her and, feeling that she must grasp the nettle, Lady Jane decided to withdraw her window and take the air.

It was then she saw it, in a crumpled heap at the side of the road. At first, she thought it was just a pile of discarded dirty old rags – until it started to move and Lady Jane noticed a head of matted hair.

'Driver. Driver, quick.'

But the driver ploughed on in the direction of the Edgeworth estate. Lady Jane crept a little out the window and had another go at stopping her man. But, with the whistling of the wind in her bonnet and the sound of the horses' hooves on the dirt-road, she could not hear her own voice, never mind be heard by the driver. So she pulled at the bell until they came to a halt.

'What's up, m'lady?'

'Driver, did you see what we passed fifty or so yards back?'

'Fifty or so yards back? No, m'lady.'

'It was something strange, like a mass of twisted hair betwixt a ball of old clothing.'

The driver gave out a chuckle and then collected himself.

'Pardon, m'lady, but that sounds like an otter. There's loads of them down by the Green River. Sometimes they leave their holts and go scavenging among the rubbish. It's a dangerous indication when you see them wandering like that – a real sign of terrible wet weather.'

'Nevertheless, Driver, I think we should backtrack.'

The driver gave out another chuckle.

'We'll be late if we go back, m'lady.'

'Late? How can we be late when I am the host? Just walk back and take a look. There's no need to turn the horses around. It would really put my mind at ease, Driver.'

He sighed to himself before flinging his driver's hat in the perch and sauntering back down the Longford Road.

It wasn't long before the driver was racing towards his carriage again, shouting *m'lady* at the top of his voice. A lifeless body dangled from his outstretched arms. Despite her alarm, Lady Jane Teale was quickly out of the carriage to retrieve the water bag from the boot. They laid what looked like a young girl on the coach seat and poured some water on her face and head. Lady Jane produced a hanky and cleared away the mucus from her mouth and nose. They wetted her lips. The driver slapped her face while Lady Jane rubbed her arms and legs vigourously. Slowly, they managed to bring the little girl around. She shivered uncontrollably as Lady Jane forced her to take a drink. She began to cry and Lady Jane told the driver to turn the horses around immediately. She assured the little girl that everything was going to be alright now. She tore away her ballgown and wrapped it around the little girl as the horses thundered back down the avenue towards Lacken House.

'Hurry, Driver. Take her inside and wrap her in blankets. Send for the doctor immediately.'

The driver did everything that was asked of him. He had the girl wrapped up and nestled beside a roaring fire in no time. He sent a boy on horseback to fetch the doctor. Then he went to check on his boss woman.

Lady Jane was putting on another dress when she heard the gentle tap.

'M'lady, I'm here to look after your wellbeing too. I hope you are not overly perturbed ...'

His eyes fell to where she had hurriedly covered her corset.

'Splendid, I see that you are fully attired once more,' he continued, as his cheeks lit up. 'May I compliment your new frock.'

'Good heavens, Driver,' replied Lady Jane, 'I'm not perturbed in the least. Have I not spied on worse than yon poor creature these last five years of dreadful famine?'

'I was told the housemaids have retired for the night, so I instructed a stable-hand to remain with the girl until the doctor arrives,' said the driver, 'now, I shall escort you back to your carriage and take you to your festivities.'

Lady Jane Teale lifted her latest-edition book of *Castle Rackrent* and proceeded towards the door. Then she stopped and weighed up her thoughts once more. Was there really any point to it after all. The men at the celebration in Edgeworth's manor house were never going to give her proper consideration in any event. And the women would be worse – unable to survive without their husbands' opinions. Lady Carrington – despite her persona as a figure of ridicule – would be the only woman there with the courage to think and speak for herself.

'No thank you, Driver. I'm going nowhere.'

Now, it was Lady Jane's turn to hope the driver was not overly perturbed.

'But m'lady, what about your pivotal role in the celebration of Maria Edgeworth's life?'

'Never you mind about that. I have decided I shan't go after all. My place is here, looking after our unexpected guest, not in Edgeworth House. Send a rider to inform my husband of my withdrawal, with explicit instructions to remain on to enjoy himself and have a very late night.'

'But m'lady, I should rouse the domestics. How hard could it be to clamber together a housemaid or two to keep watch?'

'No, Driver. I have made up my mind. I find it distasteful to *rouse the domestics,* as you so eloquently put it, from their deserved rest after a long and hard day.'

'Are you sure, m'lady?'

'Quite sure, Driver.'

'I'll go and uncouple the horses so.'

'You do that, Driver. Well done young man, you excelled

yourself this evening. I shall recommend you for a nice bonus.'

'Delighted to be of service,' he chirped, bowing and smirking with delight.

'One last thing,' said Lady Jane, as the driver skipped towards the door, 'if you tell a single soul that you happened to see me in my undergarments, I shall have your guts for garters.'

Suddenly his skipping was over. The smirk had disappeared as well. He turned and bowed again.

'Of course, m'lady.'

'Driver, you are dismissed.'

'Very well, m'lady. Thank you, m'lady.'

Three – The Road to Damascus (Part 2)

Doctor Kiernan's prognosis was a bad dose of bronchitis which was only caught in time before pneumonia set in. He decided against a medicine from his shiny black bag, but asked Lady Jane Teale did her husband keep goats. He gave a glowing endorsement of how goat milk had once cured a bad chest his grandfather had as a boy. When he heard there were two nanny goats on the premises he was delighted.

'There's nothing better for a chest complaint than milk from goats, the warmer she can stomach it the better,' the good doctor affirmed.

'Well, I had better give her something more substantial to aid this goat milk,' said Lady Jane, 'would you look at the size of those arms and legs, Doctor.'

'A wee drop of broth,' he suggested, 'but no bits in it. Her stomach won't be up to much at the minute. She's badly malnourished, the poor crater. Wherever she was hanging out, there wasn't much in the way of sustenance going to loss. But it's water for the scabs on her lips – and bed for at least three days.'

And so, Lady Jane watched and waited. She had her housemaids prepare the soup and warm the goat milk. Everything was in place for when the little girl would wake up. But she slept and slept. The following afternoon the little girl was still asleep, although not so soundly. She turned and twisted and began to say things – things like *leave me be* and *Sheila* and *don't go* and then *Sheila* again. The sight of *Castle Rackrent* brought Lady Jane's mind back to the night before. She picked up the book and leafed through its pages. She thought she would have felt more disappointed at missing out, but she didn't. Another *Sheila*, this time a roar, prompted Lady Jane to cool a sponge and wipe the sweat from the little girl's brow.

'There now,' she whispered, as the patient turned again in the bed and began her pleading and calling anew.

Just then the little girl said something that Lady Jane thought rather odd. She roared out the name *Constance*, followed by *I'm sorry*. Then she went back to pleading to be left alone and calling for Sheila not to leave her.

Two full days later and there was still no sign of Annie McKeon, the little girl who had been picked off the roadside by Lady Jane Teale's driver, to eat a morsel of solid food. She wouldn't touch the goat milk either. But she couldn't get enough of the hot soup. She drank gallons of the stuff. She volunteered her name – the only thing she had said knowingly – to one of the housemaids while being given a sponge bath. But her shyness apart, Annie was making progress by the hour. She was now sitting up in bed, throwing the covers here and there, as the fire blazed away. The time had come for some hard questions.

As soon as Lady Jane opened her mouth, Annie withdrew – pulling the sheets around her neck.

'There's no need for alarm,' said Lady Jane, 'nobody's going to hurt you. And nobody's going to force you to drink the goat milk either.'

When Lady Jane smiled Annie looked confused and then smiled back faintly.

'My name is Lady Jane Teale. I'm the mistress of this house. My girls tell me your name is Annie. I presume you speak good English, Annie?'

Annie recoiled again and then nodded in the affirmative.

'There's no need to be scared of me,' Lady Jane reaffirmed, 'I'm only here to look after you.'

Annie released the sheets and climbed out of bed before Lady Jane could stop her. Then she pulled the nightdress quickly across her head and stood there naked.

'Do you want to have sex with me,' she asked, as matter-of-factly as if she wanted to know if Lady Jane would accompany her for a walk in the country.

The mistress of the house was shaken by the question, but not too shaken to reach for the screen and ask Annie to put her night clothes back on. Then she tucked the bedsheets around the little girl and asked why she had said and done such a thing.

'Is that not why you are helping me,' returned Annie.

The question unsettled Lady Jane deeply.

'Certainly not,' she exclaimed. 'In this house we help people because we feel it is our duty and privilege, not because we want something – and especially not to have *relations* with them.'

'But I thought…'

'You thought poorly, young lady. So, here is what we shall do. We shall go back to before you discarded your nightwear and start again. Deal?'

Lady Jane stuck out her hand. Annie shook it and said *deal*.

'Now, I know your name is Annie McKeon. But that is all I know. I do not know where you are from or where you were attempting to go when my driver picked you off the road.'

It was clear to Lady Jane that Annie was so much more at ease then. And once she got into her stride, she was a right little chatterbox. She told the good lady that she was from Aughnacliffe, just inside the Longford border with Cavan. She had been working at Cranley House – tending to Herbert and Hilda Ivens, nephew and niece of Viscount de Bromley – under the stewardship of a Miss Sheila McAndrew, before the estate was sold. Annie was promised a new position on the Tunbridge estate but had been left behind when the viscount moved lock, stock and barrel across the Irish Sea. Instead, she had to settle for a hovel in Ringowney, where she survived on her resourcefulness and the kindness of neighbours. Despite her appearance, she was no longer a little girl but had turned eighteen the summer before.

'This is the Sheila of your dreams?'

Annie reddened when she heard this.

'Yes, we had a special bond – or so I thought. Bigger fool me. I was coming from the police barracks and going to the workhouse when you rescued me the other day.'

'The police barracks? The police barracks in town?'

'Yes,' confirmed Annie. 'And I was heading out to…'

'Hold on a moment,' replied Lady Jane. 'What were you doing at the Edgeworthstown police barracks?'

Annie went quiet and blushed again, so Lady Jane had to push the issue.

'Are you in some sort of trouble? Listen to me carefully now, Annie, honesty is always the best policy.'

'No, I'm not in any trouble. I was at the barracks to report a crime. But it doesn't matter now. One constable just laughed and the other threw an apple butt at me and told me to be on my way.'

'Report a crime? What crime?'

'It's not important – silly, really. As one of the constables said, nobody wants to hear anything I have to say.'

'He said that? An officer of the law? Why that is just downright disgraceful,' said Lady Jane. 'So, you came away from the barracks and decided to walk to Shroid workhouse. And that's where we met in with you.'

'Yes, madam,' said Annie.

Then a frightful feeling came over Lady Jane. She got up and walked around the bedroom. She sat in behind the dressing screen, so Annie couldn't see her worried face. She told herself it couldn't be, that Annie's brush with death had left her in an over-imaginative state – what Lord Teale referred to as *feminine excitability*. But no matter how she tried to quell it, this dastardly doubt kept gnawing away at the good lady. In the end, she just had to come out with it.

'Annie, I'm going to ask a very important question now and I implore you to answer with honesty.'

Annie nodded and Lady Jane reaffirmed the importance of honesty.

'Who is the Constance you were referring to in your sleep?'

Annie couldn't hold Lady Jane's stare. She looked down to the foot of the bed, then across at the window. Lady Jane took her hand and told her she had nothing to fear.

'Annie, heed me very carefully. The Constance you were calling, is it a girl called Constance Ryan?'

She touched Annie's chin, tilting her head towards her. Annie nodded slowly.

'Why were you saying sorry to Constance – in your sleep? Why do you need her forgiveness?'

'Because of the other day,' answered Annie, 'in the barracks.'

It was clear to Lady Jane that Annie didn't want to speak about it. But it was just too important to ignore.

'The crime you were there to report,' continued the good lady, 'it had something to do with Constance Ryan. Annie, look at me. Annie, you must report everything you know about this crime. It is the right thing to do.'

'What's the point,' cried Annie, pulling her hand from Lady Jane's grasp, 'look what I got last time for trying to do the right thing.'

She retook Annie's hand and cupped it in both of hers.

'Last time, you didn't have me for help and protection,' said Lady Jane.

'I don't want to go back there,' insisted Annie, 'those policemen were horrible to me. I can't do it, I just can't.'

'Annie, you must go back. I must go back with you.'

Annie turned away and placed her head on the pillow.

'Annie, sit up and listen. I have a prayer I say every day. It goes like this: *God, give me the strength today to do a little more than I think I can.* I'd like us to say that prayer together. Do you think it would give you the strength you need? Constance Ryan needs you now, Annie. She needs us both. Will we ask God for the strength to do the right thing?'

Slowly, Annie's head turned on the pillow. She sat up and Lady Jane dried her face with a napkin before rubbing cool water on her scabbed lips.

'I knew you would do the right thing,' said Lady Jane, cradling Annie's head in her arms, 'I can see the goodness shining in your eyes.'

'So, let me get this straight, you're not just here to report one crime, but a series of crimes?'

Lady Jane watched as Annie fidgeted with the cuff of her new dress, trying desperately to stop her trembling hands.

'Read her statement back to her and then get a signature,' said the policeman with the moustache, barely able to conceal his laughter. 'That's, of course, if she's able to write her own name.'

'I, *Anne Theresa McKeon, of no fixed abode, but formerly a nursemaid of Cranley House, Edgeworthstown, in the county of Longford, do solemnly swear to the following testimony. I was told, in good faith, by Miss Sheila McAndrew, domestic manageress to Viscount de Bromley, that the disappearance of one Miss Constance Ryan from said Cranley House was unlawful as she was procured for the purposes* of marriage to Mister Shaun Burke, formerly of said Cranley House, against her will. Viscount de Bromley and Shaun Burke drugged, kidnapped, falsely detained and transported Constance Ryan for the said purpose, for a fee agreed and paid between both parties. I was also made witness, by Miss Sheila McAndrew's words, that a Mister Shay Gorman, of Lacken, Edgeworthstown, County Longford, was set up for a robbery at Cranley House by a Mister Walter Pollach, then manager of Cranley estate, leading to a conviction and transportation to Van Diemen's Land, and for which sentence Shay Gorman is still serving at the pleasure of Her Majesty, Queen Victoria. I was also made witness, by the said Miss McAndrew, that the evidence received from Master Peter Hogan, deceased, in relation to a burglary of foodstuffs at Cranley House basement, and for which the criminal court made an ex-parte ruling against the Sugrue Gang – namely Messrs. Patrick Sugrue, Joseph Farrell, James Gorman and said Peter Hogan – was the result of severe duress after a circumstantial find of a wine bottle at premises in Granard, County Longford. Finally, I was made aware, also by the above Miss McAndrew, that the death of a boy called Turk O Nuallain, an employee on one of the Public Work schemes at Cranley House and estate, which was cited by the coroner as a suicide case, was in fact the result of foul play. Those responsible for his death are alleged to be the said Walter Pollach and Shaun Burke.'

The policeman took off his spectacles and rubbed his eyes.

'What say you, Constable,' he enquired from his mustachioed colleague.

His colleague was leaning back on his chair, giving his legs a rest on the table.

'What a fanciful load of pig slurry,' he retorted, as he threw a cold eye on Annie. 'Who do you think you are, the female version of Edgar Allan Poe? On second thoughts, don't get her signature. Book her instead for wasting police time, not to mention slandering the good names of Viscount de Bromley and his management team.'

Annie turned away from his contemptable stare, finding warmth and security in the arms of Lady Jane.

'I told you we shouldn't have come back here,' she whispered.

'There now, stay strong,' replied Lady Jane, as she stroked Annie's hair.

'I'll tell you what I'm going to do,' said the policeman, scrunching up the statement and throwing it in the paper basket, 'I'm going to pretend you didn't come here today. I'm going to pretend I never heard any of your nonsense. Now get out of here before I throw the book at you.'

Annie made for the barrack door. Lady Jane held her ground. It was her turn to speak.

'*Before you throw the book at her,*' the good lady mimicked, with a stare that forced the mustachioed policeman to look away. 'Well, that would make a change from throwing the core of an apple at her.'

'Have you taken leave of your senses, woman,' snapped the policeman, replacing his spectacles.

'On the contrary, young man. Annie was in this very barracks three days ago and you hounded her out, throwing insults and apples at her.'

The bespectacled policeman looked to his mustachioed friend, who stared on blankly.

'I don't know what you're talking about,' he replied.

'Well, your colleague will enlighten you,' said Lady Jane.

The mustachioed policeman then took his boots off the table and warned Lady Jane that if she didn't get going quickly, she and her young friend would be up in front of a magistrate.

'Yes, that is exactly where we intend to be,' answered Lady Teale.

'She's nothing but a little troublemaker,' growled the

mustachioed policeman. 'She hasn't as much as a date for any of these wild allegations. And where is her witness to all these heinous crimes? I've seen girls like her before, young sluts who think that by making up some pitiful tale against a high-ranking member of society like Viscount de Bromley she'll get a pay-off. I know what she should get – the fat end of my truncheon and no mistake.'

Lady Jane Teale was blushing with anger.

'Listen to me very carefully,' she said, ignoring the mustachioed policeman and addressing his colleague instead. 'I would be taking her statement back out of that basket. Because while you may be able to intimidate young girls like Annie, I assure you that I am quite a different proposition. In fact, my husband's legal team, Mister Thornton and associates, will be taking up this matter with your chief constable on the morrow.'

The mustachioed policeman was like a bull. But his bespectacled colleague was more concerned than angry.

'Look,' he said softly, 'can common sense prevail here. You have to see this from our end. Why would the head of domestics of a distinguished household confide such matters in a lowly nursemaid?'

Everyone looked at Annie, who remained silently tucked up in Lady Jane's shawl.

'Would you confide in your hired help,' he asked, turning to Lady Jane.

As much as the good lady didn't want to admit it, the policeman had a valid point. Something wasn't right and Annie's withdrawal wasn't making matters any clearer.

'All we want to do is corroborate your story,' continued the bespectacled policeman. 'But your story doesn't add up. If you can give us one good reason why Miss Sheila McAndrew, manageress of Cranley House and estate, would confide such vital information in you, then I promise, we will treat this matter with the utmost care and seek out all parties concerned.'

Annie wanted to curl up in a ball and die. This was the moment she had dreaded – the moment she had promised herself would never be spoken of. She thought of the shame it would bring on the family. Her mother and father would be outcasts in their own parish of Aughnacliffe. They would be shunned forevermore. All Annie had to do was keep quiet for five minutes more and she would be safe and warm in a coach on the way back to Lacken House. But then, she remembered Lady Jane's prayer. She recited it to herself: *God, give me the strength today to do a little more than I think I can.* Annie needed that strength now. Besides, Lady Jane was right – Constance needed Annie's help. So did Shay and Turk and the Sugrue Gang. She took her head out of Lady Jane's shawl and wiped her face.

'We were lovers,' Annie announced, and for the second time that evening the mustachioed policeman took his boots off the table. 'She told me all her secrets in bed. She said it would bind us together and make us inseparable. We were so in love – until she took off to England without me.'

Lady Jane hugged Annie tightly as she broke down in tears. The bespectacled policeman searched in the basket for the scrunched-up statement.

'It's all over now,' Annie cried, as she looked for her old hiding place in Lady Jane's shawl.

'No,' said the good lady, 'not over at all. On the contrary, it is only just begun.'

Four – The Double Pardon

I was hunkered down among a few stray barrels the Maguires had left lying around. I watched a hen take a dust-bath in the outfield – not a good sign – while keeping an eye on Missus Ryan's cabin. She wasn't in when I knocked. But what was I doing on my haunches. I had no reason to fear the law – not any longer. Since Annie McKeon had poured her sweet little heart out, not to mention the gracious testimony of one of the policemen involved in the paddy-wagon crash, I was free to show my face whenever and wherever I chose. But old habits really do die hard. And this was not the first time since my exoneration that I had found myself behaving like an outlaw in the public domain.

Three days earlier – August 10, 1850 – I finally decided to bite the bullet and do the right thing. So I said goodbye to my old comrade, Jeb Turling, and goodbye to the easy life in Maynooth. I couldn't have imagined the changes the countryside had been forced to endure in the three years of my absence. On the way back, in Jeb's pony and trap, we saw hovels all over the place. The joy of the great outdoors was gone. The birds didn't sing anymore. There was no wildlife in the fields. I didn't see one fox. I looked into watery patches and gripes – not even a snipe to be seen. The silence of the countryside was eerie and unsettling.

When I reached Mostrim things only got worse. I headed straight for my old home in the Cranley cluster. Broken down cabins – without ceilings and sometimes without walls – were everywhere, their remnants dotting the outfield. Now I'm no prude when it comes to the odd eviction, but this was something else again. I thought of Aidan Skelton and the day they pulled his house asunder. There were many more like it now. Of the thirty lived-in cabins during my time there, only three remained fully standing. Two looked to be idle and the other was converted into a shed of some sort. I checked out my old house. Missus Sugrue wouldn't like to see it now, marked out only by stone stacks here and there. Viscount de Bromley did his work well. There wasn't a tenant nor a beast to be seen.

When I eventually reached the clachan in Lacken there was a strange noise – like a she-cat at nighttime – coming from one of the cabins. Micheal Mooney's house was still standing – sort of. I could have cried when I saw it. Even though it was an act of war, I still felt in some way responsible. He was tending to us, after all, when it happened. The roof was gone, but the walls were still mostly standing. With everything that was going on, they must have forgotten to scatter the rest. The *Freeman's Journal* reported that an army of police wagons surrounded the house. He was followed from where we were hiding out in the haybarn. They ordered him to come out with his hands up. I didn't know he had a rifle. He must have taken it from the Ribbonmen's bunker. But Micheal was never about to come out with his hands in the air. Instead, he kissed his wife and children and walked out with the rifle aimed. The peelers ran for cover – they didn't know he had no bullets. They didn't care. Then they discharged their guns. Poor Micheal, God rest his soul, was shot to smithereens.

I was watching a clatter of snails when Missus Ryan came along. They were almost to the top of one of the barrels. Another bad sign. I watched the door swing shut and waited. She opened the top for light. I inched my way across and rattled the bottom half. Where we came from, knocking was only for strangers and peelers. Shaking the half-door meant a friend or at least an acquaintance. Therefore, I was pushing my luck and I knew it. What peered out from the darkened kitchen both sickened and saddened me. Missus Ryan, the eyes sunk in their sockets and with large swathes of her hair missing, was retying her headscarf as she made her way towards me from the open hearth.

Everything rehearsed in my brain over the previous three days suddenly didn't matter anymore. I had been toying with the idea of putting her straight about Finbar, letting her in on the real story behind his sudden flight to Scotland. And also letting her know that I had left specific orders on the night in question for Finbar and his column which they disobeyed, putting them in the wrong place at the wrong time and in serious trouble with the law. If it was hard to read Missus Ryan's face before, it was impossible now. But I wasn't expecting a gun salute from her in any event.

'Hullo, Missus Ryan. It's been a long time.'

She turned her back to rake the fire. It added to the awkwardness.

'I think there's going to be weather, maybe even a storm. I saw a hen brushing her feathers. And the snails are up the walls.'

'You're a regular William Molyneux,' she replied coolly. 'The twenty-second day of June, eighteen and forty-five.'

'Excuse me?'

'That's how long it's been – the last time we met. You were on the Public Works with young Gorman, some wall-building scheme at Cranley House.'

'You've a great memory, Missus.'

'And why wouldn't I remember, *Mister Sugrue*. It was the same day my Constance began work in that God-forsaken place.'

There was something horrible in the way Missus Ryan spat out the *Mister Sugrue*. It was totally different from the way Missus Langan would say it. If she had called me a rotten bastard it wouldn't have sounded as bad – and I'm not one for bad language.

'So, you got my letter,' she continued.

'I have it here,' I answered, taking it out so that when she turned from the fire she would see it.

'You thought about it for a while.'

'I had a few loose ends to tie up in Maynooth,' I said.

'What *loose ends*? You were making your mind up, you mean – wondering should you help the old bitch or let her stew in her own misery.'

'I assure you, Missus Ryan, I would never refer to you or any other lady in such terms. I don't care for that sort of talk.'

'No, but it wouldn't stop you from thinking it. That letter was sent four months ago.'

'I know, Missus. But I'm here now and, rest assured, I'm all in – whatever it takes.'

'Rest assured, you say.'

She took off her headscarf right in front of me, then pulled a clump of hair away in her fist.

'How's this for resting assured.'

'I'm sorry, Missus Ryan, I didn't know....'

'Never mind that, I didn't ask you here for your sympathy,' she stated bluntly. 'You know what I want, don't you?'

'Constance.'

'Yes. And despite our differences, I need you. I sent a letter to Finbar as well. He's already in England, waiting for you. Finbar can't do this on his own. He might be good but he still needs your help.'

'I'm in your service,' I replied, and for the first time in a long time I could feel the blood pumping faster in my chest.

'As you can see it's a race against time,' Missus Ryan confessed. 'I pray to Saint Agatha every day, Mister Sugrue, not just for myself but for Constance too.'

This time the *Mister Sugrue* was softer and more appealing.

'The patron saint of breast cancer,' I said. 'My mother used to pray to her too.'

'Breast cancer and sexual assault victims,' she added. 'I believe my Constance is still alive. Our Lady has told me so in a dream.'

She clenched the back of my hand. I could feel her desperation.

'Bring her back to me. Please hurry, I'm holding on here. I need to know she's safe before I depart this world. God bless you, Patrick, bring her back to the clachan where she belongs.'

'I don't think it was wise to include Finbar. He's too emotionally-involved as it is. This is a job for someone with a clear head.'

'What could I do,' she returned, 'when I didn't hear from you. Besides, Finbar is her father. He has a right to be involved – and a right to be emotional.'

The adrenalin was really flowing now. It was like old times again. I had a mission to go with my skills. I had people relying on me. As I nodded at Missus Ryan and turned to take my leave, my head was awash with confliction. I was hoping I was still up to the daunting task that lay ahead. I was fearing that time would run out on Missus Ryan before my work was done. I was sensing that what had just happened was another pardon – one to go with the absolution from the paddy-wagon crash. Missus Ryan would never say so but the way her tone softened, the way she called me *Patrick* at the end – something she had never done before – convinced me that she and I were finally at rights. I was also feeling scared because I knew, deep down in my heart, this was my final mission. I wasn't going to survive this ordeal. If only it would end well for Constance and her grandmother, then I would be happy. I couldn't have cared less about myself.

As I left the clachan behind, I worked out what the strange cat-like sound was and realised I'd been away for too long. It was old Missus Maguire, Missus Ryan's neighbour and friend, keening for the safe return of young Constance.

Five – Finbar

When I finally alighted the train, I walked up Eridge Road and onto London Road. Then I took a right into Calverley Park. I looked at Missus Ryan's handwriting again. That's what it said – clear as crystal. The house on the turn for Mount Pleasant. I uncorked my hipflask and had a nip. The rim felt strange and cold on my upper lip, where my beloved moustache used to be. I picked out a row and headed for the house at the end.

I had spent all morning wondering about Finbar – would he have changed much since his dash for Scotland almost eight years previously. I wondered would he still have that shock of blonde hair stretching to his chiseled cheekbones. Would his mad blue eyes still dart around the place, as if considering too many questions at once. And would he still want me to tell him all about the rebellion. I remember talking until I was hoarse about the Harrow and Oulert Hill and Enniscorthy and the Three Rocks and Wexford and Tubberneering and New Ross and Vinegar Hill and Needham's Gap and Father John and James Gallagher and what happened them at Tullow. And when I would finally break to draw a proper breath, there would be Finbar, picking at his lip nervously, and all he would say was *don't stop now*. So, I would indulge his amazement and begin all over again.

I knocked on the door and waited. I was preparing my apologies in case a stranger should appear before me. I knocked again and got no answer. It was only when I was walking away that I heard a familiar voice.

'Comrade Sugrue, I take it.'

When I turned again the door was still closed. Coming towards me from the side of the house was Finbar Ryan. He looked different than what I remember. His blonde hair was gone. When I say gone, he still had hair and it was still partially blonde. But it was cropped so tight to his scalp that he reminded me of something from the old days. He was thinner since the last time I saw him, and it made him look taller. But those inquisitive blue eyes still danced above his high cheekbones.

'My auld son of Eireann,' I said, taking his hand.

'As I went walking up Wexford Hill. Oh, who would blame me to cry my fill. I looked behind and I looked before. My aged mother I shall see no more.'

He recited the lyrics like a man bursting with happiness. But still, I thought it a strange thing to come out with. Especially since he hadn't seen me in so long.

He grabbed my hand again and turned my palm over.

'Long fingernails. Tut, tut, Comrade Sugrue, you should practice what you once preached. Or are you going soft in your old age?'

'They're not long,' I protested.

I had to hand it to him, he never switched off. When it came to soldiering and learning about war, Finbar Ryan was a pure topper. In all the time I spent training, he was the best military student I ever schooled.

'Look,' he said, holding up his fingers. 'My nails are chewed to the bleeding butts. If they ever catch me, it'll take a fair pliers to pluck these. The Brits love nothing better than to start with the fingernails – your words, not mine. Come on, Comrade Sugrue, let's get inside. There's webs on the bushes at the back of the house, and you know only too well what that means.'

'Another hard frost.'

He hesitated a moment, taking a compass from his trouser

pocket. Then he faced due south and looked up at the sun.

'Just getting my times right,' he said, putting the compass away again, 'you wouldn't know when you'd be without a timepiece.'

'You didn't know me with the hairdo,' he said, when we got as far as his neatly-kept kitchen.

He took a stubby knife from a drawer.

'Here, take a trip down memory lane,' he suggested, handing me the blade, 'back to the croppies. Where we're going, there's no need for style.'

'I can't,' I said, and pointed to my scar. 'Too identifiable.'

'God, but you were always a step ahead, Comrade Sugrue.'

'Not really,' I replied. 'Until the job is done, I always consider myself a step behind. Have you settled in alright?'

'Like a true citizen of an empire,' he announced. 'Even got myself a job in the local quarry, over beside Grosvenor Bridge. Start at eight, finish at four – leaving me enough time to pursue the finer things in life.'

For no particular reason, I felt uneasy when Finbar said that. The sight of a horsewhip dangling from a nail in the kitchen wall did nothing to quell this uneasiness.

'Your idea of décor? Reminds me of someone I used to know.'

'A trophy,' he admitted, 'a little trinket.'

'Did you make any headway with regard to Constance?'

'For sure,' he replied. 'I have the area where she lives staked out. The estate lies at the west of Hargate Forest. I even have a bivouac set up beside it at a place called Strawberry Hill Farm.'

I was surprised – and impressed – by Finbar's progress. He could have been no more than a month in Kent and already he had blended in nicely with a rented house, a job, and a camp not far from our target to help with our intelligence. Maybe the uneasiness I felt towards Finbar had more to do with me than him. Perhaps he was right after all – maybe Comrade Sugrue had gone soft in his old age. But one thing was for sure, I felt much better when he hung the kettle on the crossbar of the fireplace and said we'd have *tay*.

'Church of the Holy Trinity,' Finbar said, out of the blue, 'that's where himself and the missus go between eleven and one each Sunday. We could make our strike then.'

'Who? Burke and Constance?'

'No, the viscount and his wife. Burke is a harder man to snag entirely. He seems to have no set pattern. But believe me, Comrade, the place is as tight as the Tower of London, especially in the last couple of weeks. Real protective agents, not just his stable hands, doing the full twenty-four seven.'

'Someone must have told them we were coming,' I joked, and when Finbar laughed he looked just like the boy I first met playing bowls at Goshen Cross.

'Maybe you could go to Protestant mass to keep an eye on them while I sneak under the fence,' he suggested. 'As long as Cardinal Cullen doesn't find out, you'll be grand. But in all seriousness, Saint Bertha's Day would be the proper time to strike. There's a party in the parish hall after church.'

'Saint Bertha?'

'The Queen of Kent and driving force behind Christianity in Anglo-Saxon England. That's how she's described in the *Kentish Gazette*. They'll be eating and drinking and dancing to beat the band.'

Finbar still had that way with words; you never really knew if he was serious or having a jibe at you. But I didn't care, I asked the question anyway.

'And where does a fella get Catholic mass around here?'

He eyed me like it was some big secret.

'There's Saint Augustine's over on Hanover Road,' he said eventually. 'But I'd be careful of that place. It can be like the Synod of Thurles by times, with more priests and nuns than ordinary people in the congregation. Barrett's barn is a better bet. It's out on the Hawkenbury Road beside High Wood. There's a station there every Sunday morning.'

'Sure, we might take a ramble so,' I chanced to say.

'You might, but I won't,' he answered. 'These days, Comrade, I'm at my own thing. Do you still sit outside during mass? I remember that as a wain, you sitting on the wall outside Saint Mary's – come hail, rain or shine.'

'Old habits die hard,' I said. 'What do you mean, these days you're at your own thing?'

'I'd prefer an auld pattern now, instead of mass. I usually go down to the Bayham Road cemetery and do a few rounds. And there's a holy well below at Stone Farm. Although how holy it is, only God knows.'

'Are those patterns not a load of superstition?'

He laughed when I said that.

'There's no mistaking but Cullen has you by the short and curlies. Whether it's superstitious or not, I'll be doing my pattern around the cemetery on the twenty-fifth. I've never missed a Finbar's Day yet. Do you mind when we used to have benediction around Saint Barry's well in the clover field – every twenty-fifth of September, without fail. And I used to give out the Rosary because I was the only one in Mostrim called Finbar.'

'Ah, leave it to God,' I whispered and, as the memories came flooding back, I noticed the stout branch of a tree in the corner of the kitchen.

'I often belted out a tune too. Auld Master Jackson said I had a lovely voice. Ask Jim Gorman if you don't believe me – himself and myself were at the same hedge school together.'

'I see you still keep a stick,' I said.

'Little John, eat your heart out. I'd be naked without my quarterstaff.'

'Little John – as in John Naylor? Well, I hope you have better luck than he did,' I quipped. 'They say he was hanged for robbery in the end.'

'Aye, and in Dublin above all places,' he added, 'the home of robbers.'

'Is that *blood* I see on it, Finbar?'

'Oh, that reminds me, I have a little treat for you when you're finished your tay.'

I got up and examined Finbar's quarterstaff. It was always his weapon of choice, from the first day he joined the Mostrim Ribbonmen. Finbar never took to firearms – he didn't like them. And besides, he could walk about freely with his quarterstaff and the peelers couldn't say a word. As far as anyone was concerned, Finbar was away to drive cattle. This was a good stick – lightweight yet strong, with a bronze band at either end for extra heft – like two long ferrules – and grips for the hands.

'Speaking of Jim Gorman, I heard about his son. The Brits did a Stoney Brennan on him.'

'Not *even* a turnip,' I replied, in recognition of Stoney's misdemeanour, 'he stole nothing at all. It was a complete set up.'

He sat there with that look again – the *big secret look*.

'I know,' he said then, 'I got it from the horse's mouth.'

Of course, I took this to mean that his mother had informed Finbar of Shay Gorman's fate in one of her letters.

'What happened with the authorities in Australia – they wouldn't release him or something?'

'I'll tell you all about it later on,' I said, swinging the quarterstaff a little. 'A nice weapon, Finbar. It's hardly oak? The bark is very white.'

'Aspen,' he answered.

I dropped it straight away and he let out a snigger.

'Now who's been superstitious,' he argued. 'Auld piseogs.'

'I'd sooner eat the flesh of a goat than have anything to do with it,' I replied. 'You may change it, Finbar. It's unlucky and attached to unfriendly spirits. You could cut a lump of blackthorn and make a nice shillelagh.'

'Don't start with that shite, Comrade. You're a soldier – and a soldier of merit – not a crotchety auld biddy from the back of beyond. It's unlucky alright, follow me and I'll show you who it's unlucky for.'

He got up and headed for the back room. He stopped at the kitchen door and told me to *come on*.

'I told you I had a treat for you, Comrade.'

The back room was heavily bolted and it took Finbar a while to open it. Then he pushed the door through, inviting me to have a look.

If the kitchen was neat and tidy then that was the extent of Finbar's housekeeping. This room was an awful mess. Something like a rat caused a rustle and ran for cover. I inched forward carefully. There was somebody at the far end of the room, lying on a coat. He seemed to be asleep. There was rubbish everywhere and it was covered in ashes or a sand-like substance. Finbar got by me and lashed out with his boot.

'Sit up, filthy British scumbag.'

The man groaned and Finbar sewed two more kicks into him. But he remained prostrate. It was only then I saw the chord. This fella was tied to a fitting in the wall.

'Where's your big-house manners now? I said sit up, I brought you a visitor.'

The restrained man muttered something through his gag. Finbar kicked out at him again and I told him to stop.

'It's the only language the Scottish bastard understands,' growled Finbar.

Scottish. I leaned in for a closer look, hoping to dispel my own growing misgivings.

The straight black hair was no more, in its place a wiry head of grey strands. I looked for the hanging jowls. The skin seemed even looser now. Suddenly, I could feel the heat in my own jowls as I searched for his black riding boots. The steel tips on his heels were like daggers to my chest. My heart thumped so hard; I thought I was about to fall in on top of him. I turned for the door before he could see my face. I needed to get back to the kitchen and collect my thoughts. It was like his name was booming in my brain – just as it had boomed when I stood at the graveside of Turk O'Nuallain all those years ago – the name of Walter Pollach!

Six – Prisoners and Jailors

I sat on a stool and searched for breath. So that was the *horse's mouth* Finbar was referring too. I was dizzy. I tried my best to calm down. Finbar came into the kitchen, a grin on his face. He looked at me and shook his head. I was so angry I could have broken the quarterstaff across his back. Here I was, not long after receiving a pardon for a crime punishable by death, back in the thick of it again. Only this time it would be much worse. This time there would be no public sympathy. I could feel the rope tightening already. You didn't mess with someone like Walter Pollach on a whim. Pollach had some heavy hitters behind him – people like Viscount de Bromley.

'Don't tell me you've lost your sand,' said Finbar.

'Whisht up, you stupid bastard.'

'As you'd say yourself, Comrade, there's no need for bad language.'

He was right. Normally, I wouldn't have used such an outburst. But, just then, I really didn't care.

'Do you not realise what you've done? You've undermined the whole operation. And you've just signed our death warrants into the bargain.'

'*Our* death warrants? Be careful with the *our*, Comrade. After all, you were hiding in your mate's house up until a week ago.'

'I was a fugitive of the law, I had to hide away. I had no choice in the matter,' I shouted. 'This is supposed to be about Constance, not about revenge.'

'*This*,' he asked. 'This what?'

'This – us being here in the first place. We didn't need a prisoner.'

'And what about a bargaining chip,' he argued.

'This is not that sort of operation. It's supposed to be a smash and grab. We certainly don't need the responsibility of a prisoner.'

'*You* don't have the responsibility of a prisoner, I do. And as for revenge, you don't know the half of it. That fucker, Pollach, terrorised my mother for months – not to mention countless others. He beat the poor unfortunates who worked at Cranley House on a daily basis, even in my time in Mostrim. I was told how he whipped Pius Mooney to within an inch of his life. You see, Comrade, I might not be much of a churchgoing fella but even I know that if you live by the sword, you'll eventually die by it. He took a particular delight in inflicting torture, so now he can suck it up.'

'What do you mean, *eventually die by it*? Listen, Finbar, you can't kill him. Because it would be contrary to what we stand for. The Brits might call us murderers, but we know better than that. The Ribbonmen don't kill outside the rules of war.'

He leaned across the table and took a hold of my coat. I thought he was going to clout me one, so I closed my eyes in anticipation. Then he began a familiar speech.

'I, in the presence of God, do pledge myself to my country, that I will use all my abilities and influence in the attainment of an impartial and adequate representation of the Irish nation in Parliament; and as a means of absolute and immediate necessity in the establishment of this chief good in Ireland, I will endeavour, as much as lies in my ability, to forward a brotherhood – *and sisterhood* – of affection, an identity of interests, a communion of rights and a union of power among Irishmen – *and Irishwomen* – of all religious persuasions, without which every reform in Parliament must be partial, not national, inadequate to the happiness of this country.'

He let go of my coat and there was silence for a while. When he spoke again, I could hear the raw emotion in his whispers.

'Don't you dare, Comrade Sugrue, don't you fucking-well dare. They have my child – my only child. What do you not understand about that?'

He was frothing at the mouth now. I tried to hold his elbow – to settle him. But he shrugged away my hand violently.

'You sit there and tell me I can't kill him. That it would be outside the rules of war. God help them if they don't give me back my girl. God help us all. I'll choke them with their own intestines – and I'm not just saying that.'

He looked up at the neatly-slated roof. There was a wildness in his blue eyes now.

'I'll hang them from these very rafters. One by one by one. If anything has happened to my Constance ...'

He shook his head and wiped the sweat from his brow.

'I'll wage an onslaught like they never knew existed. Now, I've asked them once already, the next time I won't be asking so nicely.'

'I wasn't telling you what you can and can't do, Finbar, I'm simply thinking of Constance and what's best for her. When you say *asked them*, you mean by letter?'

He nodded gently.

'A fair trade,' I continued, 'Pollach for Constance?'

He nodded again.

'I tried to be above board about it when I got here first. I went to the peelers and asked for their help. When I went back to the barracks the next day, they told me they had been to Tunbridge House and were not prepared to interfere between a man and his common-law wife. They said Shaun Burke had produced documentary evidence of his marriage to Constance and the matter is now at an end – as if I would just walk away and leave her to that animal. So, now you know, Comrade, that was as much *above board* as I'm prepared to go.'

'And how did you come by Pollach?'

'He was as easy got as a wet foot,' explained Finbar. 'I watched him for no more than a few days at his work in Hargate Forest. He was supervising the felling of trees, and a group of men cutting and selling them. You see, men like Walter Pollach are easy prey. Their inbuilt suspicion and insatiable greed keep them at the job until all their subordinates have long gone home. One evening – after quitting time of course – I rolled up with an ass and cart, asked the all-alone Pollach for a trailer-load of timber – which he refused due to the lateness of the day – and when I got his back turned, clobbered him with my trusty quarterstaff. It was a simple matter of pegging him in the cart, covering him over and turning my donkey for Calverley Road.'

'I'm on your side, Finbar, as God is my judge. But heed a word of warning from an old, decrepit, volunteer. Don't let your head be ruled by your heart in this matter – it makes for poor soldiering.'

He acknowledged my advice with another nod.

'From now on, let me do the scouting in and around Tunbridge estate. The peelers will have put two and two together, Finbar. They'll be on the lookout for you.'

Indeed, we didn't have to wait long for the police to come looking. Fortunately, I was there to answer the door. They didn't ask me a thing, just gave me an artist's impression of Finbar and another of Pollach. They told me if I saw any of these two men to contact them immediately. I showed Finbar the drawing and it made him laugh.

'It doesn't look like me at all,' he quipped. 'But at least they got muggins in the back room correct, jowls and all, right down to the quod erat demonstrandum.'

Good prisoners breed good jailors – that's a saying from as far back as I can remember. And I believe it to be true. It was certainly the case with regard to Finbar Ryan. He got the torture treatment from the peelers on many occasions. But when Finbar was in custody, the Mostrim Ribbonmen just carried on regardless. We didn't have to move our ammunition or abandon our secret places. In the end, Finbar would grind the police down. Sometimes he even told them what they were doing wrong and how a torture method could be tweaked to be more effective. They would get fed up of him and his constant taunting and just dump him on Main Street. One time, I watched from the Granard Road stile while the peelers were letting Finbar off. He stood up on the middle of the road, dusted himself down, and serenaded them as they turned their horses for the barracks. Finbar was a master of prison mind-games and why wouldn't he be – his father before him was the best prisoner I ever had the honour of sharing a cell with. Old Johnny Ryan used silence on his jailors with the same effect as his son used mockery. More than this, Johnny went full scorched-earth policy on the peelers and the Brits who put them there. If they gave him a delf plate, he would break it before he would give it back. If they handed him an enamel cup, he found a way to put a hole in it. He would break iron if he got a chance. Often times I went without because Johnny's contempt for his captors would evolve into a hunger strike. Offer it up, he would say to me – and my belly rumbling for all it was worth – for God and for Ireland.

But if Finbar was a good prisoner, he was an excellent jailor. I watched him closely with Pollach in those first few days. He always took his quarterstaff with him into the back room – even if he wasn't intent on using it. Because Finbar knew, from experience, that the sight of a weapon was enough to cause a certain degree of mental anguish in a prisoner's head. Finbar fed him the same food at the same time each day. He gave Pollach exactly ten minutes to eat up, then he took away his plate and cup without so much as another word. If Pollach complained, or argued that he wasn't finished, Finbar sat down on the edge of the bed and stared at him. He might sit and stare at him for a long time, but he rarely said a word. Then he brought the plate and cup away in silence. When Pollach lost control in a fit of despair, I never heard Finbar telling him to *shut up* or *be quiet*. He simply replaced the gag and stared at his prisoner until he calmed down naturally. If it took one minute or one hour so be it, Finbar was prepared to sit and wait. Finbar used regularity and tedium to grind Pollach down.

Then there was the torture. Finbar made a shiv and inserted it into the shaft of his quarterstaff, close to one of the bronze bands. Sometimes he used it to wake Pollach up by making cuts in his arms and legs. The only indication Pollach would get that a serious torturing was about to be meted out was the reknotting of the gag in his mouth. Finbar had to make sure that Pollach's screams could not be heard in the public domain.

But there were times when Finbar showed his human side. On Sundays, he brought Pollach a Bible for one hour. At first, Pollach didn't bother with it. But as the weeks passed, he looked forward to having a read – even if it was only to do something different. And Finbar also brought him *cream* for his *cuts*. I thought it the strangest thing ever, especially as Finbar was the one inflicting those cuts. I couldn't help but challenge him over it.

'He may be a rotten bastard, but I still have a duty of care to him as my prisoner,' Finbar answered. 'Besides, I don't want him getting weil's disease and dying on me.'

I was relieved to hear Finbar say that. Because, up until then, I was sure he was going to do away with Pollach.

If Finbar was a clever jailor, Pollach was an equally clever prisoner. Time and again I heard him speak of his elderly mother in Scotland. She came from a place called the Isle of Jura, the youngest of ten kids. I could tell by Finbar's face that these snippets of intimate information annoyed him. They humanised the prisoner, making him into a child in his own right. But once he started, there was no shutting him up. It usually ended in Finbar holding the shiv to Pollach's neck or threatening to catch a pine marten and put it in his room.

Eventually, there was what captives call the moment of clarity. I remember my own experience with regard to this matter. It's that moment when the fog clears and you realise what's really going on. It happened for Walter Pollach on a Wednesday afternoon, about a month after my arrival. Finbar had no sooner pulled his gag down than Pollach was running his mouth off again, only this time about Finbar's nearest and dearest.

'I have you pegged now. You're the father of that bonnie wee lass from the viscount's estate, the one who coupled up with Burke. What mince luck for her.'

Finbar put the tray on the floor and held his counsel. It was time for the staring match to commence.

'I'm spot on, am I not? Why else would you want to abduct *me*? How's your mother – Missus Ryan, if I recall correctly. Her and I are old freens.'

He winked at Finbar then.

'I think she had the hots for me. You know, the auld fanny flutters.'

Finbar lifted the tray of food and warned Pollach to stop or there would be no dinner. But Pollach had no intention of stopping, he was only getting started.

'She told me all about your exploits in Scotland. Yes, you and your filthy Irish whores in your rat-infested ghettos. The Gorbals I believe, or were you strutting your stuff in Hyndland.'

Finbar lashed out and struck Pollach across the face. Then he checked his binds to make sure they were fastened tight to the bed and wall and pulled the gag back over his mouth. He brought the tray with him when he was going. I watched from a distance and I did not like what I saw. It was a clear victory for Pollach, the first time Finbar had been rattled in their psychological battle. It was a moment of clarity for me too – it was then that I realised, whether he got Constance back or not, Finbar Ryan was not going to return Walter Pollach to Tunbridge estate alive.

Seven – Tunbridge House

Below at Broadwater Down, with Hargate Forest enfolded around it like a crescent moon, stands the stately mansion of Tunbridge House. Built on an eight-acre estate, the forecourt alone accounts for a quarter of this space. What the house lacks in size – with a mere eight bedrooms, two indoor water closets and a modest all-purpose room, where Cranbrook and Tunbridge rural councils met on a regular basis – it makes up for in tight-knit comfort. Across in the back yard is the servants' quarters, its deliberate separation adding to the quaintness of the country manor, with stables attached showing two separate compartments for the work horses and those used for travel. There was never any need for a forge, the place being in such close proximity to Strawberry Hill Farm. Adjacent to the servants' quarters is another little dwelling house. This is the private residence of Shaun Burke, one of the viscount's most-trusted associates. In such idyllic surrounds, it would be hard to imagine the inhabitants of Tunbridge House as being anything but happy beyond compare. And they were, for the most part, especially in those early days since the replantation of Viscount de Bromley and some of his closest family, staff members and friends from their old base of Cranley House in the Irish midlands. This ragtag group of Kentish newbies was beginning to breathe new life into an old house as summer gave way to the autumn of eighteen hundred and fifty.

For Sheila McAndrew, the Tunbridge move was set to be her dream come true. Saying goodbye to dreary small-town Ireland, with its dirty thatched cottages and miserable tenants, and hello to the sophisticated homeland of the empire made her tingle with excitement. She envisaged high-class balls where she would shuffle about in the most fashionable gowns, being introduced as the viscount's second to the most elegant company of the day. She also envisaged cracking the whip on some new blood. The prospect of being the dominant force in the lives of a group of English girls – from their rising until Sheila had them lined up by their bedsides and checked for lice and dirty fingernails – filled her with glee.

The reality, however, was a very different matter. At the viscount's welcome-home soiree, Sheila was reduced to the role of a servant. She was mingling nicely in the great room until she crossed paths with Viscount de Bromley. He promptly told her to give the serving girls a helping hand, as they seemed to be rushed off their feet.

'And while you're at it will you take off that dress. You'll feel much more comfortable in one of their pinafores,' the viscount added.

Of course, the viscount was spot on – the girls *were* rushed off their feet. And it didn't take a genius to work out why; there weren't that many of them to begin with. The big house was always short-staffed. Five girls lived on the estate – not in Tunbridge House, but the servants' quarters. Therefore, Sheila's fantasy of having complete control of their lives – as she had done in the good old days with her subordinates at Cranley House – had not yet come to fruition. On the one occasion that she had attempted to set foot in the servants' premises unannounced, the door was soundly shut in her face. When she took her case to a higher court, Lady Ivens told Sheila that the girls had every right to their privacy.

'It is none of your business what our girls get up to outside of their working hours,' said Lady Ivens, 'or would you like a move to the servants' quarters on a more permanent basis? You are not in Ireland now, my dear.'

Sheila was also yearning for her lost love. Annie McKeon had been her faithful friend and confidante. The fact of the matter was that they were more than friends. Annie had done everything Sheila ever asked of her without question. And in return for her loyalty, Annie was promised a move to Kent and a position in Tunbridge House. But such a move never transpired as Viscount de Bromley sought to cut his staff and his wage bill. Annie was simply turfed out onto the hard road during the big mobilisation for England. Now Sheila was regretting Annie's absence. Her bed was all the colder for it. And besides, Sheila was left to *babysit* little Aoife Burke and Lady Ivens' two brats – Hilda and Herbert – not once, but on a number of occasions. With due regard to indignance, being a part-time nanny was the last straw for Sheila.

'Get one of the housemaids to do it,' she eventually raged at Lady Ivens. 'I'm head over domestics, as you already know.'

'You are head over what I say you are head over, and right now it is quite late and I need a babysitter at short notice,' Lady Ivens replied loudly. 'I have no intention of rousing the girls at such an hour.'

'And what about Constance Ryan? Did she not used to be their nanny?'

'You mean Constance Burke? I have asked for her already, but her husband refuses to release her. If only you had seen fit to bring the other little scrubber, Annie what-is-her-name, with you to Tunbridge, then we would not be in such a state. You let her go, so you will take her place. And that is all there is to it.'

As well as being a part-time nanny, Sheila was expected to look after Colonel de Bromley. Ever since the stabbing of one of the servant girls with a bayonet – a vicious arm wound requiring a dozen stitches – the viscount had appointed Sheila to *call in* on him daily. The threat of being stabbed or shot was one thing, but what

Sheila couldn't put up with was hearing the same stories again and again. The old bat, as she liked to call him, had dementia. But Sheila considered herself more a victim of the disease than the colonel.

'See this,' he would say repeatedly, whenever he found the silver medal in his greatcoat pocket, 'this is a coronation medal. It was presented to me in Saint Edward's Chapel by none other than Lord Melbourne himself. The date was ...'

'The twenty-eighth of June, eighteen thirty-eight,' interjected Sheila.

'My heavens, lassie, you are spot on. Are you some sort of military brainbox,' he gushed, astounded by her historical recall.

'Oh shut up, you old bat.'

'What do you say, lassie? Speak up.'

'Nothing, Colonel. Will I press your fatigues for tomorrow?'

'Yes, yes indeed. Fatigues. I shall want them at my hand. Who knows when one would need to go into hiding, the way that dog Napoleon is trying the lines. Are you Irish, lassie? I know they are a shower of miscreants, but I never minded the Irish too much – as long as they know their place within the empire. Great field men – the Irish can smell an ambush at a hundred paces.'

And such was Sheila's life in Tunbridge House. But after a summer of disappointment, good times were on the way as she counted down the days until the Marquis of Salisbury's party and the arrival of her father.

'There was a full moon, just like tonight. Papa, Lord rest him, was putting the scythes away, so I decided to walk on ahead. It was then that I saw her, on Forest Road, heading towards the cemetery. Her coach rumbled along, a black dog running at its wheels. Then it stopped and the dog bounded in among the headstones, returning with a single blade of grass from an overgrown grave.'

'Oh Brother, do stop. I cannot take much more,' gasped Lady Ivens while steeling herself with the drink, but the viscount had no intention of quitting now.

'She stepped out of the carriage. I was only a lad, but I shan't forget the sight of her. She was dressed top to toe in black, with a veil covering her face. She plucked the grass from the dog's mouth and pressed it between the pages of her Bible. Then, turning her back to me, she thrust a long, bony, finger in the direction of Benhall Mill Road and shouted: *Okehampton parish church*. She disappeared through the open door and the carriage sped away. The woman I saw that night was, as true as there is brandy in my glass, Lady Mary Howard's ghost.'

'Oh heck, why do you have to be so mean,' cried Lady Ivens, before lighting up her cigarette and fleeing the drawing room to the sound of the viscount's laughter.

After a few puffs, she realised that she had abandoned her drink. But she couldn't face her brother all over again. Remembering where she had hidden a bottle, Lady Ivens hurried to the parlour and sat down alone. The insensitive wretch knew just how nervous she had been, especially since the disappearance of Walter Pollach. And he cackled uncontrollably when she forwarded her opinion on the matter.

'We should never have come back here,' Lady Ivens had argued, 'the locals are spot on – it was cursed then and it is still cursed. Was Papa's body ever found? We had a right to stop at Cranley House, but oh no, you just had to sell up and drag us all back to Kent. How do you account for poor Walter just vanishing into thin air?'

'What curse are you on about? Pure poppycock. You were talking the same gibberish when we lived in Ireland. Walter Pollach did not just vanish into thin air, as you so eloquently put it,' the viscount had countered. 'He collected up enough of my hard-earned money, the blighter, and went off with some disease-ridden trollop. He was always a horny little bucko. So good riddance is what I say.'

That was only an excuse as far as Lady Ivens was concerned. She knew Walter Pollach as well as she knew anyone. Many a night she had sat with him, listening to the colonel's war tales. He was a loyal servant to her brother. He would never abandon the viscount or his estate – not in a million years. And that was not just the good lady's view, but the chief constable's – and he had been out to *Loch Lomand*, Walter's private residence, a number of times. Since the abduction, not a thing in or around the cottage had been touched.

The whole sorry business had Lady Ivens thinking again. With trembling hands, she poured another gin. She cleaned the holder and lit another cigarette. If someone or something could take a grown man like Walter Pollach so easily, then it could certainly take Hilda and Herbert. What was to stop it – especially with the numb-skulled nannies and pitiful protective agents Lady Ivens had at her disposal. She would have been better off guarding the children herself. If only Constance had been allowed to take up her old role. She was the only babysitter Lady Ivens could really depend on – even if she had filled her little darlings' minds with myths and fairy stories.

The mistress of the house walked slowly to the parlour window. She looked out at the dark and gloomy forest. She studied the blue craters in the shining, voluptuous, moon. It seemed so eerie. What was out there, God only knew. What chance had Lady Ivens against the supernatural. But, then again, what chance had Constance Burke or Walter Pollach or anybody else for that matter.

Finally, the tie was to his satisfaction as Colonel de Bromley looked into the long, gilt-framed, mirror.

'It is the full Windsor or nothing at all,' he turned and said.

Sheila McAndrew didn't bother to reply. She often let him ramble on, especially when she was busy sorting his stuff out.

'If Brigadier Sale caught one reporting for duty in anything other than a full Windsor, he would crack the whip severely. And proper order is what I say. These young bucks do not know the half of it. How can one be expected to win a war, if one is not even able to dress properly? I learned that as a trooper, back in fifteen at Waterloo. You can load those flintlocks, my dear.'

Sheila unwrapped the blanks that the viscount had given her and slid them into the guns.

'I think I will hold off with the brown bess today. Intolerably slow contraption. These Afghans would have one's snout off before one could even get a reload. No, I shall take my bayonet instead – just in case I meet a Ghilzai along the way.'

'You're getting no bayonet, Colonel. Remember what happened to your last nurse?'

'*No bayonet,* for a lieutenant-colonel of Her Majesty's forces? I shall have you court-martialed and hung for treason. What nurse are you talking about?'

Sheila shook her head. What was the point in saying anything at all. It wasn't the old colonel who she was annoyed with anyway, but his nephew. It was Viscount de Bromley who was sending her into the firing line each day. And on this particular day, Sheila had already dodged the danger. On her arrival to the colonel's room, she had to withstand a surprise offensive from the old codger. Taking a poker from the fireside, he had made several swipes at her ginger head while cursing and calling her an opium-fuelled Chinese whore.

'Make sure you even out those epaulettes,' he snapped. 'Did I mention the Brigadier-General is fussy on neatness?'

Sheila escorted the colonel down the grand stairwell and out onto the front porch of Tunbridge House, where he stood to attention as she went to get him a chair. He looked splendid in his red cut-away jacket, white trousers and shako hat.

'Fetch me my bayonet while you are at it, my dear,' he shouted back into the house, 'I am expecting Sir Robert to advance on Jellalebad any day now. If the Shah Shuja don't get a move on, the Afghanis will steal the march.'

The colonel combed his whiskers with the tips of his fingers as he looked out into the empty field, expecting the Thirty-fifth Bengal Native and his own battalion at the sound of a bugle.

After a difficult start, it was all coming together nicely for Viscount de Bromley. There were the usual complainers – those who would have complained anyway, even if the viscount had moved them into the Taj Mahal. The viscountess had all but swooned in horror at the thought of being uprooted and replanted in an eight-bedroom shoebox. Sheila McAndrew's face was getting graver by the day. If her mood did not improve pronto, the viscount was thinking of cutting her adrift altogether – just as he had done with so many other spoilt Irish brats of servants who didn't know when they were on to a good thing. And then, of course, there was his dear old uncle. The silly old fool should have been transferred to a retirement home years ago. And that is exactly where the viscount would have landed him, only he had powerful military friends still looking out for his welfare.

But those were all just teething problems as far as the head buck-cat of Tunbridge House was concerned. After a settling-down period, Viscount de Bromley was quite glad to be back in the genteel town of maiden aunts and retired servicemen. The Wells was equipped with the finest reserves of servants and artisans a body could want, and it was often the viscount's carriage was seen clip-clopping its way over to the stately homes on Sandrock Road or back from the mansions of Ferndale.

What gave the viscount most satisfaction though, when he wasn't hob-nobbing it with his illustrious friends, was his weekly call to the Holy Trinity Church. After Sunday service, he liked nothing better than to hold court in the shadow of Lord Abergavenny's statue, discussing the finer points of architecture with Decimus Burton or picking apart the Bishop of Rochester's earlier sermon.

'Is it true what they say about the manager of your estate,' asked Mister Barrett, a grand-nephew of the man who constructed the building they had just worshipped in, 'a fellow named Walter Pollach, I believe. Was he really abducted in broad daylight?'

'An interesting tale indeed,' replied the viscount, 'and I dare say a false one. I could never get a word in sideways when Mister Pollach was in my vicinity. An hour in that man's company and a kidnapper would be only too glad to hand him back – him and the ransom money.'

Despite making light of Pollach's disappearance, the viscount spent many a post-service carriage ride home wondering just what had really happened his trusted second. He didn't believe, despite what he said to his sister, that Pollach had vanished with some floozy. A man who begged for his job the way Pollach had done at Cranley House didn't just up and leave at the drop of a hat. He also didn't believe the policemen's theory – that Pollach's disappearance may have had something to do with an Irishman who came to their barracks looking for his long-lost daughter. What had Walter Pollach to do with Constance Ryan – or Burke as she was now known. Would the Irishman not have abducted Shaun Burke instead – or at least dealt with him in some other way. And, saying the police were right and it was a kidnap, where were the demands of the abductor.

The viscount afforded himself a little chuckle. Why was he bamboozling himself with such foolish questions; it achieved nothing except to get his mind all wound up and into a state.

Instead, he should have been enjoying the luxury of his carriage seat and the wholesome sights of the countryside. Because, when all was said and done, it didn't really matter what had happened to Pollach. Burke was now installed in his stead while the viscount looked high up and low down for a permanent replacement. It was all the same to Viscount de Bromley who managed his estate, as long as it was done in a competent fashion.

As they neared Tunbridge House, the viscount looked out into Hargate Forest. What an inspired decision his latest venture had been. Clearing away the trees at the south side of the forest and selling its firewood to the townspeople was going down a treat. Not only was it making him a vast amount of money, but soon there would be land to rent to local farmers as well – so much beautiful, reclaimed, land and not a shareholding in sight. The thought of it made the viscount feel good inside. Nobody with excuses instead of rent money and nobody with their hand out looking for assisted passage. And the greatest thrill of all – no Board of Guardians looking to raise the rates and overcharge the viscount so an idle public could lounge about in a poor house or pretend to be working a scheme on his estate. The problems which had dogged the viscount in Ireland were finally where they belonged – in the past.

'Get that carriage out of there this instant,' came the shout, as soon as the viscount had opened his door.

The sight of his old uncle, standing to attention on the front veranda in full military attire, was a bitter reminder that the viscount was not the real head of the household at all, but merely a scion. It was enough to fill him with resentment and loathing.

'Major General Ponsonby's arrival is imminent,' continued the colonel, drawing his sword and pointing it at the horses, 'him and his Second Cavalry Brigade. Now move that carriage before I have it torched.'

'What are you saying, you old fool? Sir William Ponsonby died thirty-five years ago at Waterloo,' replied the viscount, before sending his footman to retrieve Sheila McAndrew.

'Advance at your peril,' warned Colonel de Bromley, as he searched in the holster for one of his flintlocks.

Sheila appeared with the footman.

'Why on earth is he armed with a sword,' growled the viscount. 'What did I tell you, Miss McAndrew, *no bayonets* and *no swords* – except on special occasions.'

The colonel fired his flintlock.

'Die, you dog, die.'

But his nephew didn't die. He stayed standing while Sheila stole around to the back of the veranda and crept up on the one-time commander.

'What the blazes is wrong with this firearm,' shouted the colonel, as he produced his other flintlock and let the viscount have it again. 'Stay back I say.'

Sheila whipped the sword out of the colonel's gloved hand while he was examining the guns and put him sitting in his chair.

'Mad as a March hare,' said the viscount as he stomped up the steps and into the house, his old uncle's protestations still ringing in his ears.

Shaun Burke's life was really taking off since his big move to Kent. He had recently bought out a dwelling house on the grounds – part of an arrangement in which he paid one thousand pounds to his employer, Viscount de Bromley. He had a new wife – the other part of the thousand-pound arrangement – who, as yet, had not taken to married life. But Shaun was confident that marital bliss was about to blossom any day now. He also had a new job as acting-manager of Tunbridge estate – the viscount's pleas for a more permanent nature to the position falling on deaf ears because of Shaun's determination to concentrate on other projects. So, things were really looking up for Shaun Burke as he resettled into a summer of content in his adopted home town of Tunbridge Wells and the most comfortable seat in his new office.

There was a gentle knock and then the sallow features of Hernandez appeared through the door.

'Sir, John Smith pay money.'

Burke, who had been looking forward to mulling over his letter – the ransom note – yet again, stuffed it back in his pocket and took hold of the gun under the table.

'How many bloody John Smiths are there in this country,' he said, beckoning them in, 'it's almost as common as Paddy-me-arse where I come from.'

'Nice new lodgings,' said John Smith, 'your predecessor, Pollach, had nothing like this.'

'My predecessor is none of your business – and neither are my new lodgings. Now show us your money and be gone.'

'What, no small talk for your customers,' asked Smith, leaving his shilling and two pence on the table and throwing Hernandez a farthing for good measure. 'Old Pollach would have us rolling on the ground by now.'

'Well, *old Pollach* decided to terminate his contract. He won't have you rolling on the ground no more.'

'That's not what I heard, gov,' said Smith, the trace of a smile on his lips.

'Who cares what you've heard,' answered Burke, 'is that your trailer at the front? It's rather large – too large, I dare say. Go on, Water Pig, get to work.'

Hernandez bowed and set about filling John Smith's cart with freshly-cut lumps of timber.

'*Water pig?* Is that not a little insulting?'

'It's supposed to be,' Burke pointed out.

'Why not call him Hernandez like everyone else?'

'Because I can call my squire whatever I like. I don't need your approval on the matter. And besides, water pig is an appropriate name for him.'

'How so,' asked Smith, getting a bit hot under the collar.

'Well, he comes from South America for a start,' explained Shaun Burke, 'stands at four foot nothing, weighs nine stone, has no tail, doesn't know his own strength and is easily tamed – all the very same characteristics as the world's largest rodent. What else could you call him but a water pig?'

Smith shook his head and said no more. As he was on his way out of the nice new shed which had been specially commissioned in record time, Burke let go of the concealed weapon and rose to his feet.

'As I've already said, that trailer of yours is a bit on the big side. I'll be expecting a shilling and four next time.'

This enraged John Smith, who spat on the ground and complained that it was Pollach who had set what both parties agreed to be a fair price.

'Well, that's too bad then. Because Pollach isn't in charge now, is he? It's too large a trailer for a shilling and two. Oh, don't worry, you can dispense with the water pig's farthing – call it my discount to you.'

'There won't be a next time,' growled Smith, before going off to give Hernandez a hand with the filling.

'As you wish,' concluded Burke, before slamming the door shut.

Finally, his office was private again. Shaun took out the letter and began to read: *To Mister Burke, I have your friend, Pollach. If you want to see him again you will do what I say. I know you kidnapped my Constance and forced her to marry you. Let her go now and there will be no more about it. This is your one and only warning.*

'*My friend, Pollach,* indeed. And he hadn't even the manners to sign off like any civilised person – *Yours sincerely, Her Father,*' said Burke to himself, laughing at the good of it.

Every time Shaun read that letter it filled him with delightful fantasies. Receiving it from a servant girl in the big house was like receiving an unexpected present. It was a lovely surprise. If only his father-in-law had taken the time to scribble a forwarding address, then Shaun would surely have sent him a thank-you card and an invitation to dinner – where the old man could have reacquainted with his daughter and met his granddaughter for the first time. They could have pretended to be like those fine English gentlemen who the viscount invites to dinner – with morning suits, cigars and brandy. Then Shaun would have had the opportunity to thank his father-in-law personally for ridding him of the despicable presence of Walter Pollach, while bagging him a lucrative position – for which he had demanded double of what Pollach earned – into the bargain. And, after an agreeable plate of pheasant and spuds, Shaun would then have had the opportunity to blow his father-in-law's head off, in the presence of his daughter and granddaughter, with the gun which was under the table – a gun Shaun kept close at hand ever since the day the peelers had come calling and nosing into his marital affairs. But, alas, this fantasy would more than likely always remain unfulfilled, for Shaun's father-in-law hadn't bothered his big bogman's head to jot down a forwarding address on the letter.

The sight of Hernandez throwing what looked like a whole tree trunk into Smith's cart brought Shaun Burke out of his daydream. He glanced at his pocket-watch, then gathered the money up off the table. Securing the gun inside his weskit, he checked to make sure he had his letter. The last thing Burke wanted was to leave that lying about for the viscount or the police to get their mitts on. It was time to head home to his family, to mind the child while his wife got herself ready for the evening's entertainment.

'That's it for the day, Water Pig,' he hollered at Hernandez, who was securing the trailer door while John Smith waited patiently in the perch seat. 'When you're finished here, couple up the horses and get the carriage ready. We've enough done for a Friday.'

Eight – The Blushing Bride

The baby nodded peacefully as Constance cradled her in the big armchair. It wasn't called the *soft chair* for nothing – so soft and comfortable that it was moved away from the old piano and replaced with a hardback for those who wished to concentrate while tinkling the keys.

'Aoife was her name, just like you,' she continued, as the baby's eyes grew heavier all the time. 'And this Aoife was a bold girl, not like you. You're a good little Aoife. But the bad Aoife was jealous of Lir and Bodh Derg's love for Fionnghuala, Aodh, Fiachra and Conn. One day she took them to Loch Dairbhreach and while they were swimming cast a spell over her stepchildren. She turned them into four white swans.'

Constance looked down at the child's face. She had fallen asleep to the sound of her mother's voice and the pitter-patter of raindrops on the tin roof of the stables outside. Constance checked the pendulum clock – it was time to get out of the soft chair, time to do this thing once and for all. She put the baby in her cot and glanced over at the floor tile.

'We'll be beautiful white swans one day too. I promise you, Aoife, my love. And we'll spend nine-hundred years together on the lovely lakes of Ireland, just you and me, never to be parted.'

She kissed her daughter's forehead.

'But mammy has to go away now, pet, to a place all by herself.'

Constance removed the floor tile. The knife was waiting for her – she could hear it calling out her name. It was going to happen this time for sure. In a few more minutes Constance would be as free as a bird – as free as the children of Lir. She couldn't stop her body from shaking as she went into the privy. She tried to steady her hands. She had chosen the time carefully – Aoife would not be alone for long. Burke would be back soon. He always came home – it was his home, not hers – early on Fridays. She opened the window and felt the cool breeze on her face one last time. Then she took a deep breath and began the cut. The blade pierced her left arm. It was time to cut across. She was going to give herself a count of three.

'One,' she said, and grimaced.

The bad things flashed before her eyes. They were mostly confined to the latter years of her life – since that awful day her grandmother had led her up the great avenue to Cranley House. She saw their faces then, floating towards her – Sheila McAndrew, Walter Pollach, Viscount de Bromley. They sneered at her. Shaun Burke. He laughed loudest of all. Constance looked down again and moved the point of the blade. Blood began to run more freely.

'Two ...'

She flattened the edge against her wrist. One quick slice is all it would take. The drops of sweat tickled her ears. Constance braced herself once more. Then she saw a blinding light – a flash of gold. The sun had come out for the first time all day, catching the Saint Anthony's medal around her neck. Constance saw more faces, friendly faces – the good faces of her life. Her grandmother floated towards her, a beautiful smile on her face. Her father followed. She missed him so much since he had to go to Scotland. Jim Gorman came towards her, his wife Mairead by his side. Behind them, the face of Shay smiled back at her.

'Put down the knife,' Shay whispered.

'But I want it all to end,' said Constance.

His face was moving on, like the others had done.

'This is not the way,' she heard.

Constance looked down at her arm. She could see the black spot from where the glare of the sun had blinded her. She wanted to say *three*, but she hadn't the strength. She fiddled absentmindedly with her Saint Anthony's medal – Shay's Saint Anthony's medal. How many times had she held it and prayed. Hopelessness washed over her again. It didn't matter anymore. Even if Shay did ever come back, he wouldn't want her now – she was married, with a child. Worse still, she was damaged goods. Burke had beaten her down as far as she could go. His friends had raped her at his invitation. He had looked on with delight as they ravaged her again and again. Constance burned with humiliation and rage. Then she heard Aoife crying in the other room. What was she thinking – she couldn't leave her daughter to that monster. She wiped the blade of the knife with a cloth. Then she wiped the blood from her wrist. The voice was right – there had to be another way.

The Gosnell's set on the shelf in the privy served as a constant reminder. The perfume and face cream and powder. Their famous cherry toothpaste and soap – with its image of a smiling queen of England. It was the second last present he ever bought her – a present for her wedding day.

'For the Victorian obsession with cleanliness and white teeth,' he had told her, reading the words from the side of the box. 'And now we're just like them, my love – Victorians too. With the help of a good finishing-school teacher, we'll have you transformed to a lady in no time. Then, the world is our oyster. We can attend all the best parties in London. We'll travel the world, just the two of us.'

If she hadn't been so miserable, she'd have laughed in his face. He just didn't grasp it. Or maybe he *couldn't* grasp it. Perhaps he really was delusional. For if she told him she was engaged to another – whom she loved dearly – once, she told him a hundred times. As she sat there in the privy, with her arm raised to stem the blood, it all seemed so long ago now – long before the return of Viscount de Bromley and his entourage. Three years to be exact, but it seemed like thirty-three.

'Go easy with the rouge,' she remembered him saying as he gave her the gift, 'it's not Ireland you're in now. Over here, an overly made-up face is considered a dirty face.'

The marriage took place a week later. And what a week it was. Burke plotting and planning their nuptials and Constance resisting at every turn. He started by laying on the charm. He ordered the servant girls of Tunbridge House to wait hand and foot on his soon-to-be wife. He had them tend to her every need. He had dressmakers and hairdressers call to the house. He organised caterers and musicians. He rooted out a priest from the tiny Catholic community. The ceremony would take place in Saint Barnabas' Church, the reception in the great room at Tunbridge House. On the eve of the big event, Shaun bought Constance a jewel-encrusted necklace to mark the occasion.

'For you, my love,' he said, opening the purple velvet box to reveal the stunning piece of jewellery, 'money is no object.'

She refused to accept, telling him that she had a necklace already.

'Enough of this nonsense,' he declared, 'how could any girl refuse such a pendant. It will complement your wedding gown.'

Even the mention of a wedding gown made Constance sick to her stomach. She turned her back. She couldn't bear to look at him.

'I'm telling you for the last time, there's not going to be a wedding. How many times do I have to say it – I love another man. I'm engaged to be married to *him*.'

Shaun Burke stood for a few moments, the purple velvet box held aloft. It was like he was frozen in time. Then he flung it away violently, bouncing it against the wall. He grabbed Constance by the shoulders and spun her around, before punching her in the face. He punched and punched and, when she lay on the ground pleading with him, got down on his knees and punched her some more. Blood spewed from her two eyes, her nose and her mouth. A tooth was broken and her bottom lip was already swelling. He had a wild look in his eyes and it appeared as if he was going to start into her again.

'Okay, okay,' she cried. 'Please, stop.'

He got off his knees and wiped the saliva from the corner of his mouth. Then, before he took his leave, he turned and pointed a finger of warning down at her.

'You're going to be married tomorrow or you're going in the Grom. You decide.'

The next day Shaun Burke and Constance Ryan were joined in matrimony at the church of Saint Barnabas. They travelled in the same carriage to the chapel. Burke had warned her ladies-in-waiting – the servant girls at Tunbridge House – to make sure the bruises were hidden with make-up. Constance had Gosnell's rouge dripping off her chin. Just before the vows were to be exchanged, Burke leaned in for a kiss on her cheek.

'Remember, the Grom,' he whispered.

He needn't have bothered his head whispering any threat – the old priest who Burke had unearthed was as deaf as a post. Besides, there wasn't a word of dissent from Constance. She never doubted her new husband for a moment. She knew she was going in the river if Burke didn't get his own way.

The trauma of her wedding day had never left her. Time could heal the wounds on her face but not the wounds in her heart. It was still so vivid to Constance, so raw when she recalled it. She ran her tongue across her broken tooth. It still felt strange, long after the pain had gone. There was noise in the forecourt. It was Burke. She ripped a piece of rag and tied it around her cut. Burke came into the house and went straight to the cot.

'I'm taking the child to Sheila McAndrew,' he barked, 'have the dinner on the table when I get back.'

That was it then. It was to be another night of *entertainment*, as he called it – another night when Constance would be violated by one of his drunken friends. When he brought Aoife away to the big house – it was then that Constance knew. But this night would be different. This night would be a sorry one for whoever Burke brought back from the tavern. She wrapped the knife in the rest of the rag. Shay's voice was right – there was another way after all.

She nodded bashfully and if she could have crawled under the carpet to get out of our sight, she would have. Before Lady Teale could embarrass her further, there was a knock at the door and a heavily-built servant informed Lord Teale that a visitor awaited his attention in the parlour.

'There are some coins with my pocketbook in the drawing room, Carruthers,' replied Lord Teale pleasantly, signalling for his wife and Annie McKeon to sit down and have tea.

Carruthers loitered at the door awkwardly.

'It's not that kind of visitor, Your Lordship,' he mumbled.

'We'll leave you boys to it,' said Lady Teale, and Annie McKeon needed no invitation to bolt for the door.

'He's here about a Shay Gorman. He said it's important, Your Lordship, that he speak with you alone.'

As soon as she heard the name on Carruthers' lips, Lady Teale halted in her tracks. Even his lordship was more than a little intrigued by this. He wiped his mouth with a napkin and pushed his plate away.

'Do fetch him, Carruthers. Mister Sugrue, stay seated. Please stay, my dears, I'd like all my present company to hear what this man has to say for himself.'

A few minutes later, Carruthers presented Terence Barry to the room. He was tall and thin, his bony elbow protruding through a hole in his hunting jacket. The boots he wore had seen better days, which suggested to me that he was an outdoors type. He fidgeted constantly with the cap he held in both hands and behaved as though he was in a rush to be somewhere else. He looked at the women as though he had never seen one before, and at me like I was about to run him through at his lordship's request.

'State your business,' said Lord Teale, reading Terence's worried eyes, 'and don't be so concerned – we've had our meal, we're not about to feast on your leg.'

Terence Barry twiddled his cap some more and looked down at his boots while searching for words.

'Oh, do hurry on man,' snapped his lordship.

'I'm here about a friend of yours, boy,' said Terence Barry, in a distinctly non-Midlands accent, 'a Mister Shay Gorman.'

'To whom are you calling *boy*?'

'I'm sorry, sir, I didn't mean any disrespect.'

'Where are you from,' asked Lord Teale, 'and how do you know Shay? And, while you're at it, how do you know the lad is a friend of mine?'

It was only a simple series of questions. But Terence's face grew so grave it was as if Lord Teale had just donned the black cap and condemned him to death.

'Hurry on, man,' continued his lordship.

'I come here from Rio,' stated Terence Barry, 'and I too am a friend of Shay Gorman. I have been sent here by Shay to …'

'Hold on there, young man,' interjected his lordship. 'What do you mean, Rio? Are you trying to take a lend of me in my own home?'

'I mean Rio in Brazil. And I assure you, sir, I am in no way trying to take a lend of you.'

'Now, you listen up. I may be getting on a tad, but I am not so gullible just yet. Your skin is as white as snow and you speak, from what I can discern, with a southern Irish accent. You will not dupe me as nicely as all that.'

Terence Barry's face turned bright red. He almost tore his cap in two halves.

'Assuredly, sir, in no way do I intend to mislead you. In fact, I only agreed to travel here as a personal favour to Shay. He asked me to come on his behalf to talk with you alone, on account of you and him being such good friends.'

'Say whatever it is you came here to say in front of my party. And if I was you, young man, I would start talking fast. Take care not to exhaust my patience with a tissue of lies – I will not be trifled with.'

'Indeed, sir, I know that. Shay has told me all about you. He speaks so highly of Lord Harold Teale, otherwise known as Lord Lacken. Now, as you already worked out, I have a southern accent. I was born in Cork, raised in Cork, and jailed in Cork. I was sent the short distance from my home in Blackrock to the lock-up in Sunday's Well for stealing provisions from a respected landed family in the area.'

His lordship looked at me while lighting his pipe, then turned his attention back to Mister Barry.

'I hope you are not here to cause rebellion or lift anything,' he said.

'Indeed, sir, I am not,' Terence Barry assured him, the hurry he had seemed to be in a short time earlier completely gone off him. 'Because of the overcrowding which existed in Cork jail, myself and about fifty others were sent to a place called Spike Island to await our trials and help out the convicts. You should have heard of it – the Brits consider the island vital for trade, military and naval purposes.'

'I'm well aware of the place, young man,' returned Lord Teale, 'and how the so-called Brits perceive it. The question is are you really aware of it, or are you telling us what we want to hear?'

'Please, sir, if you will allow me… we were housed separately from the convicts and enjoyed a small amount of leeway. They're building Fort Westmoreland in memory of the old lord lieutenant, a massive star-shaped fortress with six protruding bastions – each housing guns which can fire huge six-inch diameter shells – connected by ramparts and surrounded by a dry moat. Outside the moat is a glacis – a smooth slope extending outwards, built to leave attackers nowhere to hide. It's a specially-designed defensive structure from where you can see the only entrance to Cork Harbour, and it's being constructed in such a way as to withstand cannon attack.'

'Have you come here to give us a running commentary on British defensive stratagems or have you come to talk about young Shay?'

'Oh yes, sir, excuse me,' continued Terence. 'I remember the first time I ever saw Shay Gorman, among the scattered stones which are thought to be the remains of Saint Mochuda's monastery. He was collecting rocks for a wall on the south bastion, where a few of the other prisoners were using pickaxes and shovels to fill earth into carts so big that it regularly took all eighteen of a crew to shift them.'

'I don't understand,' declared Lady Teale, 'how could you have met Shay when Counsellor Thornton tells us he is languishing in a penal colony in Taz...'

'Please, my dear,' said his lordship, 'let the young man speak. We shall talk then.'

'I assure you, madam, we met on Spike Island while awaiting the prison ship. By then, I had a ten-year transportation to face into after the landed family's lawyers and the trial judge were finished with me. I soon learned that it's no defence in a court run by the British to point out it was the only time in my life I had taken anything belonging to another – and that the famine made me do it. My sentence was upgraded to burglary. From then on, there was no more soft-living leeway. My life would be spent in a frightening place full of hard criminals. I had to survive on my wits. Therefore, I decided to make friends on the island – being a loner was a dangerous occupation. I teamed up with Shay and another prisoner called James Cleary. They had also been incarcerated at Cork jail, but I didn't know them then. Shay told me he had been brought there from Galway Bay in August of forty-five, on the *HMS Success*. We were among the first convicts to arrive on Spike Island in October of forty-seven – with bazzers on us like a baboon's behind – aboard the *Minerva*, which was moored at the island and where we slept each night.'

I threw an eye on Lord Teale, hoping to grab his attention. This Terence Barry certainly had his dates correct. But his lordship was smoking away absentmindedly, looking into the fire.

'The only time we were chained was at night while we slept. Amid the biting cold, I'd huddle with Shay Gorman. It's then that I'd work up the nerve to study the other convicts – all mixed in together as they snored – and wonder how the hopes and dreams of our young lives had come down to a floating jail. And, believe me, a floating jail can be even more dangerous than a regular one. The hulk of the *Minerva* was one such example, with its boredom, overcrowding and lack of supervision. And then there were the gangs. Convicts from Ulster usually stuck together and God help anyone without an ally who crossed their path. The Dublin gangs were just as bad. Much of the violence was centred around strength in numbers. We kept our heads down for the most part. We didn't invite trouble but that wasn't to say trouble didn't come looking for us. I remember the day the *Minerva* arrived back from Cork Harbour with Thomas Francis Meagher, the famous Young Irelander, aboard. Myself, Shay and James befriended him straight away. He was so motivated and so organised in everything he did. And our lives changed from then on. Thomas Francis Meagher opened our eyes to what was ahead of us. He made us aware that if we thought a floating hulk was difficult, it was nothing compared to what the trip to Australia held in store. Storms, suffocating heat, coarse food and tainted water meant prison conditions like we had never experienced for a journey of up to nine months lay ahead. With all this in mind, there was only one thing to do according to Meagher. We had to move first. We had to escape Spike Island before they readied the ship that would take us to Van Diemen's Land.'

Ten – The Man from Rio (Part 2)

Finbar refused my hipflask – or should I say Roger Giles's powder flask – and said he'd put on the kettle instead.

'There's a grand drop of whiskey in it,' I told him.

He agreed that some of the good stuff in his *tay* would be nice.

'What are you stopping for,' he asked, obviously enthralled with my story. 'They were about to attempt an escape.'

I had a good wallop of the whiskey; he wet the tea. Then I got on with it, casting my mind back to Lacken House and the revelations of Terence Barry.

'Spike was getting fuller by the day,' he said, clutching at his cap again. 'The *Minerva* was soon at bursting point, so the jailors sent for another ship to hold the newest prisoners at night. We decided to enlist a fifth man to help in our escape – a newbie called Thomas Jordan, who, we were reliably informed, had considerable expertise in the building of rafts. Once it was done, we hid the raft at the back of the old Tower House ruins, covering it with seaweed. Thomas Francis Meagher did all of the planning. We were to escape on a Sunday. Meagher had a few reasons for this. For a start, a Saturday was one of the better days for grubbing. At least we got bread, meat, vegetables and milk on Saturdays, which is more than can be said for Wednesdays, Fridays and Mondays – when there was no dinner recipe at all. Therefore, we'd be at our most nourished for an escape on a Sunday. Secondly, there would always be lots of people hanging around on Sundays – we wouldn't be as easily missed. Our chaplain, Father Timothy Lyons, considered religion essential to the reform of convicts. Therefore, we all had to attend church on a daily basis. We spent many a long mass listening to the lambasting of hulks from the pulpit – where, in the chaplain's opinion, the greater part of a prisoner's time was spent recounting his adventures in vice and infamy. Father Lyons invited a civilian population to his Sunday chapel on the north-eastern side of the island – mostly family members and friends of the convicted – and encouraged the prisoners to mingle freely with them after mass. Thirdly, many of the jailors and custodial administrators were of Protestant persuasion and attended Reverend Henry Woodruff's Sunday morning service on the south side of the island, thus rendering them absent for a good part of our sabbath day. Finally, Meagher's network of intelligence made him aware that the *USS Jamestown* was set to make a trip to Spike Island to carry out inspections. It had been moored at Cork Harbour since April of forty-seven – over a whole year lying idle – since it was used to provide food relief for the needy of County Cork. This would present our jailors with just the kind of distraction we needed. The four-gun salvo from the saluting battery on bastion three would act as the ship's welcome and our signal to make the break for freedom.'

Lady Teale held up a bottle of cognac but her husband was too invested in the story and in his smoking to notice. She had one of the serving girls bring Terence Barry a *nice* cup of tea and seated him down by the fireside.

'They're all nice cups, Your Ladyship,' I remarked, draining mine before flipping it over to reveal the stamp underneath, 'pure toppers – the best of bone china from Indonesia.'

I wasn't speaking out of turn or being cheeky. I knew my place as a man of straw in the manor. I also knew Lady Teale – and respected her enormously. She took great pride in having the best of everything in her house, and the smile which followed my comment told me so. That pride extended to the plantation and the residents. Not one of her tenants had been lost to the famine. That's not something one could say about every landed estate in the parish of Mostrim.

'What happened then,' asked Lord Teale, 'how did the escape go?'

'Not well, boy,' answered Terence, after taking a gulp of his tea. 'As the shots hailed the arrival of the *Jamestown*, an off-duty prison guard just happened to be talking with one of Thomas Jordan's relatives outside the church after mass. They decided to bring Thomas in on their conversation, only Thomas wasn't there to be brought in – he was driving on for the Tower House site and the hidden raft in the company of myself, Shay Gorman, James Cleary and Thomas Francis Meagher. After a scout around, the off-duty prison guard wasted no more time. He climbed the stone parapet of the nearest rampart and waved the red flag, signalling to bastion one. As we were placing the raft in the water, the emergency bell was echoing in our ears. I thought I was going to gawk. Cleary wanted to scuttle the raft in an attempt to avoid an escape charge but Meagher was having none of it. Jordan bolted for Fort Westmoreland, to hide among the civilian population. As I was about to follow, I noticed Shay's hesitation. He said he was thinking of taking his chances on the raft. I warned him it would be suicide to do so – Meagher was a sitting duck for the twelve-pounders from the Smooth Bore cannons which were no doubt being flinted up at that very moment. Instead, we made it as far as the flanking galleries without detection. The sally ports were open. Shay made a dart, but I stopped him just in time.'

'In time,' said his lordship, 'in time for what?'

'Before walking into a hail of bullets, sir. I told Shay I didn't like it – that sally ports were not normally left wide open with an emergency bell ringing out. As we were debating the issue,

Thomas Jordan came out of nowhere and, before we could stop him, ran through an open sally port and into the dry moat. Amid a cloud of smoke, as the emergency bell was drowned out by the crackling of rifles, poor young Jordan was riddled to pieces. Myself and Shay gave ourselves up to the quartermaster immediately. Thomas Francis Meagher surrendered on the water – the raft caught in the crosshairs of a hundred muskets. James Cleary was found in the famine graveyard, hiding among the headstones, before nightfall. We were sent to the unforgiving punishment block.'

'How much more unforgiving could it have been,' Lady Jane Teale asked, 'from being chained in a ship's hulk with a horde of miscreants?'

'It was much worse,' admitted Terence Barry. 'First of all, we were publicly lashed. The authorities were determined to make a lasting impression on the other prisoners. Also, there could be hope – however faint – and companionship in the hulks. The punishment block was a lonely, rat-infested – and a filthy, disease-ridden, rat I most certainly did not want to share my bread with – prison within a prison. It was doubly-guarded at all times, with specially-designed narrow doorways and two-foot-thick walls as added deterrents to rebellion and escape. We were held separately, in cells furnished merely with a stool. We had to sleep on the floor. We were also heavily chained at all times and clothed in black from head to toe, with only a small hole in our hoods to see through. At night, you could hear the hysterical laughter of the insane. The suicide rate in there was much higher than out in the hulks. Many of the punishment-block inmates were found hanged in their cells. The authorities covered up everything.'

Lord Teale shot out of his seat. A dreadful thought had just come on him. The eyes bulged in his head with fright.

'Shay didn't ...'

'Didn't what? Oh no, nothing like that,' Terence assured him.

'Are you quite sure,' asked the perturbed head of Lacken House. 'Because the penal authorities would rather pretend to keep an inmate in custody than have to detail their suicide.'

'I don't know what happened to Thomas Francis Meagher or James Cleary, but myself and Shay were eventually taken from the punishment block. We left the largest prison in the British Empire aboard the *USS Jamestown* on the twenty-eighth day of May, eighteen forty-eight – the day before the arrival of a certain Mister John Mitchel – and were ferried into Cove. From there we were put on the *Phoebe Dunbar* and sent beyond the seas.'

'*Beyond the seas!* You mean Australia? Well then, what's all this nonsense about coming here from Rio? I warned you earlier, young man, do not take me for a fool.'

'Bear with me, Your Lordship, and I'll tell you all. Myself and Shay may not have been successful in our first attempted escape but our fortunes were soon to change. Twenty days after leaving the shores of Ireland we sailed into Bridgetown – that's some going – and we were only ever made row when there was no wind. One hundred of our three hundred prisoners were to serve their time in Barbados. Then we headed on for the South Atlantic, stopping off for provisions in Rio de Janeiro, Brazil. It was there that we eyed a second chance at freedom. During loading and unloading, the ship's guards would always use some of the healthier convicts for heavy-lifting purposes. So, myself and Shay were commandeered and let loose from our chains. We had to make our way repeatedly between the ship's storage compound and a bakery close to the quay, carrying sacks of flour past merchants and hawkers selling everything from turkeys to tarantulas. The ship's guards, with muskets at the ready, watched our every step. On our last trip to the baker's – just when it seemed like we'd be heading for the Cape of Good Hope after all – Shay Gorman, dropping his sack of flour, grabbed the money from a merchant's table and flung it up in the air. Well, all manner of sweet pandemonium broke out. People flocked from all directions – the poor, the maimed and the otherwise afflicted – diving on reals and dollars, sacks of flour and anything else which wasn't nailed down. The merchants and hawkers tried to beat them back. And the ship's armed guard was caught up in the melee. It was the quickest bit of thinking I ever witnessed. Myself and Shay were down the road and out of sight before our guards knew what was going on. After that, we hid ourselves in a favelas in Rocinha, on the outskirts of Rio, until we were sure that the guards of the *Phoebe Dunbar* had given up the search and sailed on to Van Diemen's Land. We adapted quite well to life in Brazil. Nevertheless, once a week we went to the Biblioteca Nacional do Brasil – where the newspapers of the world are held – to read the *Freeman's Journal*. The latest copies in storage were always three months behind, but at least we got to keep abreast of what was going on in the homeland.'

'And that is where you saw my legal representative's notice concerning the Australian authorities' refusal to release young Shay,' said Lady Jane Teale.

'Correct,' confirmed Terence Barry, producing a piece of paper. 'This newspaper cutting, here in my hand, is the reason myself and Shay came back to Ireland. Mister Thornton, BL, is your counsellor?'

'Yes,' replied her ladyship, 'he is working on the acquittal. So, you are telling us Shay is back in Ireland?'

'Closer than that,' answered Terence, 'he's back in County Longford. But you understand why he couldn't come here with me today – his face is known in these parts, mine isn't.'

Lady Teale covered her eyes with her hands. This news threatened to overwhelm her, but then she regained her composure.

'Terence, this is the Annie McKeon of your newspaper clipping.'

Annie was back where she dreaded – at the centre of the attention. Terence Barry handed the clipping to me and, I have to admit, my heart skipped a beat. Lord Teale, whom I imagined would have been doing cartwheels by then, was less impressed.

'Why did Shay not correspond with us directly? It is not as if he is unaware of where I reside – or his parents for that matter.'

'With all due respect, Your Lordship, it was a risk we were unwilling to take.'

Lord Teale couldn't disguise his annoyance at such a comment. Sensing this, Terence Barry tried to make amends.

'Oh, that's not a slight on your good self or his dear mother and father, do ya know like. But we were hiding from the law, Your Lordship. We still are.'

'You were not about to be extradited from a place like Brazil,' Lord Teale pointed out.

'That's true, my lord. But if our letters – or yours – had been tampered with or fell into the wrong hands, it could have proved disastrous to our position and safety. The British go to great lengths to retrieve their runaway convicts. Anyway, that's why I sought an audience with you today. I'm here on behalf of Shay Gorman, to make sure this paper clipping is not a trick of the British government to flush us out into the open.'

Lord Teale puffed away on his pipe, deep in contemplation.

'Seize him,' he said eventually.

We were all taken aback, even Carruthers – who Lord Teale was talking to. Nobody was more shocked than Terence Barry.

'I said seize him, Carruthers. Put him in the lock-up and alert the police.'

Carruthers put two strong restraining arms around the thin young Corkonian and arrested him on the spot.

'I assure you, sir, I'm telling the truth.'

'Save it for the constabulary,' answered Lord Teale. 'Oh, you are the clever boys – you British spies I mean. One of your government's most famous tactics – the old double-bluff. I might even have swallowed your tale – up to a point. The Australian authorities may well be saying they will not release young Shay – because they may not want to admit that the young man has escaped.'

'Sir, I appeal to you ...'

'I am not finished,' added his lordship. 'And what do the British politicians go and do once their Australian cousins report back? They dress up one of their Irish sleeveens in tattered clothes and boots, brief him on the layout of Spike Island, and send him into Lacken House, thinking I have the boy in my care. Well, your little plan has just backfired, Mister Terence Barry – or whatever your real name is.'

Personally, I didn't think Terence Barry's clothes were too shabby – but then I'm not from the upper echelons.

'Please, Your Lordship, you're making a big mistake. How can I convince you of the truth?'

Carruthers began to drag the struggling Terence Barry towards the dining-room door.

'You cannot, Mister Barry. Now, if you would, please go quietly.'

'No, wait. Check out my story. I'm telling the pure truth. Please, don't call the peelers.'

'Your story is a story of common knowledge. Now, be a good chap and accept your lot with manners,' Lord Teale concluded.

Despite his considerable bulk, Carruthers had a tough job ejecting the wiry Terence Barry from the room. But, after a struggle in the doorway, it seemed as if they had finally gone. Until the shout – that final, desperate, plea – echoed through the hallway. To the rest of us, it was just some gibberish – something

Latin-sounding or prayer-like. But it was enough to bring Lord Teale to his feet. It really shook him up – tears beginning in his eyes as he emptied out the pipe with trembling fingers. Stumbling to the door in a hurry, his lordship called out to Carruthers to stop and return the escaped convict to the dining room.

'What did you just say,' he then asked Terence Barry.

'Faber est quisance fortunae suae.'

Lord Teale went as white as snow. He retreated towards his chair, his head lowered as he wiped his eyes and his forehead.

'Every man is the architect of his own fortune,' explained Terence. 'It's something Shay Gorman used to say to me.'

'You – and me too,' said Lord Teale, taking Terence Barry from Carruthers' vice-like grip and embracing him warmly.

Eleven – Annie's Allegations Come Home to Roost

The sight of Eleanor the housemaid only heightened the tension Lady Ivens had been experiencing since the ringing of the bell. When the door of the dining hall swung open, there stood Eleanor with two policemen in full uniform. When they saw the lady of the house they removed their hats and tucked them under their arms. Viscount de Bromley, standing by the fireplace, couldn't hide his amusement at his sister's exasperated expression.

'Eleanor, please, where is our manners,' he prompted, before placing a sherry to his lips.

Eleanor curtsied towards the viscount and apologised, then asked the policemen if she could take their coats.

'No, mam, but thank you all the same,' one of them replied. 'We're not here on a social call.'

'Oh, that sounds very officious indeed,' said the viscount, 'and what does bring the constabulary out and about on such a chilly evening?'

Only the talking policeman moved forward. The other stood to attention where he was at the dining-hall door.

'For pity's sake, come in and sit down,' urged Viscount de Bromley.

'As I said already, this is not …'

'Suit yourselves,' interjected the viscount, 'what is it you want?'

'First of all, we're sorry to be bothering you at all,' stammered the self-appointed speaker.

'Oh, come on, Andrew, spit it out man.'

'Well, you see, my lord, it's somewhat of a sensitive matter,' he continued, throwing a bashful look in the direction of Lady Ivens. 'It might be better if we took this matter down to the barracks.'

'Better? Better for whom?'

'Better for all of us,' said Andrew the policeman.

'Well, not better for me,' returned the viscount. 'I have nothing to hide or be ashamed of. If you gentlemen have a bone to pluck, then by all means, pluck it. Whatever you have come to say can be said in front of my sister – and Eleanor, for that matter. Please stay.'

Eleanor, who was bowing so as to return to her chores in the kitchen, had to wheel around and stand awkwardly in the dining hall. Andrew the policeman was not comfortable with this arrangement.

'Well, my lord, we wouldn't be bothering you at all if we had our way. But the chief constable insisted we speak with you – purely on an exploratory basis, of course.'

Lady Ivens was so edgy she reached for the sherry again.

'Good idea, Sister. We should all have a drink. Eleanor will pour. Andrew, sit down and do not look so serious. You boys are among friends in this house.'

Putting his hand up as if to direct traffic, Andrew informed the company that neither he nor his colleague partook in alcohol while on duty.

'How about a cup of tea then?'

'No, mam,' he answered, 'but thank you just the same. We're here on a matter concerning some allegations that were made in Ireland.'

'*Allegations? In Ireland?* Well, come on. Let us have a full report,' said the viscount.

'Yes, my lord. These allegations concern yourself and a number of persons linked to you. Some of the matters under investigation are the subject of an ongoing case before the Irish courts.'

'*Irish courts,*' repeated the viscount, who was clearly losing his smug exterior, 'what *matters* are you on about?'

'Matters concerning ...'

Andrew the policeman gulped audibly before continuing.

'Matters concerning kidnap – the abduction and unlawful purchase and detention of a named female for forced matrimony. And other matters concerning false imprisonment, collusion to frame a member of the public in a crime and false witness in court.'

Lady Ivens reached for her glass and sank the remainder of her sherry. Eleanor the housemaid picked nervously at her fingernail and Andrew's colleague studied the carpet's design around his boots. Viscount de Bromley wiped his face with a napkin, then blew his nose.

'These are indeed dreadful allegations. The question I would like to know is who is doing the alleging?'

'A Mister Thornton is pressing the matter on the instruction of a Miss Annie McKeon. The case has already gained some momentum, my lord.'

'Momentum?'

'Yes, my lord. It has already been heard at a number of court sittings. Mister Thornton is most determined to see it through. Those cited in the proceedings include Mister Shaun Burke, Mister Walter Pollach and Miss Sheila McAndrew.'

The viscount turned his back to look out the window.

'Tell me again. Who exactly are thee ... *persons* bringing these allegations?'

Andrew the policeman pulled at his collar before continuing.

'Well, Miss McKeon is a former employee of Cranley House in

a place called Edgeworthstown. I believe this residence was once belonging to you, my lord.'

'Yes, I thought as much. I cannot recall this young troublemaker, but she obviously has an axe to grind over losing her job. Alas, I should not be expected to transfer my whole workforce when moving to a new country. Tell me, Andrew, who is this Thornton fellow?'

'Mister Thornton is a senior barrister and legal representative to a Lady Jane Teale, also known as Lady Lacken, of Lacken House in Edgeworthstown also.'

Viscount de Bromley clapped his hands so loudly he gave his sister a start.

'Ah,' he shouted, 'say no more, my good man. That explains the whole affair. Lady Teale is only doing her husband's bidding. Lord Harold Teale – or Lord Lacken, as he was known to us on the Board of Guardians – has a gripe against me ever since he tried to set up a fever hospital in the locality. He was unhappy with my contribution – or the lack thereof. Well, that certainly is Ireland for you. They billed me to keep the locals alive and then they expected me to pay to watch the blighters die as well. What a country, I say.'

'With all due respect, my lord, there may be ulterior motivations at work here but we are legally obliged to carry out a thorough investigation regarding all aspects of these allegations.'

The viscount turned from the window and bowed in the direction of Andrew.

'Indeed, gentlemen, I understand you have a job to do – and may I say what a wonderful job you are both doing.'

'Is Miss McAndrew in the house,' asked the policeman then.

'Of course. Miss Eleanor, would you be so kind as to fetch her please?'

'We would like you to release her for the duration of our deliberations. She will be required to come with us to the barracks,' said Andrew.

The viscount mopped his brow again. Lady Ivens was fit to burst out in tears.

'Now, now, gentlemen. Is there any need for such a fuss? I am sure whatever Miss McAndrew has to say, she won't mind saying it in front of the rest of us. We are all on our honour in this house,' explained the viscount.

'It would be for the best if you released her into our custody,' confirmed Andrew.

'I do not think it would be *for the best* at all,' growled the viscount. 'May I warn you fellows that Miss McAndrew will not be taking one footstep outside the door of this house without my full legal representation escorting her to your barracks. If you are intent on making a big deal from this tissue of lies then I do not mind making a deal of it myself. Now, what is it to be?'

Just then, Eleanor arrived back in the dining hall with a nervous-looking Sheila.

'Here she is now,' declared the viscount. 'Miss McAndrew, these policemen are following up on an ...'

'We'll take it from here,' said Andrew.

'As you wish,' returned the viscount, 'provided you *take it* under this roof. As I have already said, where she goes, my legal team goes too.'

'Miss McAndrew, would it be true to say that Miss Annie McKeon is known to you,' asked the other policeman, taking over from Andrew.

'He speaks,' hailed the viscount.

Sheila pulled at an eyelash and nodded.

'Could you speak up,' the other policeman urged.

'Yes,' she said, and looked away.

'It has been alleged that you and she were *friendly*. Would that be correct?'

'Yes,' Sheila said again.

'Then why, *Miss McAndrew*, would somebody who was *your friend* go to the constabulary in Ireland issuing such abhorrent complaints about you – and, believe me, she has dropped you right in the middle of some serious allegations in her affidavit.'

Sheila McAndrew's cheeks burned with embarrassment.

'I don't …'

'She does not have to say another word,' shouted the viscount, taking his seat once more, 'at least not without the full backing of a legal team. Now fellows, if that is all you came here for – to parley with allegations and mistruths – then I suggest we have nothing more to talk about. Eleanor will see you to the door.'

Andrew's colleague put on his hat. But he wasn't finished just yet.

'We're looking to speak with a Mister Shaun Burke regarding this and other matters. We have reason to believe he resides on this estate with his wife. Also, we are following a number of lines of enquiry in relation to the disappearance of one Mister Walter Pollach. We sincerely hope, my lord, that he has not employed a third party – an Irishman who, we have reason to believe, came to the area in recent months looking for his daughter – as a decoy to stage his own disappearance in the light of these charges.'

'Do not be so foolish,' the viscount groaned. 'Why would he do such a thing? Need I remind you boys that Mister Pollach is a free agent – free to come and go as he sees fit. He had no knowledge of this ridiculous fantasy story, and neither had the rest of us before today. If this is pertaining to the legality of Burke's marriage then, boys, let me assure you that I was present at the ceremony and everything was indeed above board.'

'Good day to you, my lord.'

Andrew's colleague fastened his hat strap and bowed in the

direction of a distraught-looking Lady Ivens.

'My lady, if your handmaiden would be so kind as to point out Mister Burke's residence, we will bid you all good day.'

Suddenly, the viscount sprung from his seat by the fireside.

'Gentlemen, there is no need for us to be at loggerheads over some silly tale with no foundation,' he said, his tone softening and his face breaking into a smile. 'Now, I will not allow those responsible for the upkeep of law and order in Tunbridge Wells to leave my house without a nice stiff drink. Eleanor, please.'

Andrew looked at his pocket-watch and said they had better be on their way to visit Mister Burke.

'Nonsense,' replied the viscount. 'The day is young yet, gentlemen.'

'Miss McAndrew can pour the drinks,' insisted Lady Ivens, obviously in need of one herself after all she had heard. 'Miss Eleanor will depart and fetch Mister Burke.'

'No need, no need,' announced the viscount, snatching his cape from the hanger and popping his stove-pipe on in a hurry. 'I will fetch him myself. I am sure Eleanor has enough to be doing within the four walls of this house.'

The viscount hurried away from the dining hall, ordering the first housemaid he met on the grand stairwell to keep the booze flowing and the glasses topped up.

Twelve – The Bivouac and the Queen's Arms

'Terence Barry. Now there's a proper friend, Comrade. I wouldn't mind a pal like that,' admitted Finbar, running a stone up and down the shiv in his quarterstaff. 'He took a queer chance turning up in Lacken House like that. I know he wouldn't be a household name on the flat rolling plains of Longford, but he could have been nabbed just the same. I'm going to take a leaf out of his book and branch out too – when hiding away from the peelers it's hard to get anything done. I've thought about it and I'm prepared to take a chance on following Burke to the *Queen's Arms*. That's where he drinks, you know. The bivouac is grand for keeping an eye on Tunbridge House, but I'm not getting anywhere close to him.'

I wasn't paying him much attention, my mind being on Walter Pollach instead. Since realising his big mistake – that abducting Pollach had been a complete waste of time because nobody was going to swap him for Constance – relations between Finbar and the prisoner had been at their lowest ebb. And, to tell you the truth, I was becoming more annoyed with Finbar all the time. Gone was the code of ethics which he used to abide by – the respect he was duty-bound to afford Pollach as his prisoner of war. A respect that I took a certain pride in, seeing as it was me who trained him as a soldier. Gone were the basic human rights, things like the provision of a bucket for toileting purposes. Too many times – for my liking – Pollach was found in an unacceptable state, lying in his own excrement or having wet his trousers due to a lack of attention. And then there were the punishment beatings. Within a month of my arrival, these went from one or two a week to a daily basis. Punishment beatings should only be carried out in the pursuit of some goal, some end-product, and not because the jailor is in bad humour with the prisoner.

Not that Walter Pollach was an innocent party in all of this. He was very much the architect of his own misfortune. Once his gag had been removed – for eating or drinking purposes – he never shut up provoking and inciting his torturer.

It was all done to a routine. The sharpening of the shiv would be the start of it. Then Finbar would go into the back room with a bowl of gruel and a tankard of water. More and more often, I'd find myself standing at the door, a snood at hand, ready to intervene if things got too out of control. The gag would come off and then Pollach would start – shouting obscenities or calling Finbar and his mother names. I heard him call Missus Ryan everything from an *Irish-born period-faced bitch* to a *loose-fannied auld besom*. Sometimes he'd eat what he was given, other times he'd chew it a while and then spit it back at Finbar – preferably straight between his eyes. That's when the quarterstaff came into play. Finbar would answer a volley of insults with blows to the face and digs to the body. He'd run the shiv up and down Pollach's hanging jowls. By times, it was as brutal as anything I've ever seen in the peelers' interrogation room or a Ribbonmen's bunker.

Then there was the time it all became too much – that moment when Pollach finally wore his jailor down. In the days leading up to it, I could sense Finbar was about to break because he had started to do strange things – like going fishing and bringing back the weasel from Dunorlan Park.

'I heard she gave every wee braw in Edgeworthstown a dose of the clap,' said Pollach.

It was nothing out of the ordinary by his high standards of shit-stirring, but it was enough to tip Finbar over the edge. He stopped lashing Pollach with his quarterstaff and rushed to the kitchen. He returned with the cage, whipping off the cover to reveal the weasel. When Pollach saw it he went into hysterics, so much so that Finbar was forced to put his gag back on.

'You're not so fucking smart now,' quipped Finbar, as Pollach struggled to retreat in fear while uttering some unintelligible plea.

Finbar held the cage close to Pollach's petrified face.

'This little fella's looking for a place to stay,' continued Finbar, 'think he could bunk with you for a while? He could do with a good feed – he hasn't had a bite for a week.'

Pollach began to drool on his gag. He was hyperventilating by this stage. He held his hands up in a praying motion, imploring Finbar not to release the weasel. But his pleas were going to be in vain. Finbar fed a few strands through the bars, letting the weasel smell the straw. And that's when I pulled the snood over my face and rushed into the room. I grabbed the cage just as Finbar was about to open its latch. I took it to the kitchen. Finbar followed in a rage. Then he pulled the snood right off my head.

'Don't you ever interfere in my fucking business,' he fumed.

'This is not right,' I tried to explain.

'And this is not the Ribbonmen,' he snapped. 'I'm calling the shots now.'

'You're in no fit state to be calling anything,' I told him. 'Where's your composure gone? Where's that measured silence? Don't you see, Finbar, Pollach has dragged you down with him. You'd rather be in there debasing yourself as a soldier, than doing what you're supposed to do – and obligated to do – when you take a prisoner.'

'The only thing that bastard understands is fear, Comrade.'

'Maybe so, Finbar. But you can't just set a weasel on him like that. At least not yet.'

'What do you mean, *not yet*?'

'Send Tunbridge House another threatening letter. Tell them

you're going to set the weasel on Pol...'

'But he's not a weasel. He's a ferret,' explained Finbar.

'Okay, *ferret then*, going to set the ferret on Pollach if they don't release Constance at once. Tell them Walter Pollach's blood will be on their hands if they fail to act next time.'

Finbar thought about this for a moment. Then he smiled and admitted that I just might be onto something with such a suggestion.

'And another thing,' I added, 'once you send your new ransom note, I want you to keep a low profile. We've a better chance of getting Constance home this side of Christmas if I concentrate on the *Queen's Arms* and you continue surveillance from the bivouac. Is that agreed?'

Finbar seemed happy enough with these arrangements. He didn't say as much, but I grasped it by the way he put me in a headlock and gave me a skulling while reciting a verse of his favourite song.

'*As I was mounted on the platform high, my aged father I chanced to spy; my aged father did me deny, and the name he gave was the croppy boy.* Will I put the kettle on and wet a sup of tay, Comrade?'

'A mug of tea would be just grand, my auld son of Eireann. Wait a minute, where's your quarterstaff?'

He scanned the kitchen before returning to the back room to retrieve it. As he was leaving, he looked in on the prisoner. Noticing the Bible beside him on the ground, Finbar squatted where Pollach lay.

'You better pray that your friend, Shaun Burke, pays more heed to my next ransom note than he did to the first.'

He bent down fully and tucked the holy book into Pollach's breast pocket.

'Because if he doesn't,' Finbar continued, squeezing his hand around the throat of the prisoner, 'you'll be having my little furry friend for Christmas dinner. Then again, maybe my little furry friend will be having you.'

Shaun Burke leaned across the stile at the entrance to Strawberry Hill Farm as Hernandez rushed about the yard looking for the blacksmith.

'Forge vacante, sir,' he shouted, as Burke had a stretch and a yawn for himself.

'Take your time, Pig,' he replied. 'You'll bust a blood vessel the way you're going on.'

They were due to go to Maidstone, on the business of the viscount, but Burke was half-hoping the blacksmith wouldn't be found. He had to force himself out of bed in the first place but, since they had broken a wheel, he felt like abandoning the trip altogether. Besides, with the meeting coming up, Shaun was too excited to go anywhere. And now that he had received another letter concerning Walter Pollach, he was doubly excited. He sat on the stile and wondered about the evening ahead of him. He tried to picture what Doctor Egon Mortuland would look like. He wondered what this *most lucrative venture* could be, as the surgeon-cum-lecturer from the University of Science and Anatomy in London had put it in his correspondence. It seemed a little strange that the doctor would insist on meeting in a tavern – somewhat lowly for such a high-ranking academic. But what on earth could Shaun help him with that was so important – or so secretive. If Mister Prenderville – their mutual friend – knew, then he was most definitely keeping it to himself. Burke took out his pocket-watch and did a quick calculation. There was no way he was going on a five-hour round trip on this day of all days.

Finbar Ryan's eyes almost jumped out of his head. He couldn't believe his luck. Not thirty yards away from where he was camped was his long-lost son-in-law, sitting quietly on the turnstile at Strawberry Hill Farm. He turned the other way and looked up at the big house. There was no one on sentry duty. Wherever the guards were, they weren't on the forecourt.

'High time for an introduction to the family,' said Finbar to himself, as he gathered his quarterstaff and prepared to attack.

But, after running his hand along the stick, Finbar got a nasty surprise. The shiv was missing from his quarterstaff. He searched the ground of the bivouac – nothing. He would have to look for it later. It was time to strike while the iron was hot. Finbar readied some rope and a strong cloth gag. Then he left the bivouac and made his way along the hedge that bordered the stream, parallel to Eridge Road. He was going to creep up from behind and stun Burke with a poke-blow to the temple. The blow would have to be accurate and damaging to the point of disorientation, especially in light of what I had told Finbar of Burke's skill in taking down the unfortunate Turk O Nuallain. The hedge finished short of the stile where Burke was resting. There was about a ten-metre clearing which had to be negotiated. Finbar decided he was going to make a run for it and hope Burke didn't hear or see him until it was too late. Finbar got as far as the end of the hedge. He hunched down and kissed his quarterstaff. This was it.

Suddenly, just as Finbar was about to take off, there was a rumbling of wheels. A horse-drawn carriage pulled up at the stile. He got an awful shock. Two seconds later and Finbar would have been exposed in the clearing. He made a hasty withdrawal along the hedge. While returning to his bivouac he had a terrible thought – what if Shaun Burke was deliberately drawing him out of his hiding place. What if the peelers were already in the bivouac, awaiting his return. Abandoning his retreat, Finbar headed down Saint Mark's Road and on for Rumblers Hill. He was free to fight another day – but only by the skin of his teeth.

The carriage door shot open and the smiling face of Viscount de Bromley looked out at Shaun Burke.

'I see you're taking things nice and easy,' said the viscount, 'especially as you're expected to be half way to Maidstone by now.'

Shaun Burke looked over his shoulder sleepily.

'We're having problems with a broken wheel,' he answered. 'A warp in the rim just as we were coming out the avenue.'

'And surely you've a spare above in the imperial, or maybe in the boot?'

'No,' replied Burke.

'And why the blazes not, man?'

Burke shot the viscount a look of contempt.

'Because a certain someone ordered his footman to remove it from my boot last week. Or have you gone as forgetful as the colonel?'

The viscount nodded and flashed a sheepish smile.

'Our footman and the pig have gone up to rouse the blacksmith,' said Burke, pointing to Strawberry Hill Farm.

'And what about switching carriages,' asked the viscount.

'No can do. From now on I only ever travel in my own carriage. I took your old Brougham to Groombridge last spring and had a sore arse for a week.'

'That was your own fault, my young man. There are plenty of cushions about the place, if you care to look them up. Where's Hernandez now?'

'Above in the forge,' answered Burke, while the viscount took the watch from his pocket.

'It's getting on in the morning. Perhaps you and Hernandez could go to Maidstone another time? Head over to the office instead. Make sure they have those trees cut up – the batch felled yesterday. There are a number of large wagons due in today.'

This was music to Shaun Burke's ears, although he wasn't going to let the viscount know that.

'Whatever you think,' was his reply instead, 'you're the boss.'

The viscount closed the carriage door. But, just as Shaun Burke thought he was free to pore over his letter once more, the viscount unhinged the window and stuck his head out again.

'I've received numerous complaints from our customers,' he said, 'what do you have to say on this?'

Burke uncorked a bottle of water and shook his head. He was fed up with the viscount at this stage.

'About the sudden surge in prices. They're saying you're being unfair with them, and asking when will Mister Pollach be back.'

'If they don't like the price they can fuck off and get their timber somewhere else,' was Burke's reply, once he had finished gulping down the water.

The viscount hid a smile of satisfaction. He always enjoyed winding the young man up. But behind all the codology, he loved Burke's no-nonsense approach to money.

'By the way, any news on poor old Pollach?'

Then it was Shaun Burke's turn to hide a smile. He put his hand in his pocket to make sure the ransom notes were safe and sound.

'No. No news at all,' he retorted, 'he's probably on a beach in Mexico by now, sipping tequila and running his chubby little fingers through some busty senorita's long hair.'

The viscount laughed at the thought of it.

'Speaking of *senoritas*,' he continued, 'we haven't seen much of your other half since you tied the old knot. The viscountess is anxious that you bring her to dinner in the big house.'

'Yeah, maybe so,' Burke answered, getting annoyed and wishing the viscount would just go away.

'Well, what shall I tell her? You heard that she and my sister are organising some players for an opera to celebrate the Marquis of Salisbury's homecoming at the Saint Valentine's ball? *Maria de Rohan* – it was supposed to be my batty old uncle's favourite before he lost his marbles. The viscountess believes it may be good for his long-term memory. If you ask me, it's all a load of poppycock. But she's going to insist on you and your lovely wife being there.'

'Maybe. Tell her I'll be in touch.'

This made the viscount laugh all the more.

'Be in touch! Are you on the level? You only live across the courtyard, you young scoundrel, and you'll *be in touch*. How is the beautiful Constance these days?'

'She's grand,' replied Burke, preoccupied with thoughts of his upcoming meeting in the *Queen's Arms*.

'*Grand*. Well, take care not to give too much away,' said the viscount sarcastically.

'And what would be wrong with her,' snapped Burke, remembering the beating he had given Constance the previous weekend.

'Nothing,' answered the viscount. 'It's just that Miss McAndrew tells me there was a lot of noise coming from your place last Saturday night. I was just wondering if everything was okay.'

'You can tell the nosey little busybody that things were never better. If you gave her more to do, she wouldn't have as much time to be interfering in other people's lives.'

'Now now, Shaun, is that not a little strong – even by your standards. Miss McAndrew was in no way interfering. She was merely talking as a concerned neighbour.'

'Yeah, well, if she was more hands-on with the colonel, and less concerned about my affairs, she'd be better employed. It's a pity but he didn't give *her* a good run-through with his bayonet, instead of that other poor unfortunate. Now, I'm away to get the water pig. I've no time to be standing around chatting when there's work to be done. I'll be leaving the office early – I have to see a man in the tavern this evening.'

'Oh, that's another thing,' quipped the viscount. 'I hear you've been spending copious amounts of time in a certain tavern on the London Road – odd for a man who has never even taken a drink. Alas, you wouldn't want to get a name for rubbing shoulders with the riff-raff below in the *Queen's Arms*.'

'And who told you that – Sheila McAndrew? Let me worry about the riff-raff. I'll go where I like in my own time.'

'As you wish, young man,' concluded the viscount, giving the go-ahead to his driver, 'I'm only for your own good.'

The *Queen's Arms* is a small enough tavern in the Mount Sion area of Tunbridge Wells. Outside its London Road entrance, on the stylish wooden front, hangs a peculiar flag – a white horse on a red background, and the butcher's apron itself – the Union Jack. Inside, there's only one bar – no snug or *lounge*, as they called it in England. Like most taverns, the stools are lined up side-by-side at the counter. The tables and their cushioned seats are pushed tightly together due to the limited floor space. It is the perfect layout for a night's eavesdropping – and I intended on using the intimate atmosphere and the ever-growing crowd to do just that.

'What's yon flag outside in aid of,' I asked the barmaid, as she pumped a handle for all she was worth.

'Wot flag, the one wiv thee 'orse? That's the flag o' Kent, mate,' she informed me.

A bell on the tavern door tinkled every time it was pushed open. Upon my arrival, the place was already buzzing with conversation and that suited me down to the ground. The barmaid looked as tough as leather, with a matchstick between her teeth and the sleeves of her low-cut dress pulled up to her elbows. But she was pleasant in everything she said and did. I was careful not to get holed-in at the corner of the bar. I kept my drink in my hand and my feet on the move, stopping at a table here and there and talking with the other customers every now and then.

I looked at the timepiece Finbar had lent me. It was well after seven by then and still no sign. So much for his *sound advice* on how you could set your clock by Burke.

'You 'ave ants in your pants,' joked the barmaid as I came back for a refill, and two men in the line propping the bar had themselves a laugh. 'Are you Welsh, love, or maybe Irish?'

'Right second time,' I replied.

The bell tinkled again and a small stocky sallow-skinned man held the door open. Behind him was Shaun Burke. He looked too well-dressed for his surroundings, sporting a black morning suit, top hat and cane. Nonetheless, he acknowledged some men at the bar and they returned his greeting.

'Alwight, my darlings,' said the barmaid, but Burke was obviously more concerned with getting a table.

As he surveyed the floor, his sallow-skinned associate bowed, said something in a strange accent, and vacated the premises. A man wearing a gold-coloured cravat, seated behind a talkative old couple at the fireside, held up one gloved finger. Burke didn't look at all pleased to see him.

'Wot'll it be then,' asked the barmaid, placing her matchstick on the counter.

Shaun Burke acknowledged the question with a turned-on smile.

'Same as last time – a chilled water.'

'Bloovy terrific,' she sighed, 'talk 'bout last o' thee big spenders. Iced water in middle of winter. You're Irish too, if I 'member correctly?'

Burke gave the barmaid a curious sort of look.

'What do you mean *too*?'

'Same as 'im,' replied the barmaid, pointing at me. 'I thought you Irish boys were all big drinkers.'

'Where in Ireland is he from,' I heard Burke ask.

The barmaid shrugged her shoulders.

'Where you from, Paddy?'

Instead of answering her, I turned away and had my drink.

'The cat must have his tongue,' quipped Burke to the barmaid. 'And a jar of whiskey for that man over there.'

'Who? The man in thee cravat,' asked the barmaid. 'You'll 'ave to bring it down yourself, my lovely. I'm up to my eyes in it 'ere.'

'Your boss will have to get you help,' said Burke.

'New girl starting soon, darling, and not before time. An American, if you don't mind. She's gonna 'ave you fancy boys who like a piece o' crumpet biting at your bottom lips.'

As he walked away from the counter, Burke looked me straight in the eye. I wasn't worried because I had the advantage of him. I knew his face but he didn't know mine. I watched him bring the drinks across and sit down with the cravat-wearing gent. I gave them a few minutes. Then I manoeuvred my way through the crowd, zig-zagging towards the fireplace and a table behind them. It was time to sit tight and focus. I concentrated on drowning out everything else.

'Where's the doctor,' asked Burke. 'He was supposed to be meeting me.'

'No,' said the man in the cravat, 'he never said that. He's a busy man. That's why he sent me in his place.'

Burke got up to leave, saying that he was a busy man too.

'I'm no fool,' he snapped, 'and I won't be treated like one. Prenderville told me, face-to-face, that Mortuland was coming here tonight to talk with me in person.'

'Nobody thinks you're a fool. But if you walk away and neglect to hear me out, you most certainly will be. And as for Mister Prenderville, he's a delivery boy. He doesn't know his arse from a hole in the wall.'

Burke sat down again and then some people at a nearby table started telling jokes and laughing. I couldn't hear what was being said, so I moved a little nearer.

'Ten pounds a go,' said the man with the cravat, 'and, you can ask around, that's almost twice the going rate. The doctor will pick your men.'

'Nobody's picking nothing until I meet Doctor Egon,' replied Burke. 'How can I be sure everything is above board until I talk to the man himself?'

'Shaun, aren't you talking to me? How much more *above board* do you want it?'

'What does he want for his ten pounds anyway?'

'Just cadavers,' answered the man with the cravat.

'*Cadavers?* What the fuck are ...'

'Bodies – dead bodies, to be precise. He needs them for his students – for their practical and research.'

'Where am I supposed to get bodies,' asked Burke.

'Use your imagination – graves, churches, hospitals, asylums. Get them where you will, Doctor Egon doesn't care. As long as you can provide him with a dead body every fortnight, nobody gives a fuck where you get them. Can we do business – yes or no?'

'Yes, I think we can,' answered Shaun Burke optimistically, 'on two conditions. I want to meet Doctor Egon Mortuland in person.'

The man in the cravat turned his head slowly from side to side.

'That's not part of the arrangement. He's a senior surgeon at the Royal London Hospital as well as a lecturer at the university.

He hasn't time to bless himself, let alone come down to Kent to meet you. But I can give him your address and ask him to write. And the second condition?'

'Ten pounds is nowhere near enough – I want twenty.'

'*Twenty pounds!* Come on.'

'I want twenty or no deal,' confirmed Burke. 'Do you understand the risks involved?'

The man in the cravat sipped his whiskey and agreed reluctantly.

'And now I have a condition of my own,' he added. 'I'll get you your twenty pounds a cadaver if you can get me another night with that tasty little wife of yours. What's this her name is – Con…'

'Poontang,' Burke interjected. 'That's what you'll call her. I told you before, no names out of school. Have you got that?'

The man with the cravat nodded slightly and mouthed the word *poontang* to himself.

'What does it mean anyway,' he asked.

'That's what my boss's mad old uncle calls members of the fairer sex. It must be something he picked up out foreign – at one of his wars.'

'So, you don't mind me having another helping of your tasty *poontang*?'

'No problem. We've a deal then,' said Shaun Burke, offering his hand.

'We do indeed,' answered the man in the cravat, shaking it and licking his lips in anticipation.

Thirteen – Poontang

The tick of the pendulum clock throbbed in Constance's ears. It seemed to be getting louder as the night went on. It was all built in to the sense of foreboding – and Shaun Burke knew how to build it more than most. Taking away the child was the first step. Not long after coming home from Hargate Forest, Burke had taken Aoife to the big house. Constance knew it wouldn't be long now. It was almost midnight and the *Queen's Arms* was already closed a half hour. Something stirred in the forecourt. Constance put her ear to the door. A second set of footsteps brought back the pain in her chest. She tried to control her breathing. She clasped her Saint Anthony's medal and thought of Shay.

'O gentle and loving Saint Anthony, whose heart was ever full of human sympathy, whisper my petition into the ears of the sweet Infant Jesus, who loved to be folded in your arms. The gratitude of my heart will ever be yours. Amen.'

Constance listened at the door again. Maybe it was just her ears playing up. Maybe it was just the one set of steps after all. Then the talking stirred her worst fears. Unless he had brought back a woman again. But why would he, when it hadn't worked for him before. How could he make Constance jealous when she didn't care how many women he brought to the house. She wasn't in love with him and never had been. She backed away towards the floor tile – at the other end of the kitchen. The door swung open. She faced them like a cornered animal. It was one of the men from before – the man who wore the cravat.

'Hullo, Missus,' said the man, embarrassed by her show of fear.

Constance lifted a stool and used it to fend off her so-called husband and his friend in the cravat.

'Put it down,' warned Burke, 'or it will be all the worse for you.'

Constance inched her way back towards the floor tile.

'Go on to the room,' Burke instructed, 'I'll bring this mad bitch in with me.'

'Ah, I don't know. Maybe I should leave it tonight. She might be a tad wound up,' said the man in the cravat.

'It was you who suggested it, Gerald. Now you can go and fuck yourself if you think you *should leave it tonight*. Get in there I said. Don't worry about this whore, I'll take care of her.'

Constance had reached the floor tile. She held out the stool with one hand and pulled the tile up with the other.

'Stay back,' she threatened, thrusting the legs of the stool in the direction of her husband as she searched the hole where the tile had been.

'Are you looking for this,' sneered Burke, producing a small knife from his jacket pocket.

As Constance's heart sank, Burke swept the stool from her grasp. He held her wrist with his right hand, forcing it behind her back. He took hold of her hair with his left hand, pulling her like a rag-doll towards the bedroom door. He let go only to strike her three hard blows across the face before dragging her the rest of the way by the hair of the head.

Gerald stood in his long-johns on the cold bedroom floor, his cravat and suit before him on the bedspread. He would have loved to call the whole thing off, but he was afraid of what Burke might do to his wife – or what he might do to him – by that stage.

'So you thought I wouldn't find it, you fucking bitch,' Burke growled, as he tried to get the knife to Constance's windpipe. 'Thought you'd cut my throat while I slept. You dirty trollop. How would you like a taste of your own medicine?'

Constance stopped crying; she stopped struggling. She became still in his grasp, presenting her neck to the blade.

'Go on then, what are you waiting for,' she said in a calm tone.

'Don't try me,' he roared, 'I'll do you in a second, you filthy bitch.'

'You haven't got the guts,' she answered.

It looked for all the world as though he was about to slit her throat. Gerald's heart was in his mouth as he struggled with his trousers. If that maniac was to kill his wife then Gerald knew the game was up for all of them. He stuffed the cravat in his trouser pocket and made a beeline for the bedroom door.

'Where do you think you're going,' rasped Burke and, taking the blade away from his wife's throat, slashed at the dress she was wearing. 'You leave now and her death is on your conscience.'

Gerald was in a serious situation. He didn't want to be anywhere near this madman. But he knew that if anything happened Constance, then he was finished too. And not just him – Doctor Egon would be implicated. Their lucrative body-snatching scheme would surely come to light. They would all be bound for Newgate prison, never more to see the light of day.

'You wanted her. Now here, have her,' said Burke, ripping away the remainder of Constance's dress to reveal her breasts. 'It's all the slut is good for.'

'Okay,' agreed Gerald, as calmly as he could while undoing his flies once more, 'I'll take it from here.'

Burke gripped Constance by the forearms and fired her onto the bed.

'Poontang,' Gerald heard him say as Burke pulled up a seat to watch, 'whoever heard of poontang saving herself for a fiancé?'

Fourteen – Heartbreak!

Rooted to the spot by what I had just overheard, I stayed in the *Queen's Arms* after Shaun Burke and the man in the cravat had gone. I will admit I was scared. And I will also admit I didn't know what to do. I felt like stopping them, like beating the shite out of them, but I couldn't. In my heyday I'd have gone through them both for a shortcut. But not now. I'm too old now. Burke would have handled me on his own, let alone with the help of his pal. Besides, where would fighting have got me – what would it have done for Constance, only landed her in even deeper trouble. And the peelers were no use – they had proved that already. No, there's a time for fighting and a time for talking. I had to talk this out with Finbar. But I also needed to be diplomatic – something that does not come easy to a man who has spent too long in battle.

'No 'ome to go to, love,' said the barmaid, picking up the empty glasses from the tables around me.

'Sorry,' I replied, noticing for the first time that the tavern was empty apart from the two of us.

'Normally, you could sit awhile longer. But I don't want no policemen tonight,' she explained. 'Can't get the buggers out o' the place once they start drinkin', darlin', and they don't believe in puttin' their 'ands in their pockets neither.'

I drank up and thanked her. It wasn't a long walk from Mount Sion to where I was staying with Finbar on the Calverley Road. It certainly didn't warrant the two hours I spent getting there. But I couldn't get the thoughts straight in my head. So I wandered up Pembury Road and took a seat in Dunorlan Park. What was I going to say to Finbar. I couldn't tell him I had overheard Burke pimping out his common-law wife – Finbar's common-law daughter – to the man in the cravat and that, more than likely, Constance was being raped as we spoke. The truth would only serve to drive him out of his mind entirely, and Finbar was already too emotional for the good of our ultimate aim. He would surely have headed for Tunbridge estate, all guns blazing, and undid the work we had already put in.

There was another reason why I made up my mind to keep the truth from Finbar – a selfish reason. The truth made me look weak. It made me look cowardly. Instead of stopping those two villains on the spot, here I was, sitting on a park bench, more worried about our plan being in place than about the welfare of young Constance. I bowed my head with the shame of it all.

'Would you 'ave an 'aypenny, good sir?'

An old beggar woman gave me a right start. I rummaged in my pocket and took out a farthing.

'Blessin's o' God on you, kind sir.'

She reminded me that poverty was a worldly thing and not confined to the shores of Ireland.

Missus Ryan came to mind and my shame returned. What would she think of the celebrated rebel of the 1798 Battle of Ballinamuck if she knew that he sat idly by while two scoundrels violated her grandchild.

On my way back from Dunorlan Park I decided on what to tell Finbar. I wanted to impress upon him the need for immediate action without filling him in on the real, awful, truth. Therefore, I would tell him I heard in the *Queen's Arms* that Burke was planning an imminent move abroad – something to do with the management of Viscount de Bromley's affairs in Africa. That should sharpen his mind still further and hasten our plan along.

The front door was open when I eventually reached the house.

A new adrenalin took over, filling my brain with dread. I almost made a run for it. Then I took the snood from my pocket, pulled it over my face, and had a look about. Outside, everywhere was silent. I listened at the door. The house was silent too. So, I pressed ahead.

'Finbar,' I whispered. 'Finbar, are you there?'

I remember hoping that he hadn't done away with Pollach in a fit of rage. I went to where we stored the candles. I took a deep breath as I lit one, expecting to see the shadow of a constable before me in the hallway.

Instead, I saw an empty cage and blood on the floor of the hall. The weasel was missing. I moved the candle upwards – more blood! Handprints on the wall and doorknob. I opened the door to the back room. I imagined a half-eaten Pollach tied to the bed. I was careful of where I was walking – keeping the weasel in mind. But Walter Pollach was not in the straw – he was missing too. His broken binds were still tied to the bed. I almost dropped the candleholder with sheer panic. I tried to steady my hand and my nerves. It was all so silent.

Even though my mind was screaming *get out of the house*, I continued on to the kitchen. I could feel the sweat on my brow. I held the candleholder up to the high beam, remembering Finbar's threat to hang Pollach from it. Nothing. The kitchen window was still intact. It all seemed as normal as when I had left earlier that evening for the *Queen's Arms*. Then I turned around, towards the fireplace, and got the fright of my life. It was anything but normal.

A silhouette was partially revealed by the dying embers of the fire. I moved closer. The head was slumped and faced away. I could see my quick, white-smoked, breaths in the candlelight.

'Pollach,' I rasped, 'stay where you are.'

I needn't have worried, the silhouette never budged. Hunching down, I tried to grip at the hair, to turn the face towards me – hair which wasn't a mass of black and grey curls, but cropped and fair.

Instead of a hanging jowl there was a high, lean, cheekbone. A mad blue eye stared back in horror. I released my grip and shot backwards. Then I noticed the other side of his face. His trusty quarterstaff had been driven through the other eye – his left eye. His throat had been cut across.

'Finbar,' I exclaimed, forgetting my fear and cradling his head in my arms.

I don't know how long I lay there, but when I awoke the candle had burned out and was replaced by the first light of day. I got sick on the kitchen floor. I became even more anxious then – I had to get away. I reached the door before stopping. I couldn't leave an old defender of Ribbonism – the best foot-soldier I had ever trained – like this. I went back and, using my boot to steady his head against the wall, yanked the quarterstaff from his eye. It squelched and sent more blood oozing down his face. It was coming out in purple globs. I was thinking of what I should do next. Maybe I could hide him – or maybe I could get him to the lake in Dunorlan Park.

It was while I was taking off my coat to wrap it around him that I eventually came to my senses. There was no way I could carry or drag the dead weight of Finbar almost a full mile. Besides, if I was caught attempting to dispose of him, I would be tried for murder and hanged. As much as I hated to do it, I left Finbar there and then. I closed his eyelids and walked away. It was hard. It was heartbreaking. Finbar Ryan's war was finally at an end.

Fifteen – Lousy Requiem for a Local Hero

Finbar's war was not the only thing at an end. I was at an end – the end of my sanity. My nerves were so far gone that all I could do was walk the length and breadth of Tunbridge Wells. And when I arrived back at the point where I had begun, I would simply take off again. I stood outside places and didn't know where I was. In the hours after finding Finbar dead, I wasn't aware of my surroundings. I didn't feel hungry. I didn't feel tired. The nervousness which took hold just made me walk and think. I thought about going back to the house on Calverley Road and taking charge of Finbar's body. I went by it and turned for Mount Pleasant at least twice on my walking marathon. I looked across at it. The house still looked deserted – as if there was no body there. Maybe there wasn't. Maybe the peelers had come since my leaving. Maybe they were watching the place as I strode by – waiting for the murderer to return. Or maybe they just didn't give a shite about some straggler from Ireland who had only received his comeuppance in the most gruesome of circumstances. What if there was a weasel inside, feeding on an old friend's flesh and blood.

When my mind did return to the land of the living, I found myself outside Church Road in the freezing cold. It was starting to rain. The Holy Trinity church choir was in full voice and the crowd was getting larger. They were collecting for Saint Barnabas' workhouse on Bayham Road. It dawned on me that this was the day before Christmas Eve. I listened as the crowd joined in. They were singing *O Come, All Ye Faithful*. Jabber Farrell came into my mind, as a skein of geese made their regimented way across a grey sky. It was the first time all day that I had thought about anything other than Finbar. Perhaps it was the word *workhouse*, printed in bold red lettering, which made me think of Jabber. I wondered how he was getting on in America. A boy turned in front of me and held out a brown bag of sweets. I didn't take one. But, as I smiled back, his mother gripped him by the shoulders of his coat and forced him around to face the choir. I could have been from the workhouse for all the boy knew – I certainly looked like an inmate from a workhouse. Then she turned again and flashed me a suspicious eye, an eye that said: *I know where you were last night; you were at the scene of a grizzly murder.*

A coach arrived with Santa Claus. They call him Father Christmas over there. The kids went wild with delight as the crowd rushed towards him. He had loads of small presents and sweets. After acknowledging the cheers, he left down his sack and began conducting the choir. They started into another hymn – *Silent Night*. I joined in for something to do.

Silent night, holy night; all is calm all is bright.

Despite the darkness of the day, the singing made me feel better.

Round young Virgin, Mother and Child; Holy Infant so tender and bright

Sleep in Heavenly peace, sleep in Heavenly peace.

I don't mind saying there were tears in my eyes as I croaked out the last line. Then I moved away from the crowd. I was heading for the tavern. I needed a bowl of broth and a few whiskeys to warm me. But first I had one more place to go, out of respect for the dead.

Dusk was falling when I reached the bivouac. Thank God for a hunter's moon and an early frost. The location alone filled me with yet more admiration for Finbar's soldiery. It was built in just the right place – onto the slope of the gripe and in the shade of two junipers. I have said many times that Finbar was the best soldier I ever trained. That's no lie. A galvanized sheet – which was camouflaged in foliage – disguised the entrance perfectly. I pulled open the sheet, propped it with a stake, and climbed inside. It was the perfect vantage point for spying on the comings and goings at Tunbridge House, while also affording a clear view of the stile at the entrance to Strawberry Hill Farm.

I waited a while for my eyes to adjust – my nighttime vision isn't everything it was in my heyday with the Mostrim Ribbonmen. It brought back memories of how good Finbar's see-in-the-dark vision used to be. He became so skilled in the black darkness that he would be right up in the face of the enemy before they would know it. A moon was only a hindrance to him when he went night-scouting. Eventually I saw a circular outline. The rivet-holes on the sides told me that this was once a barrel, but Finbar had used it as a makeshift table. I ran my fingers over the top. The first thing I encountered was a cold, smooth, metal ball. Immediately, I was transported back to a time and a place I didn't know still existed in my memory.

It was a sunny Sunday afternoon in the early eighteen twenties. I was walking home from the town of Longford when I stalled at Goshen crossroads for a chat and a drink with the neighbours who had gathered. No sooner had the hipflask doused my whiskers – I wore my moustache with pride, even back then – than a miniature cannonball came bounding towards me at lightning speed. It was lucky I hadn't supped too much homemade, as I was forced to duck out of the way in a hurry – the cannonball shaving my lug before belting it on for Ardagh village. Then, just as I was collecting myself, another of the score came whizzing by – missing my unmentionables this time by the narrowest of margins. I was mad as I waited for the bowlers to appear. Sure enough, two young fellas sauntered down Camlisk Lane towards us, entertaining a pair of comely maidens, if you don't mind.

'You two rapscallions should be ashamed of yourselves,' I seethed, 'if ye're going to roadbowl then you'd better get yourselves a lookout.'

'Now,' said one of the young lads turning to the girls, 'didn't I say that ye'd hit someone sooner or later. Excuse me, old man, you wouldn't lend us your hipflask. There are some very dusty roads around these parts with the good weather we've been having.'

That was my first encounter – the first of many – with Finbar Ryan. He was no more than a teenager back then, but he was already a cheeky little git. Yet, despite the impetuosity of youth, Finbar had a massive sense of place – even back then he carried a great love in his heart for the people of Mostrim. This did not wane with time or distance. Being a founder member of the Mostrim Roadbowling Association was only the start of his civic duty in aid of his fellow parishioners – a civic duty not merely confined to a sporting context. The early years of the nineteenth century were underlined by absolute Protestant supremacy in the world of politics within the county of Longford. The dawn of the eighteen twenties looked to be following suit, with Viscount Forbes and George Fetherston elected without any real challenge at the general election which followed the death of George III. Just to make doubly sure of the maintenance of this old order, the determined dowager, Countess Rosse, had bankrolled Fetherston as successor to his father, Lord Oxmantown. The Catholic majority was in serious need of electoral amendment to gain some measure of political representation. With this in mind, the Catholic Association was set up in eighteen twenty-three. I remember a youthful Finbar Ryan at the forefront of its establishment. Despite Forbes and Fetherston being returned again at the polls in eighteen twenty-six, their days of total dominance were numbered. The Catholic Associations were in the engine room which ultimately led to Daniel O'Connell's Catholic Emancipation three years later.

Even after the counsellor's greatest triumph in twenty-nine, it did not stop there for Finbar. He became embroiled in the struggle against tithe payments, helping beyond the parish where need be. Many a time he faced down a proctor's team, loaded with the leading administrative men of the day along with the muscle and firepower to match. I wasn't a half hour in his Tunbridge Wells home when he asked about Roger Giles. To his amazement, I informed Finbar that Giles was not *as dead as a dodo* or *doddering around some retirement home* but very much alive and active as a captain in the Longford Yeomanry – a captain who harried and harassed Jabber Farrell, Jim Gorman and myself all the way from Mostrim to the emigrant boat in Dun Leary port.

'It's hard to kill a bad thing,' Finbar had concluded. 'Would it not be more in his line to be praying for a happy death?'

Then he asked me all about the famine and how badly it had gone on the people of Mostrim. I told him it was bad – there was no point in dressing it up – but that we had fared no worse than any other rural parish. I knew the conversation would sooner or later revert the whole way back to the Rourkes in Lisnageeragh – our first fatalities of the great hunger. Finbar had been in the same hedge school as Gregory Rourke – a brother-in-law and uncle to Maisie and her child, who had been found starved to death in their farmhouse.

'I spent half my childhood over at auld Rourke's place,' Finbar had told me, with sadness in his eyes, 'part of a meitheal and, sometimes, just part of the crack. My mother didn't write it in her letters.'

'She didn't want to upset you,' was all I could say.

Many felt that Finbar's inclusion in the Mostrim Ribbonmen was only a natural progression of his work with the Catholic Association and Anti-Tithe League. I didn't. While he had the love and interests of his people at heart, and trained harder and more diligently than any other volunteer I ever knew, killing humans –

despite it being in the name of war – did not come naturally to him. He loved life too much to concern himself with death. And that is why, once I heard Finbar speak of his intention to kill the prisoner, I knew it was no idle threat. I knew, deep down, this business with Walter Pollach could only end badly.

I whispered a prayer and, stuffing the roadbowling ball into my pocket, closed up the bivouac for good. It was time to get out of the cold and the wet and wrap myself up in the *Queen's Arms*.

Shaun Burke was not among the large attendance in the tavern that night. I was disappointed and relieved at the same time. There was no telling what I would have done if confronted with the sight of him. But, with around-the-clock protection employed at Tunbridge estate, I was going to have to rely on his fondness for iced water and the opposite sex – he had already tried his chat-up lines on dozens of women, including the barmaid herself. A chance meeting in the *Queen's Arms* – in front of scores of witnesses – may have been my only shot but was in nobody's best interest just then. I ate a bowl of soup at one of the furthest tables from the counter. I went to the privy to clean up. I saw myself in the looking glass. I knew then why the woman at the carol-singing service had been so wary of me. I was a total mess. I racked my hair, washed my face and the blood off my neck, and returned to my whiskeys.

'That's some tree they erected on Church Road,' said a person close to where I was sitting. 'Hauled it up with ropes.'

I didn't realise they were talking to me until it was too late. I didn't mind though. I wasn't in the mood for chatting. The guilt of the previous morning had returned to haunt me. How could I have walked away from Finbar. Was it not an unwritten rule of conduct among the Mostrim Ribbonmen never to leave a colleague in the charge of the English authorities. I was fairly sure that code of conduct extended beyond the shores of Ireland and also to the dearly departed. What was I going to tell Missus Ryan. She was bound to ask the question: *where is my boy's body now?* What was I going to say to that – *oh, I just left it there on the floor and walked away.* That's not good enough, not for Missus Ryan. She had fallen out with me for so long over Finbar's flight to Scotland, how was she going to react to this. She sought my help to bring back one member of her family and I end up losing her another. But there was nothing I could do about it now. Finbar was gone and, just like his daughter Constance, he wasn't coming back. My mission had been a total failure. Sooner or later, I would have to get my head around that simple truth. So, when I returned to Ireland, I would have to look Missus Ryan in the eye and tell her exactly what happened. I owed her that much. I would have to put my pride in my pocket and face up to my shortcomings.

As more and more people milled around my table, I gulped down the last of my whiskey and made for the counter. Now I had an idea of what Maisie Rourke must have felt as she gathered her daughter and retreated to their cabin for the very last time. It was a feeling of utter defeat, of helplessness, an acceptance of complete failure. Tomorrow I would face that defeat, gather my things and head back to the old country with my tail between my legs. Tonight though, I would chase my worries away with drink.

'What's you' poison?'

'Whiskey,' I said, drawn to the strangeness of the voice. 'Where's the barmaid gone?'

'I am the barmaid – the *new* barmaid,' she said in what sounded like an American twang. 'And by the way, buste', it's bartende'. Where I come from, maids are to be found in the more affluent homes of the upwardly mobile. The othe' bartende' has withdrawn to the cella'. She will return momentarily.'

I took the whiskey and turned away. This new barmaid must have swallowed a dictionary for lunch.

'Lousy day?'

I turned to look at her again.

'Excuse me?'

'By the look of you, it's been a rough day,' said the new barmaid. 'Wanna talk about it?'

'What? No.'

What was she on about? Men might have talked about their feelings and their *rough days* in America, but she had a lot to learn about us fellas from Ireland. Instead, I decided to hold my glass aloft.

'To Finbar Ryan, my auld son of Eireann,' I declared, 'here's to a requiem for a local hero.'

She pushed the strands of beautiful black hair behind her ears as she readied herself to serve another customer.

'Lousy requiem, where's the rest of you' funeral party,' she returned, pumping the handle over a pint glass. 'You have an audacity to celebrate *local* heroes and you with an *Irish* accent.'

'A Mostrim hero then,' I announced at the top of my voice.

The new barmaid did well not to drop the glass she was filling. She looked at me as if she had just seen a ghost.

'Did you say *Mostrim*,' she asked, 'as in Mostrim, County Longford?'

'What's it to you,' I replied, looking around suspiciously.

She came over beside me when she was finished with her customer.

'Do you know Jim,' she whispered.

'Jim who? There's a million Jims in this world.'

'Jim Gorman,' she continued, 'and Jabbe' Farrell.'

A cold sensation trickled down my spine. Before I could make sense of it, or run for cover, she extended her hand and swept the hair away from the left side of my forehead.

'Oh my God, it *is* you,' she exclaimed.

'What are you on about,' I growled, expecting the peelers to come out of the woodwork at any moment and jump me.

She leaned over the counter and whispered at me again.

'You're the Sugrue guy they always speak about. You' sca' gives you away.'

Sixteen – A Tale of Three Countries

I was listening to the wheezing in my chest as the new barmaid tossed the apron and said goodbye to her English colleague. Her instructions were to follow at a distance until I met the man who was waiting to take her home. I asked if she was some sort of spy – joking of course – and she put a finger to her lips and whispered the word *later*. For all I knew I could have been walking straight into a trap, the latest in a long line of male eejits to be undone by a beautiful woman – like Samson or King George IV. As my dear old mother used to say: *there's no fool like an old fool.*

She turned right and I followed her down Castle Road. All the time I looked about, preparing myself for the peelers or a couple of ruffians to arrest my progress. But why the apprehension, I asked myself then – this barmaid knew my name, and Jim Gorman's and Jabber Farrell's. She even knew about my scar and where to find it. Then, just before where Major Yorks Road intersects the Commons, I spotted a tall young man leaning against a lamppost. I stopped on instinct as the two embraced. There was no point in trying to make a run for it, so I looked around for a broken branch or some other weapon.

'There's no need to be so defensive,' she assured, beckoning me towards them, 'nobody's gonna harm ya.'

The tall young man had a mostly Irish accent. But you could tell there was something else in it as well. He held on to the black-haired barmaid like she was a piece of gold. Whatever his faults were, his eyesight wasn't one of them. But I could tell he was as in the dark as I was, and there was comfort in that much at least. The barmaid took a last look around, as if she was about to impart the world's greatest secret, before addressing her young beau.

'Jeremiah, you won't believe who this guy is,' she said, pointing at me again. 'It's Sugrue.'

Her young man looked at me and then blankly back to her.

'Who?'

'Sugrue,' she repeated. 'Jim Gorman's *Sugrue*.'

He looked again, this time a bit more knowingly.

'Not *the* Sugrue,' he asked her.

'Yes,' she gushed, 'the very guy Jim and Jabbe' used to spend all those hours telling us about.'

'You're having a laugh, Breda,' he snapped, 'or what sort of a gobshite do you take me for?'

'Look,' she exclaimed, and swept the hair from my forehead once more as if I was some sort of show pony.

The young man laughed and kissed the barmaid tenderly again. Then he turned to me.

'When did ye concoct this?'

'What,' I said.

'This little pantomime. Did ye make it up in the pub? That scar needs some red ink to make it look more realistic.'

'It *really* is him,' pleaded the barmaid. 'I wouldn't have believed it eithe' only I heard him toasting some guy from Mostrim – the same Mostrim where you and Jim and Jabbe' hail from.'

On hearing this, I had a closer look at this skinny youth – his blonde locks combed back with oil and his shiny button nose. But those deep blue eyes gave me nothing to go on.

'Not a ghost of a chance,' he said then. 'Whose idea was it to draw the scar on his forehead? God but ye're hard up for a bit of fun.'

I thought it was about time to get my own two-pence worth in then.

'Listen, sonny, I'm as confused about this entire episode as you seem to be. So, I'll make this plain. I wouldn't have followed your girlfriend as far as the front door of the *Queen's Arms* if she hadn't mentioned certain things – things like Jim Gorman and Jabber Farrell and Mostrim and County Longford and my scar. Now, I'm finding it all a bit unsettling to say the least. I've had the most horrible day imaginable and I'm just about ready to walk away from this whole set-up. But before I go, I'd like to know how ye know my friends?'

The young fella scratched his chin and nodded.

'This sure is a good one,' he conceded to the barmaid. 'There's only one thing for it. We'll have to go back to Cabbage Stalk Lane and see what Jim and the padre have to say. But I still think the joke is on me.'

'The padre,' I said, as we headed through the Commons for a shortcut, 'not the padre as in Father Murtagh, by any chance?'

The tall youngster looked at the barmaid in astonishment.

'The very one,' she said, answering the question for him.

'And where in Mostrim are you from,' I asked.

'Croshea,' he said, 'near enough to Ardagh village. My family name is Figg, but I'm all that's left now.'

'Figg,' I muttered to myself, but the name meant nothing.

'During the famine we were forced into the workhouse in Shroid. That's where all my people died.'

'Is that where you know Jabber Farrell from?'

'Yes,' he answered. 'The Shroid workhouse was where we met first, but I got to know him properly in New York.'

Now it was my turn to be astonished. I could hardly wait to hear the rest of what these youngsters had to say.

We stopped at a small Tudor-styled house on the edge of Cabbage Stalk Lane, a stone-throw from the River Grom.

'Leave him in the hallway,' Breda – the barmaid – said excitedly to her beau, whose name I had pieced together as Jeremiah Figg. 'It will add to the surprise.'

'Good idea,' he agreed, 'then we'll spring him on Jim and the padre.'

I was so excited, tired and cold that I could hardly stand upright in the hall. But while I waited, I heard Breda build the suspense by telling those in the kitchen that she had brought home a very special old friend to see them. Then she led me in and presented me like I was Millard Fillmore himself. I nearly fell out of my standing again when I saw Jim and the padre slouched at the table. I watched as the realisation slowly played with their minds. They looked at each other in silence, until the padre turned up the wick in one of the lamps. Lifting it from the table, Jim Gorman approached slowly and steadily. He held the lamp right up to my face, then turned towards Father Murtagh again. He looked just the same as the last time I had seen him, at the boat in Dun Leary, except that his sandy hair had a sprinkling of silver now.

'Are my eyes playing up on me,' he asked the padre.

The padre arose from the table and came towards me then.

'Patrick and Bridget and Columbanus,' he exclaimed, reaching out to touch my clothes in case I was an apparition.

Jim looked sickly as he inspected the knuckles of his little hands. I thought he was about to faint at any moment. Father Murtagh – or *the padre*, as Jim had referred to him in one of his letters from America – gave me a hug, while Jeremiah and Breda looked on in amusement.

'Mind now, Father,' I said, more out of embarrassment than anything else, as he nearly squeezed me to death.

'My grace is sufficient for you. For My power is made perfect in weakness,' whispered the padre in my ear.

'Ah yes, I remember,' I replied, 'the last words I spoke before you sailed away on the *Erin's Queen*.'

'Yes indeed,' returned Father Murtagh, and I thought he was about to burst out crying and give the two youngsters even more to laugh at. 'Corinthians, chapter twelve, verse nine.'

'I'll take your word for it, Father. And what about this man,' I said, turning to the ashen-faced Jim Gorman. 'Did you miss me on your wonderful travels?'

'Every minute of every day,' he replied, as we shook hands warmly. 'New York wasn't the same without you.'

'Which means you had nobody there to carry the can for you,' I joked. 'We're a long way now from building walls on the Public Works' scheme at Cranley House.'

Then a peculiar thing happened. The talking and joking and embracing came to a halt and we all just looked at each other in silence, scarcely able to make sense of it. In my almost seven full decades on God's earth, I couldn't remember a stranger day. It was Breda who broke that long, eerie, silence. She escorted the three of us to the table, while her beau went in search of a bottle of poteen.

'I might have a drop of tea instead,' I gasped, the crackling in my chest getting worse with all the excitement.

And then came the standout question in my mind.

'Where's Jabber Farrell?'

'I'd say California by now,' replied Jim Gorman, 'did you not get my last letter?'

'I got it alright, but I thought he might have come back with ye. Did I read it correctly? He married over there – with a black woman?'

'He did indeed,' Jim assured me, 'in Saint Patrick's Cathedral,

New York City. This man here was the celebrant.'

I looked at Father Murtagh and he just nodded shyly and smiled.

'So, he finally met the woman of his dreams,' I said, and I was very glad to say it.

'He did for sure. Miss Melanie Campbell,' confirmed Father Murtagh, 'a beautiful lady all the way from a cotton plantation in Breaux Bridge, Louisiana. Opposites really do attract.'

'A cotton plantation? Is she a slave?'

I could barely get the words out with the chattering of my teeth.

'She was, Sugrue,' answered Jim, 'at one time. Now she's a free woman of the Union states of America.'

'Get yourself togethe', miste',' urged Breda, pouring me a large glass of poteen, 'and get some of this inside ya. It's gonna warm the cockles of you' heart.'

I showed her my hipflask but, on finding it empty, decided to avail of her hospitality.

'And this is another free woman of America, I take it?'

'Right again, Sugrue. Breda is a tough little city girl.'

'Less of the *little*, Jim Gorman,' she cracked.

'What about Jeb Turling,' asked Jim, looking at me nervously over the rim of his glass. 'Good old Jeb, he was fierce decent to us when we were most in need.'

'Indeed and he was,' I agreed. 'Well, I stayed with Jeb – hiding out, should I say – for almost three full years. I only left him on the tenth of August last because Missus Ryan had written to me. Jeb's living a great life in Maynooth, thank God, and having a whale of a time on his barge, trading on the Royal Canal.'

I knew what the next question would entail, once I had mentioned Missus Ryan. I wasn't looking forward to answering, but I had made up my mind that I wouldn't mince my words. I was going to get it over with as quickly as possible.

'And how is Finbar Ryan? We were told he came down from Scotland to join you in seeking out young Constance.'

'*Seeking out*. When you put it like that, it sounds so simple. Burke, the cur, has a team of protective agents minding the place.'

'Yes, we know. We've been here about a month,' replied Jim, 'we sailed directly to Southampton from New York. And we heard all about what has been happening – or in the peelers' case, not happening – concerning Constance. Those protective agents are fully stocked. The last thing we need is a bloodbath on the forecourt. So, it was decided that our best chance of getting into Burke's house is through Breda. He's a regular customer – not to mention a regular womanizer – at the *Queen's Arms*. Breda got a job there so she can get close enough to seduce him into bringing her home. Once she gets past the guards and through the front door, she's going to slip something into his drink and slip Constance out the back door. We'll be waiting by the stables.'

'This sounds a bit dangerous. Is everybody okay with it,' I asked, looking at Breda.

'Are you kidding me, miste',' she gushed, 'I live and breathe fo' stuff like this. Peril is my middle name.'

'No,' joked Father Murtagh, 'I got a look at your Baptismal certificate for your upcoming nuptials and Beryl is your middle name. But, don't worry, we'll keep that between ourselves.'

'Aw, shaddup Pops,' answered Breda, 'and just how many monikers have you had in the past few years.'

This conversation was getting a bit too light-hearted for the burden I was obliged to unload. It was time to say it out.

'I have very bad news concerning Finbar – the worst news possible. Finbar is dead.'

Jim's face was a study of disbelief in the lamplight. Father

Murtagh blessed himself in shock. Breda stopped her teapot-stirring and approached the table, Jeremiah by her side.

'I'm sorry to be the bringer of bad news, especially at such a joyous reunion as this. It only happened last night.'

'*Last night!*' exclaimed Jim.

'I found him in his house on Calverley Road, the old quarterstaff he was so fond of rammed through one of his eyes. He was already dead when I got to him – murdered.'

'*Murdered*,' said Father Murtagh.

'Yes. And I'm fairly sure I know who did it too. It was Pollach.'

'*Walter Pollach*,' shouted Jim.

'I'm afraid so,' I added. 'If you're here a month then you'll be aware of Pollach's disappearance?'

I waited for Jim's nod before continuing.

'Well, it was all down to Finbar. When he couldn't get any satisfaction from the peelers, he took matters into his own hands. And with Tunbridge House and estate a fortress, he decided to take a hostage instead. After a number of failed attempts to snare Shaun Burke, Finbar settled for the next best thing. Pollach was supposed to be traded for Constance, but Burke wouldn't respond to Finbar's ransom letters. And then, yesterday evening, Pollach must have somehow got free of his binds to kill Finbar. Believe me, I have seen some brutal scenes in my life, from the rebellion through to the famine, and what I witnessed last night was pure butchery. I won't say any more in front of a young lady.'

Jim's face said it all – shock, sadness, anger. He was already mourning the loss of his old schoolfriend. Even though there were a couple of years between them, both himself and Finbar had attended Master Jackson's hedge school in Mostrim at the same time. Father Murtagh held the glass up to Jim's mouth and made him have a drink of poteen. He was now in the same place as I had been earlier in the *Queen's Arms* – in a state of hopelessness.

'We'll have to rethink our plans. We can't put Breda in that kind of danger. If something was to happen to her....'

Father Murtagh swapped Jim's glass for his own.

'Jeremiah's right,' he conceded, 'we can't put a young woman in the firing line like this.'

'Poor Missus Ryan,' Jim whispered, 'we're finished now.'

'Hi everyone. I'm in the room too, ya know,' snapped Breda. 'O' does anyone care to listen to my opinion? We cannot abandon ou' plan. Afte' all, what did we come all this way fo' in the first place – to rescue Constance Ryan. Yeah, well, we're not gonna rescue the little mite by talking garbage about what we can't do. We've put this plan in motion already – and I'm not pulling out. I'll dangle the carrot, and Burke – the lascivious old stag – won't be able to help himself. It's not as if we've anything bette' to be going on with.'

'I agree with Father Murtagh and young Jeremiah,' I said to Breda. 'Seducing Burke is much too dangerous. But I would encourage you to remain in your position as barmaid at the *Queen's Arms*. What you see and hear may be of great value, especially as I have reason to believe he is mistreating Constance in their home.'

Then I asked Breda if there was any buttermilk to quell the wheezing in my lungs.

She looked at me all confused.

'Well, a drop of hot whiskey might do the trick instead,' I suggested, and she went off to prepare the kettle once more.

I had just thought of a possible solution to all our problems, but I needed the time it took the kettle to boil to work out just how much of the awful truth to reveal. I would certainly be leaving out anything about the current plight Constance was facing. If Jim Gorman knew she was being raped, he would have charged off to Tunbridge House there and then. No, it was time to use the information I had acquired in the *Queen's Arms* for the greatest gain possible.

'There's another way,' I said eventually, and I could feel the goodness of the hot whiskey warming my insides.

'What do you mean,' said the padre, 'another way? What other way?'

'Another way besides putting young Breda directly in danger. Shaun Burke is involved in some very shady business with a couple of hobnobs from London. He has agreed to provide a leading surgeon, a fella by the name of Doctor Egon Mortuland, with cadavers.'

'What in heaven's name are cadavers,' asked Jim, forgetting his hopelessness for a moment.

'Dead bodies,' answered Father Murtagh. 'Go on, Sugrue.'

'These cadavers are to be arranged through middlemen, a Mister Prenderville and a small cravat-wearing man, whose name I don't have but who advised Burke as to where he can attain his cadavers – from asylums and hospital morgues and graveyards. Therefore, Burke is going to need help to get his hands on these cadavers. Now, if you fellas could arrange a man to go to Burke on the pretence that Prenderville sent him from the Royal London Hospital on the approval of Doctor Mortuland, then I think ye could get an inside man to take Burke down and get us in to Constance.'

'It'll never work,' insisted Jim.

'Whisht out of that. It will work if you make it convincing enough. The doctor has been asked to write to Burke. So, anyone good at forging?'

Jeremiah put up his hand like he was still in school.

'Perfect,' I said. 'You send the letter so, Jeremiah, on the headed notepaper of the *University of Science and Anatomy*, with a clear *London* postmark on the envelope. That should provide all the convincing needed.'

'How do you know all this,' asked Father Murtagh.

'Never mind that. Well, what do ye say?'

'I love it, Sugrue,' answered Jim, a smile returning to his face.

'So do I,' admitted the padre.

'I'll do it,' announced Jeremiah, 'I'll be Prenderville's man.'

'No,' I said. 'That wouldn't work.'

'He's never seen me,' he protested, 'I'm perfect for the job.'

'No,' I repeated. 'You're not. You have too much of an Irish accent. There's no way a swanky medical man from a top London hospital would have anything to do with the likes of you.'

'Thanks very much,' said Jeremiah sarcastically.

'You know what I mean, young man. Besides, Burke would see through the ruse all too easily. We need someone else – someone who understands the mannerisms and sophistication of an English gentleman, yet has the ability to blend into the role of a blue-collared graverobber.'

Jim's smile grew even broader then as he eyed Father Murtagh.

'Will you tell him or will I,' he asked.

'Sugrue,' said the padre, 'we have the very man for the job.'

'Charles,' declared Jeremiah. 'I forgot all about him.'

Breda lifted the glass of hot whiskey and pushed it towards my mouth.

'Now drink up,' she demanded, 'you have what my mum would call the death rattle in you' chest.'

I drank the whiskey and collapsed into a bed she had prepared. I didn't wake up for two whole days.

Seventeen – In Party Mood

The colonel stacked the chairs on top of a table and pushed them against the window. When he was satisfied that the window had been fortified, he returned to his barricade in the corner. He rested his Brown Bess and mopped his brow. He inspected his red jacket, levelling out his epaulettes. What would Sale have thought if he found one of his lieutenant colonels lying dead or, worse still, taken in civilian code. Ameer Akbar Khan would have had a field day on the strength of it. The good name of Colonel de Bromley would have been the laughing stock of the Indus Valley. He couldn't allow such a thing to happen – he wouldn't. As soon as the surprise offensive began, he had acted with speed and daring. *Bang, bang, bang, bang, bang.* He had crept out of his bunk and, keeping low, dressed in his uniform. *Bang, bang, bang.* He crawled to where his firearms lay hidden. *Bang, bang, bang, bang.* He loaded his flintlocks and checked his musket and did what any military officer worth his salt who found himself alone would do – started on his barricade.

He took out his timepiece and checked. It was eighteen minutes and ten seconds since the last shot was fired. They'd be combing for him by now. What an Afghan wouldn't give to gut a commanding officer of the British realm – he and his family would be up to their armpits in pistachio nuts for the rest of their natural lives. And there would be an even greater bonus if they took him alive.

'No lieutenant colonel on Her Majesty's service is going to be taken today,' he said out loud, 'the first blighter who sticks his head through that mess door is for it.'

The colonel sat and waited. Still the silence prevailed. He hated the silence. It was then that he got to thinking about the predicament he was in. How would he explain to his field marshal the bizarre circumstances of his separation from the thousand men he was supposed to be leading. The colonel would be demoted for this, he was sure of it. If he survived, he would be a rifleman all over again by supper time. Brigadier Sir Robert Sale did not take kindly to mistakes in the field. And he was not known for giving second chances – especially not to seasoned campaigners such as Lieutenant Colonel Maximillian de Bromley.

'If only I could get back to my battalion,' the colonel told himself, before slipping out of the barricade for a look down the hall, 'I could save this situation yet.'

The coast was clear. Placing his flintlocks inside his cutaway, the colonel crawled as far as the staircase. If he was going down, he was taking as many Afghans as he could with him.

The all-purpose room was a hive of activity. Lady Ivens knew the troupe was coming, but she hadn't expected any of them until the end of the month. Nonetheless, she was delighted.

'They waste precious little time. Imagine, building the stage already. Your manageress, I dare say, could take a leaf from their book,' she told her brother.

'You leave Miss McAndrew out of this,' returned the viscount, deep in contemplation. 'I was to use that room for a meeting of the rural council on Thursday evening. It is not a good look when the chairman is forced to uproot or postpone. And as for the stage, they hammered a couple of boards together and now they are nowhere to be seen.'

'They have gone to retrieve the remainder of the timbers,' explained Lady Ivens. 'Is it not marvellous, Brother? When your

Irish guests arrive, we shall be able to thrill them with *Maria de Rohan* on their very first night. It is a most exhilarating opera. Your uncle was saying, just the other day, how exciting it will be to see it after so many years.'

'Yes, well, as long as it does not set him off on one of his fantasies,' replied the viscount. 'Speaking of guests, we need more bedroom space. Lord Colehill has taken up my invitation at the last moment.'

'The house shall be brimful,' said Lady Ivens. 'How many is that?'

'Would you give over,' snapped the viscount. 'You do not hear me harping on when you invite your bridge players around to stay. I have never heard such a shower of chatterboxes in all my time. The viscountess swears she shall retire to Essex on their return.'

'*The viscountess*,' exclaimed Lady Ivens. 'Why *she* has a hand in every conversation. My bridge girls say she could talk for England. So, with Colehill, I make it five.'

'Five what,' asked the viscount.

'Five guests from Ireland, silly – Giles, McAndrew, Colehill, the vicar and Michael Pakenham Edgeworth.'

'Edgeworth sent a telegram – he can't make it. Neither can Reverend Smyth.'

'Oh, what a pity,' cried Lady Ivens. 'I used to so enjoy the reverend's company after service in Saint John's. He had such a simple outlook on life.'

'Speaking of simple, here comes your troupe again. Although the blighters tog out more like carpenters than actors. Perhaps I could persuade them to see to the upstairs lintels when they have finished making your stage.'

Colonel de Bromley had almost reached the butt of the grand

stairwell when the shooting began again. *Bang, bang, bang, bang.* Abandoning his position, he ran for cover behind the grandfather clock in the hallway. They must have thought he was still in his barricade because then the enemy showed itself for the first time. An Afghan – it must have been an Afghan because no self-respecting Ghilzai warrior would be seen without his lungi – was coming towards him without a care in the world. In the Afghan's right hand was a peculiar-looking pulwar sword. A prisoner of war would be very useful to a man separated from his battalion. It was now or never for the colonel as he stepped out from behind the grandfather clock and pointed his flintlocks. It was time to be good or, failing that, lucky.

'Hold it right there,' ordered the colonel.

The Afghan looked on in amazement as Colonel de Bromley advanced.

'Surrender your weapon at once,' he added. 'One false move and you're a dead Afghani.'

'What are you on about,' answered the travelling actor, dropping his saw in alarm.

'Ah, yes, the oldest trick in the book,' said the colonel, 'pretend to be on the British side. You Afghans are all the same. It will take more than a half-baked English accent to get you out of this one.'

'Have you gone mad,' exclaimed the travelling actor, 'or have you been smoking too much opium, old man?'

'A different war, a different time, Afghan. I was only a major back then.'

The travelling actor lowered his arms then.

'This is ridiculous,' he complained. 'Who are you calling an Afghan? I'm as English as the rest of you around here.'

'Place those hands in the air or I shall blow you to kingdom-come. No more scouting for you today, Afghani.'

'Now look here,' said the travelling actor. 'this has gone too far.

I'm not who you obviously think I am. I'm part of an acting troupe and I'm too busy for this sort of nonsense. All we're trying to do is build the stage for the upcoming performance.'

Bang, bang, bang, bang.

'Shut your yap,' growled the colonel. 'I'm in charge here. An acting troupe, my arse. Who is doing all that shooting?'

'What shooting?'

Bang, bang, bang.

'That's not shooting,' explained the travelling actor, stooping to pick up his saw. 'That's the stage being hammered into place. Now, if you'll excuse me, I have some timbers that need to be fetched from our trailer and cut to size.'

'Get back, you Afghan dog,' the colonel warned, marching forward and discharging his pistols.

Instead of falling dead in front of him, the travelling actor breathed an audible sigh of relief and leapt on top of the colonel. He wrestled the flintlocks out of the weary ex-officer's hands.

'I told you, old man, I'm not an Afghan. And I don't take kindly to being threatened with firearms.'

The colonel looked up, shaken and helpless.

'You will have to kill me,' he panted. 'A lieutenant colonel of Queen Victoria's military command does not surrender.'

The travelling actor took Colonel de Bromley by the lapels of his jacket and shook him gently.

'I'm not here to hurt you,' he said. 'I told you before, I'm an actor and we're building a stage. That's not the sound of shooting, it's just one of our fellows hammering some nails.'

The colonel collected his thoughts as the travelling actor helped him to his feet.

'And on whose authority are you building this stage?'

The travelling actor looked hard at the colonel and scratched his head.

'On the lady's permission – Missus Ivens, the woman who's employing us.'

The colonel laughed aloud when he heard this.

'She has about as much authority in this house as that brother of hers,' he said then. 'You have to get the proper permission.'

'Now hold on there, old man. Are you saying Missus Ivens and Viscount de Bromley aren't calling the shots around here?'

The actor had been stiffed out of his wages before on his travels and he was beginning to smell a rat.

'That is exactly what I am saying, young fellow,' replied the colonel. 'The man with the only real authority around here lives in yon house across the way.'

'Which house,' asked the travelling actor, and the colonel pointed out the window to the residence of Shaun Burke.

'You have to go and ask his permission. Tell him Lieutenant Colonel de Bromley of Her Majesty's Thirteenth Foot sent you.'

Gathering himself and throwing a cautious glance at the drawing-room door, where Lady Ivens could be heard directing operations, the travelling actor asked for the name of the man who lived in that house.

'Brigadier General Sir Robert Sale,' answered Colonel de Bromley, 'and you shall find him quite the amiable chap.'

'Pegasus soared high into the sky, his taut muscular frame and flowing white mane a tribute to Poseidon, the sea god. It was hard to believe that something so lovely could have Medusa for a mother – the gorgon with the snakes for hair, her very appearance enough to turn an onlooker to stone.'

Constance sat up in the soft chair. She looked across at the piano. Burke had wanted her to learn. He even offered to pay a pianist to teach her. But Constance refused and refused again. She had never even tinkled on the keys.

'Horses,' she whispered to the little bundle in her lap, 'the most beautiful creatures God ever made.'

Then she thought she heard the door. Her so-called husband must have done a U-turn, although she hadn't heard a horse and carriage. The love story of Diarmuid and Grainne came into her mind, the same story Burke had caught her telling Aoife a few days earlier.

'I want to hear no more of that Irish mythological bullshite,' he had bellowed. 'And I certainly don't want you filling the young one's head with it – if it's not good enough for those brats next door, then it's not good enough for her. Besides, it was the limit to have to listen to that mindless babble from the auld Gahan one in the national school in Mostrim. That's enough now, Constance, or you'll feel the weight of these fists again.'

If things weren't bad enough with Herbert and Hilda Ivens, Constance was now banned from stirring her daughter's imagination with the folktales of her own youth. To circumvent this, she had decided to change to Greek mythology. Then, before she could continue, Constance heard more noise and went to the front door.

'Hello,' she said, responding to the heavy knocks from the other side.

Constance's heart began to beat faster as Shaun Burke came back to her mind. What if this was one of his *friends* calling for a cup of tea or a lie down with his wife.

'Hullo,' said a voice from the outside, 'I'm from the acting troupe that arrived at Tunbridge House this morning. Is the general home?'

'The general,' replied Constance. 'What are you on about?'

'Excuse me, miss,' continued the travelling actor, 'but we want to erect our stage for Missus Ivens' performances. The old fellow in the army uniform told me I needed permission from General Sale. He told me the general was living here.'

'What old fella in the army ...'

Suddenly, she thought of Colonel de Bromley and an idea formed in Constance's brain.

'Oh, yes,' she gushed, 'that would be correct. The general lives here alright.'

'Well, miss, if you wouldn't mind sending him out, I would be much obliged.'

'He can't go out,' answered Constance, still trying to piece together her great plan of escape.

'Well, can he at least come to the door,' asked the travelling actor. 'Or maybe I could go in to him? I wouldn't disturb him but a moment.'

'I can't get the door open,' said Constance. 'We seem to have mislaid the key.'

'Oh, that's a shame,' replied the travelling actor, 'perhaps you could ask his permission for me?'

'I can't ask him,' conceded Constance. 'He's not conscious at present.'

'*Not conscious*,' repeated the travelling actor, 'are you sure he's okay? Should I raise the alarm in the big house and have them fetch a doctor?'

'No, not at all.'

'And why not, miss? If he's not conscious surely he needs medical care of some description?'

'No, he's grand,' Constance assured him. 'He falls into a state of unconsciousness on a regular basis. It's all to do with the shellshock he suffered in one of the wars. I usually just put him in his wheelchair and take him for a nice walk. The country air always brings him around. But, unfortunately, I can't find the key of this door.'

The travelling actor was wondering what sort of an asylum this Tunbridge House and estate really was when he heard Constance's voice again.

'You say you're erecting a stage?'

'Yes,' he replied, 'in the all-purpose room of the big house. Missus Ivens is quite excited at the prospect. She was the one who employed us in the first place, but the old man says she had no authority to do so. He reckons General Sale is our man.'

'Yes, that's right. The old man is right,' Constance reiterated. 'My husband – General Sale – is the only one who can give the proper go-ahead.'

'And who will be paying us when the performances are over,' asked the travelling actor.

'Oh, don't worry, your wages are safe,' said Constance. 'Listen to me now. If you're making a stage, I presume you have tools.'

'Of course,' he returned.

'A clawhammer of some description?'

'Yes, missus. Why I have one right here in my toolbelt.'

'Good. Could you use it to break into the house?'

'*Break into the house*,' exclaimed the travelling actor. 'Indeed and I will not. This door is made of expensive-looking timber. It's wages I'm after, not a bill the length of my arm.'

'I promise,' Constance added hurriedly, 'you are doing nothing wrong in breaking the lock on the door. In fact, I will make sure you are handsomely rewarded for helping General Sale in one of his moments of weakness.'

'Well, okay. If you say so,' uttered the travelling actor unconvincingly. 'But I find this sort of request somewhat odd.'

'Please. I'm the woman of the house and I'm asking you for

your help. There's nothing at all to be feeling odd about.'

'Alright, missus. Stand back from behind that door and I'll have you and the general out in a jiffy.'

The travelling actor walloped the door with the heavy hammer until he got a good wedge to work with. Then, inserting the claw, he hinged away at the lock until it was about to snap.

'Just another inch,' urged Constance, as she gathered Aoife into her arms and prepared to flee.

The claw sank into the lock again. Instead of the snap Constance was waiting to hear, there was a yell from across the forecourt.

'Hey, you. What do you think you're at?'

One of the protective agents came running.

'I'm trying to open the door, mate,' said the travelling actor.

'Get back at once,' ordered the protective agent, producing his firearm, 'I have a good mind to shoot you on the spot.'

'Shoot me for what,' asked the travelling actor, 'I'm only trying to help the general.'

'What general?'

'The general who lives here. General Sale. He's unconscious and has lost his keys.'

'There's no General Sale here,' said the protective agent. 'Mister Shaun Burke lives in this house. What's more, he left strict orders that this door is to remain locked at all times while he's away from the premises.'

'Well, why is the general's wife inside? I'm only going on her instructions,' explained the travelling actor. 'I'm belonging to the acting troupe that Missus Ivens sent for.'

The security guard shook his head, then drew out and gave the travelling actor a kick up the arse.

'If there's no general, then there's no general's wife,' he

snapped, 'you'll be lucky if you're not paying for the door. Now get back to your acting buddies, before I call in the police or the white coats from the nearest funhouse.'

The travelling actor went back to Tunbridge House more confused than ever. Constance sat slumped on the other side of the almost-broken lock, Aoife in her arms and tears in her eyes, her freedom so near and yet still so very far away.

Eighteen – No News ... Good News?

On the first Thursday after my arrival at Cabbage Stalk Lane, Father Murtagh burst into the kitchen and flung the *Gazette* onto the table.

'No news of him in that paper either,' he complained.

'The *Kentish Post* is a better bet,' said Jim Gorman consolingly, 'the *Gazette* isn't as intimate with the happenings of Tunbridge Wells.'

'Well, the *London Times* isn't as intimate to Tunbridge Wells either, but it had a piece on Finbar last Monday.'

'No it didn't, Father,' I argued, 'it had a piece on a man who was found murdered in Calverley Road. It didn't name anyone.'

'Yeah, but we all know who the man is.'

'But *they* don't,' I explained, 'not one journalist has published a name. So, even though the peelers have already met Finbar, they may not be able to identify him formally.'

Breda put a hot mug of tea in the padre's cold hands.

'Fellas, I still think we should do the decent thing and go down to the police station. At least if we claim his body and bring it away, we can give him a Christian burial.'

'Whisht now. The peelers will have to see to the burial. That's the way of the world.'

'Ah, Sugrue, will you cop yourself on. The peelers will keep him for a while and then throw him into the first paupers' hole available.'

Jim was trying to stay out of it. I knew as much by the way he was turned towards the window. Maybe he was right. Maybe he was just trying to avoid yet another heated debate on the matter. Or perhaps he didn't really know what to make of it all. But the padre was determined to have him as an ally.

'Jim, will you talk a bit of sense into Sugrue?'

'Leave me be,' said Jim to the padre, 'I don't want us to be at each other's throats like yesterday and the day before.'

'I won't leave you be,' snapped Father Murtagh, 'I won't let any of you be until we take responsibility of this. You know I'm right, Jim, I can see it in your face. Or what class of pagans have we become? Even Stone Age man, with all his brutish behaviour, looked after his own with some sort of primitive burial observations. We must go down to the police station and claim Finbar's body. We owe it to Missus Ryan and, Sugrue, you owe it to the Mostrim Ribbonmen. We have to see to this in the proper fashion.'

'And what if they don't have Finbar,' asked Jim. 'Who's to say his body isn't below in some morgue in London?'

'Bullshit, Jim, and you know it. That's an excuse, if ever I heard one. In the immortal words of Saint Matthew – let us render to Caesar the things that are Caesar's; and – with due regard to the recently deceased – to God the things that are God's.'

I was fed up with this argument. We were only going over old ground.

'Listen to me now, Father,' I said. 'You're forgetting the most important man in all of this – Walter Pollach.'

'You keep saying he's responsible for Finbar's death. But you have no proof, Sugrue. For all we know something else could have happened.'

'Pollach still hasn't been accounted for – not since the evening of Finbar's murder. Nobody seems to know where he is. Now, you're an intelligent man. Does that not say something, Father?'

'He could be half-way around the world by now, for all we know. Maybe he's back in Scotland?'

'Maybe, Father, but not likely. It's far more reasonable to believe that Pollach is out there, waiting to pounce. Just biding his time, along with the peelers, for someone to come looking for Finbar and then ...'

I clapped my hands together and a dozy Jeremiah got a fright.

'If he *is* a free man, why hasn't he showed up at Tunbridge estate,' asked the padre.

'Because Pollach knows there was someone else in that room, besides himself and Finbar, and he wants to find out who that someone was. He also knows that Finbar sent Shaun Burke two ransom letters, both of which were ignored. He's playing a very clever game – and we must be as clever. But if you're so determined to go down to the barracks and claim Finbar's body – and leave yourself open to arrest – then by all means, Father, be my guest. But I'm not about to join you.'

There was a silence in the kitchen then, before the padre asked Jeremiah and Breda what they thought of our present predicament.

'I'm with Sugrue on this one,' said Jeremiah, 'it would have been good to give Finbar a nice send off, but we can't take the risk.'

'And as fo' Missus Ryan,' added Breda, 'we're all really sorry fo' the lady but Finba' is still gonna be dead whethe' we retrieve his body o' not.'

'I don't know,' said Father Murtagh, trying to convince himself, 'I'd still like to get the body back. Any rumblings below in the *Queen's Arms*?'

'*Rumblings*,' answered Breda, 'with regard to this Pollach guy? As fa' as his disappearance is concerned, some say he absconded with a fancy-woman – a broad with an expensive taste in furs and a bad taste in guys. Others claim he robbed his boss blind before taking off into the sunset all on his lonesome.'

'That's old talk,' I said.

'Well, that's a good thing – is it not,' observed the padre. 'At least he's not linked to Finbar in any way. I mean, no news is good news.'

Jim turned away from the window and stood up.

'That's not always true, especially when we're talking about Walter Pollach. With all due respect, Father Murtagh, that swanky education you got at the seminary won't give you much insight into such a man. You don't know Pollach like myself and Sugrue do. We had to serve under him on a Public Works' scheme at Cranley House. He's about the nastiest bastard ...'

'Jim,' I interjected, 'language, please. There's a lady – and a man of God – present.'

Jim apologised before continuing.

'...nastiest *man* you could ever hope *not* to meet. And he's nothing if not persistent. If you only understood the way that fella hounded us the whole way to the boat in Dun Leary, Father, the night you came away with us to New York. He's a nightmare to have in your business. So, with all this in mind, I don't agree that no news is good news. We had better sit tight and watch how this develops. Because, like Sugrue, I don't think Walter Pollach has gone away. He would never be so kind.'

Nineteen – Raising the Dead

The new barmaid was a *little stunner*. That's how Shaun Burke had described her to Doctor Egon Mortuland's business representative. Gerald eyed her like a hungry dog, fidgeting with his cravat as he battled to keep his mind on the business at hand.

'He's meeting us here this evening,' continued Burke. 'Doctor Egon said so in his letter. Charles Langley is his name. The doctor wrote that the chap did a number of jobs for a surgeon buddy of his, and he's rated very highly – a *consummate professional* – in the doctor's own handwriting.'

The new barmaid was on the move again, taking drinks down to the people who were seated at the table next to where Shaun Burke sat. Gerald moved his chair so he could get a better look.

'You have had correspondence with Doctor Mortuland then,' said Gerald. 'He didn't bother letting *me* know about this new grave-robber. But he did send a telegram instructing me to meet you here and that you would fill me in.'

'*Resurrection man*,' Burke pointed out. 'Grave-robber sounds coarse.'

'Grave-robber, resurrection man, whatever. We're not going to argue over the terminology now, are we,' stated Gerald suspiciously.

Burke produced a folded envelope and threw it on the table.

'Read for yourself,' he said.

Gerald opened the envelope and took out the page. His attention was torn between the letter and the barmaid. But then she was only yards away, taking the family at the next table their change. He could smell her perfume. She turned around and smiled at Shaun Burke.

'Are you guys okay fo' everything,' she said in a sing-song accent while displaying her pearly, American, teeth. 'Y'all just holle' if you need me.'

Burke smiled and raised his glass in appreciation. Gerald checked the postmark on the envelope. But he just couldn't open the letter, so lost was he in her emerald eyes.

'Shall I compare thee to a summer's day,' he asked, taking her hand for a bold kiss.

'Oh my,' she exclaimed, fanning herself with an empty tray, 'what a gentlemanly thing to say.'

'Just something an old professor of mine used to recite,' Gerald admitted, then watched her long legs stride confidently back to the bar and disappear behind the counter before showing the envelope once more. 'Well, it's all the way from London alright.'

'You're a mistrustful old dog,' quipped Burke. 'If you bothered to look at the letter, instead of the barmaid's arse, you'd see the headed notepaper – sent straight from the doctor's office.'

'I'm sorry, Shaun. I don't mean to be suspicious. It's just that it's more like the doctor to run things – you know, to do with this business – by me first. But I see now that my misgivings are unfounded and I apologise.'

'You wouldn't apologise if the barmaid gave you a go. Your tongue was practically hanging out, you dirty little git. Now that's what I call a tasty piece of poontang.'

Gerald shook his head and puffed out his cheeks.

'I'll call her over for the fun of it,' teased Burke, and Gerald turned bright red with embarrassment.

'Hullo,' shouted Burke, ignoring Gerald's pleas to leave it be. 'Can I get some service here?'

The barmaid visited their table once more.

'What kindda service would you like,' she purred, batting her long dark lashes in Burke's direction.

Shaun smiled and winked over at Gerald.

'That all depends,' he quipped. 'What kind of service are you offering?'

'Want anothe' drink?'

'I want a lot of things,' he replied, and then licked his lips, 'the question is am I going to get them?'

'I'll get you guys anothe' beverage. Iced wate' and a whiskey, I take it.'

'And do you,' asked Burke.

'Do I what?'

'*Take it?* My friend here wants to know.'

'Does he now,' answered the barmaid. 'Well then, you' friend is outta luck. Because a lady should néve' divulge whethe' she *takes it* or not.'

By then Gerald was so turned on, his reading glasses were in danger of fogging up.

'*Divulge*, now there's a nice word,' he panted. 'You're obviously learned. Tell me, what's an educated girl like you doing working in a place like this?'

'Is you' friend always this uptight,' the barmaid asked Shaun Burke. 'It was my intension to follow my mothe' into public-house servitude.'

'Your *intension*,' replied Gerald, 'or your *intention*?'

'Both,' answered the barmaid, 'where I'm from, a good intention springs from a firm intension.'

'Speaking of where you're from, your accent,' said Burke, 'I like it. It's what a gentleman might call *alluring*.'

'You don't say? Well, in that case, you call me when a

gentleman enters the tavern and we'll all find out togethe'.'

Funny and intelligent – Burke's admiration was growing all the time. This young lady had what his boss's mad old uncle would call *spunk*.

'You're American?'

'I am fo' certain,' answered the barmaid. 'And while we're talking accents, yours is the strangest English voice I've heard since I've come to these parts.'

'That's because it isn't an English voice,' replied Burke, 'it's an Irish one. Well, a half-Irish one. My name's Shaun, what's yours?'

'Bea,' said the barmaid.

'*Bea,*' repeated Burke, 'as in Bernice or Beatrice?'

'Bea as in anything you want it to *be*,' purred the barmaid.

For a conservative individual, Gerald lost the run of himself completely when he heard that. Even Shaun Burke was getting hot under the collar at this enchantress and her subtle innuendoes.

'Bea as in Breda,' she said eventually. 'And you' friend here, does he have a name?'

Gerald, who had been disrobing her in his mind, snapped out of his fantasy.

'Gerald,' he said, and taking her hand he placed another kiss on her elegant fingers.

'Oh, I stand corrected. We do seem to have a gentleman in the house afte' all,' said Breda.

'I can be a gentleman too,' returned Burke, taking Breda's other hand and getting to his feet, 'it all depends on the lady.'

But instead of kissing her hand, Burke planted a big sloppy smooch right on her full, crimson-waxed, lips. He searched for a spark of attraction. Breda's green-eyed stare gave no indication of how she was feeling. Privately, it unsettled him. Publicly, the boldness he had displayed in breaking the ice would have to be backed up. Therefore, he would continue to act the playboy until she was just another notch on his bedpost. He had already made up his mind – he had to have her. It was as simple as all that.

'What's the stuff on your face,' asked Gerald.

'Where,' replied Burke, patting around his mouth and cheeks with a napkin.

'It's still there,' said Gerald, pointing to the exact spot. 'It seems to be a white powdery substance.'

'That would be my fault,' confessed Breda, 'and it serves you right, Shaun Burke. Afte' all, you did go in fo' you' kiss unannounced.'

'And it's not the only kiss I'll be going in for, unannounced or otherwise,' Burke retorted.

'Cheeky brat,' quipped Breda.

'You'd want to be careful with all that rouge and powder,' warned Gerald, as Breda was walking away to serve another customer, 'over here in England, a made-up face is considered a dirty face.'

'She's a rare beauty all the same,' Burke pointed out. 'Real poontang – she's practically begging for it.'

'I don't know,' whispered Gerald. 'I'd take great heed with that one.'

'Well, she had you pegged from the moment she set those gorgeous eyes on you,' snapped Burke in return. 'You *are* an uptight little bastard, Gerald. And all because I made progress with her.'

'It's not that,' replied Gerald. 'She called you Shaun *Burke.*'

Burke looked at Gerald like he was about to choke him with his own cravat.

'She did, and why wouldn't she? That's my name, isn't it? You cooled off her quick enough – you that was bursting at the seams to have a go.'

'You're not listening to me, Shaun. How did she know your surname?'

'Because I introduced *myself*. And then, she introduced *herself*. You should try it sometime, Gerald. It's the first step on the road to getting into a girl's drawers.'

'But you only introduced yourself as Shaun. You didn't ...'

'Oh, forget it. It's not my fault if you can't pull a young one. But don't be so miserable just because I have the sand to pull one. Now you can go out to the privy and pull something else, for all I care. That's the problem with all you city boys, you pussyfoot around the good-looking ones like they're made of bone china. Down here in Kent, we don't mess about, we grab them by the arses and they love us for it.'

Minutes later, a young man in a grey fedora appeared through the door and flitted his stick-thin body in and out through the tables to where Shaun Burke and Gerald were seated.

'Are you the doctor's men,' he whispered, looking around while combing his little ginger beard with his fingers.

'We are,' answered Shaun Burke, 'you Langley?'

'At your service,' he answered, extending a long scrawny arm and shaking hands hastily with them both. 'Charles Langley. And you are?'

'Shaun Burke.'

Then he turned swiftly towards Gerald.

'And what might I call you,' asked Langley.

'Gerald is my name.'

'Gerald, who?'

'Just Gerald. Gerald will do you for now,' he replied.

Breda left the bar and came towards them again.

'What will you have,' she said.

'Another one of you,' answered Charles, as he took off his hat and bowed.

'And what, may I ask, is wrong with the original,' quipped Burke.

'A dollface this beautiful has to be married,' replied Charles.

'If I was you, I'd put my hat back on my head,' cracked Burke, 'married or not, she'd hardly go for a ginger.'

'Excuse me,' said Breda, 'but I find ginge' hai' such a turn on, especially when he's got the freckles to match.'

'I'll have whatever he's drinking,' declared Charles Langley, pointing at Burke's glass.

'Not anothe' *iced wate*',' moaned Breda, 'talk about the last of the big spenders. What a bacchanal affai'. At least Gerald has got some moxie about him. A nice strong whiskey – now that's a real man's drink.'

This brought a smile to Gerald's worried face. But his reservations were growing by the minute – why would a lowly bar wench use a word like *bacchanal*. Some of his former Oxford classmates might not have had the wherewithal to use such a word.

'I'm afraid the doctor will have to increase my wage if I'm to start drinking whiskey,' said Charles. 'I'll have an ale instead.'

'Carling alright, darling?'

'Still a tad rich for my station in life,' returned Charles, 'any Carillon's in the house?'

'Carillon's Ginge' Pale it is then,' confirmed Breda.

'*Real man's drink*, my hole,' snarled Burke, still smarting from her iced-water remark, and Breda afforded herself a secret smile on her way back to the counter.

'Wow, look at the hips on her,' exclaimed Charles, 'I wouldn't mind giving her ten inches of prime Essex sausage meat and making her bleed.'

'What are you intending to do,' asked Burke, 'put it in four times and give her a box on the nose?'

Everyone, including Gerald, laughed then – but it wasn't long before he returned to his natural cautiousness.

'So, you're from Essex,' he probed, with the first chance he got.

'Yes,' Charles confirmed, 'Chelmsford to be exact.'

'And how do you know the doctor,' persisted Gerald.

'I don't,' returned Charles bluntly, 'I never said I knew him. I work for him – the same as you. But I've never met Doctor Egon in person.'

'You *work* for him, but you've never *met* him,' continued Gerald. 'Is that not rather odd?'

'Listen here,' said Charles aggressively, 'I'm not here to answer your questions. I don't know you from Adam – for all I know you could be a peeler?'

Gerald stared hard at Charles when he said that. It was Shaun Burke who attempted to lighten the mood.

'Now girls, don't start with the hissy fits. There's no need for all the questions, Gerald, or the accusations, Charles. I assure you, there are no policemen present.'

'That's good to know,' replied Charles, as Breda came back with his pint of Carillons. 'But you could never be too careful.'

'A ginge' ale fo' a ginge' male,' she joked.

'Relax and blow the froth off that,' said Burke.

Charles settled in his chair and took a slug of ale.

'Okay,' he said apologetically, looking at Gerald, 'maybe we got off on the wrong footing here. Now, let's get down to business. Where can we get the freshest cadavers with a minimum of fuss?'

'Peeler,' mouthed Gerald, under his breath.

'What's that,' asked Burke, turning suddenly in his chair as Breda stooped to lift some empty bottles from a nearby table.

'Nothing,' answered Gerald, and as he listened to Charles's suggestions his eyes narrowed with suspicion.

'Look at the tits on that, boys,' gasped Shaun Burke. 'Where has she been all my life?'

'In America, by the sound of her,' uttered Charles.

'Never mind her now,' snapped Gerald, 'Doctor Mortuland's business comes first. We can look at the wench when our work is done.'

'Here, here,' agreed Charles. 'Never was a truer word spoken.'

Twenty – The Great Escape

It was a day of such rarity – a day when Lady Ivens could be found in the kitchens.

'Miss McAndrew, there you are. Why I have riddled the house in search of you. Mister Burke requires your attention this instant.'

'Well, Mister Burke will just have to wait,' responded Sheila. 'I'm watching over this new girl while she makes dinner. I have to be sure she's doing everything correctly. Then, I have a time-management meeting with some of my more seasoned housemaids.'

'You go ahead,' said Lady Ivens, 'I will see to her. I mean, how hard could it be?'

Even the new girl – who was but a week in the job – wondered at what she was hearing.

'He seems to be in an outrageous fluster for a babysitter,' Lady Ivens added. 'He came into the drawing room like a tornado. I believed he was about to strike one of the poor maidens, such was his temper. That man really ought to control his emotions. Do go ahead, my dear, for I do not want a repeat of his earlier tantrum.'

So Sheila went ahead, but only to tell Shaun Burke she wasn't available to look after his daughter that same evening. As soon as she arrived next door, she learned that it was not about babysitting at all.

'Do you see any child for minding,' he roared. 'Go on, have a good route around the house.'

Then he took a banknote from his coat pocket and held it out to her.

'I'll give you twenty pounds, right now, if you can find a child for minding. And I'll double it if you can find the mother of a child for minding.'

Sheila was almost afraid to speak, such was the ferocity with which Burke flung things about his sitting room.

'With all due respect, sir, why send for me?'

'Why send for you? Are you serious? Or are you just having a laugh at me like the rest of the women around this house?'

He grabbed her by the arm and pulled her.

'Ye're all in on it. I know ye are.'

'In on what,' replied Sheila. 'Mister Burke, let go of my arm, you're hurting me. Have you gone mad?'

Then one of the protective agents appeared at the door.

'You fucking numbskull,' growled Burke. 'You were supposed to lock the door, you silly little bollocks.'

'Please, sir, I'm sorry. I was sure it was locked. I mean, I thought I locked it.'

'Oh, you were sure it was locked, were you? Well then, maybe she just walked through the wall like a ghost. Is that what you're trying to say? Are you saying I married a ghost?'

'No sir,' answered the protective agent, 'I'm not saying that at all. I just want to apologise. We'll find her, I promise. At the moment, we're searching every inch of ground from Strawberry Hill Farm right over to Ramslye – and we've deployed some men to the forest.'

'You wouldn't find your arse in the bath,' said Burke, crossing the floor and taking the protective agent by the scruff of his collar. 'You better pray that they're found. Because, if they're not, your job will be the least of your worries. Now get your lazy hole out there and start looking.'

Burke returned his attention to Sheila.

'Miss McAndrew, did Constance share anything of her plans to leave?'

'No,' Sheila retorted, insulted by the question, 'this is the first I've heard of it.'

Burke placed his soft hand around Sheila's slender throat.

'Are you sure? Because if I find out that you're keeping my business from me – and it is most certainly a man's business when his wife is plotting against him – the viscount won't save you.'

'Stop, will you. I told you I never ...'

Sheila took into a fit of coughing and Burke retracted his hand.

'Good girl,' he said, and winked at her. 'We can all have our little secrets now, can't we, Miss McAndrew? Some secrets that are best kept hidden, and some secrets that are best told back to a husband. Wouldn't that be right, Miss Mc...'

Burke's attention was broken again. This time he raced to the window, opened it and shouted at his servant, Hernandez.

'Get in here, Pig. I've been looking for you for over an hour.'

'I hear what happen, Senor Burke. Que mal negocio. I look for wife and chile for you.'

'You obviously haven't been looking hard enough, Pig. Go and bridle a couple of horses. Take out the Brougham and search the roads. And Pig, read my lips – do not return home without them. Do I make myself clear?'

Sheila could hear a *si senor* before the window was snapped shut and latched up again. She was feeling aggrieved at having her neck squeezed. It was nothing to do with her if Constance and her daughter had taken flight. When he turned around again, Burke was still in a state of agitation. But he made an effort to be nice this time.

'I'm sorry, Miss McAndrew, this whole business has really got to me. I'm worried sick about my wife and child, but I shouldn't have taken it out on you.'

She signalled her forgiveness with a nod. He took out a handkerchief and wiped his brow. Sheila thought he was going to start crying by the way he looked into the hanky. But he blew his nose instead and returned it to his pocket.

'You see, Miss McAndrew, they could be anywhere by now. In danger, who knows? My darling dote of a wife and a daughter barely old enough to walk. They could be lying in a gripe somewhere, stone dead in some freezing field. Oh, I just don't know what I'll do if they're not found soon. I'd give anything, you know, to have them back here with me – safe and sound. Money doesn't matter at a time like this. What is money anyhow, without the ones you love? Do you know where I'm coming from, Miss McAndrew?'

She nodded again and made for the door. He held out an arm, halting her progress.

'If you think of anything – anything at all – or anywhere they might possibly have wandered off to by mistake, I'd be very grateful,' he whispered.

He took a gold sovereign from his breast pocket and pressed it into her hand.

'Very grateful, indeed. But don't say anything beyond in the house, I don't want the viscount thinking I can't control my own wife.'

Sheila nodded again and left him there – a forlorn figure staring out a window.

On her way back to the big house, Sheila took a detour through the stables. Knowing Constance as she did, and her love for animals of the equine variety, Sheila thought it worth her while to take a peek. She didn't even have to search. All she had to do was look at the bolts on the stable doors. They were all closed – as they should have been – except for the one at the far end of the stable yard. She tiptoed her way across and pushed the door gently. There was Constance, on her knees in the straw, and her daughter Aoife cradled in her arms. It reminded Sheila of the Nativity scene – with horses instead of cattle and sheep. All that was needed was Saint Joseph, three wise men and a shepherd or two. Constance couldn't see her, as she was turned the other way.

Sheila stepped away from the door and had a think. It would have been proper order for Burke if Constance did escape. She deserved to escape. And Aoife deserved to be brought up in a world without her father – if indeed he was any blood relation to her. If this life held any justice worth noting, then Constance would have held out until nightfall. Then, when Hernandez had parked the Brougham, Sheila would have hidden mother and daughter inside the carriage while she herself drove into the night – leaving the occupants of Tunbridge estate to eat her dust in the process.

Sheila worked it out in her head as she continued on for the big house. She could have had Constance and her baby dropped at the train station in Maidstone and the Brougham back home in its garage and the horses in their stables in less than three hours. Come the next morning, nobody would have been any the wiser. As she neared the steps of the front entrance, Sheila turned on her heel. She had given this enough thought. It was time to do the right thing.

On the way back to the stables, Sheila found herself reminiscing about days of old – days when she and Constance had shared everything from belladonna, rouge and moisturisers to a dressing-room and work schedule. Well, almost everything. The one thing Sheila craved more than anything else was something Constance had refused to share. That was her bed. The first moment Sheila had laid eyes on her – as Constance stood trembling in the hallway of Cranley House with her grandmother by her side – she had fallen deeply in love. And Sheila had never fallen out of love. Even when Constance rejected her advances, Sheila still secretly pined for her affections. And when she took another – a girl called Annie McKeon – for her lover, it was of little comfort to Sheila. She eventually pushed Annie away. Because the simple truth was that there was just no substitute for Constance.

'We could have been so good together, so happy and fulfilled,' Sheila heard herself say, as she gripped the door by the open latch and prepared to spring her plan into action. 'But then the bitch had to go and ruin it all on both of us.'

With a loud thud, Sheila pushed the latch closed. As she walked away, she brushed a tear from the corner of her eye and steeled herself against the banging and pleading from inside the secured stable door. As she marched on towards the Burke residence, she felt something in her coat pocket. It was a gold sovereign piece – the one Shaun Burke had given her a short time earlier.

'What is money anyhow, without the ones you love,' she said, echoing Burke's own words. 'We'll see about that, won't we.'

It was time to do the right thing for sure – and the right thing was not to separate a husband from his wife. Burke could have Constance back, safe and sound. But he would have to pay Sheila for the pleasure, and pay her handsomely at that – a single gold sovereign bit was only the tip of a very lucrative iceberg.

Twenty-one – Old Friends and Foes

'I love to see yon words,' confessed the viscount, pointing out the window at the *River Grom* signpost. 'They let me know I am but a few miles from home. No doubt, you gentlemen will be glad too. It must have been a long haul from Liverpool – not to mention the boat across.'

'It has indeed,' agreed Lord Colehill, 'but your cheerful disposition and these comfy leather seats have shortened the journey from Maidstone station.'

'She's a beautiful carriage, Your Lordship.'

'Why thank you, Mister Giles. The Marquis of Salisbury was likewise impressed when we drove him from London yesterday. The Brougham is the only way to travel long distance in this country. My road wagon would pull the heart out of the poor horses and add some hours to an already arduous journey.'

The viscount then leaned in, as if to tell his guests a secret.

'And if it is good enough for the marquis and marchioness, it is certainly not too good for my esteemed Irish guests.'

'Splendid,' said Lord Colehill, 'I must source one of these lighter buggies, they are all the go these days.'

'I must warn you,' quipped the viscount, laying a hand on Lord Colehill's arm, 'I paid a king's ransom for this little beauty – forty guineas, if memory serves me correctly. But it was worth every farthing.'

'You pay for comfort,' Lord Colehill pointed out, as Viscount de Bromley uncorked the cognac and passed it across once more.

'No thank you, Your Lordship, I've had my quota,' admitted Roger, retracting his cup.

'Come on, Giles, let us be having you,' insisted the viscount, 'it is time for you to relax. After all, you *are* on holiday, are you not, from all those jobs and responsibilities – captain of the Longford Yeomen, the militia, your tithe-proctor duties.'

Roger thought for a few moments and offered his cup across with a smile.

'How is Walter Pollach these days,' asked Roger then, 'is he still cracking the whip as your estate manager?'

The viscount's face turned sour.

'With all the excitement I forgot to mention,' he answered. 'Alas, poor Mister Pollach is no longer with us.'

'*What, is he dead,*' exclaimed Roger.

The viscount regained his cheery disposition before putting his guest's mind at ease.

'No, not dead, Giles. The scoundrel is missing. But knowing Pollach the way I do, like a bad penny he is sure to turn up. I thought you fellows would know all about this. The *Times* gave his sudden disappearance significant coverage.'

The viscount looked at Lord Colehill, whose blank expression said it all.

'Are you boys keeping abreast of what is happening over here at all? Anyway,' continued the viscount, 'some months past, Mister Pollach went missing without a bye or leave. The local constabulary have drawn a blank in their investigations.'

'Very peculiar,' said Lord Colehill. 'I met him briefly during the search for Sugrue and his villainous friends, about four years or so ago, and his application impressed me then.'

At the very mention of my name, Roger Giles shot a curious look in Tom McAndrew's direction.

'Pollach headed up the militia on that occasion,' added Lord Colehill, 'if my old grey matter is still in working order.'

'He was *with* them, not *heading* them,' snapped Roger, 'and a bloody hindrance at that. Are you still going ahead with the performance in the absence of Walter, Your Lordship?'

'Why not? You talk as if he is deceased,' replied the viscount. 'Mister Pollach never liked opera to begin with. Speaking of absentees, it is a darn shame about poor old Duxbury.'

'Oh yes, I forgot all about Lord Duxbury,' said Lord Colehill, 'his advanced years prohibit his ability to make the journey. Yet he sends you warm regards and appreciates your invitation, Viscount.'

'Indeed, he was a grand old topper,' continued the viscount, 'stone mad after skirt, he that would hardly poke the fire. Edgeworth could not join us either, and I had so much to ask him on seed planting.'

'Unfortunately, Michael Pakenham had to return to India,' replied Lord Colehill. 'He was called back unexpectedly due to his expertise in the field of botany – concerning some sort of excavation being carried out by the military – but he assured me that he will call on you the next time he gets home. He asked me to present you with this, Your Lordship, as a token of his goodwill and appreciation.'

Lord Colehill produced a camera from his travelling portmanteau and handed it to the viscount.

'Marvellous. The viscountess will be delighted with this,' uttered the viscount, sitting the camera beside him on a cushion. 'She has the local artists' hearts broken painting portraits of her in all her finery.'

Lord Colehill had a good laugh and said the camera would save all concerned a great deal of time and expense. The viscount looked out again as the carriage skipped onto Eridge Road.

'Not far now, chaps. A left at the Broadwater and I dare say we are home and dry,' he said. 'Tell me, Mister McAndrew, have you forgotten how to speak the queen's jargon, or has the cat got your tongue?'

Tom McAndrew, who had been sipping his cognac, reddened slightly.

'I'm sorry, Viscount de Bromley, I'm not much of a conversationalist.'

'That may be so, yet I have heard a world of good things about you.'

Then the viscount turned around to Lord Colehill again.

'He certainly has rewarded our faith in him, Colehill. I am told eighteen and fifty was a record year.'

'Indeed,' answered Lord Colehill, 'he has more than doubled our overall collections since his appointment six years ago. And you were told correctly, Your Lordship, last year was the largest collection of tithes since records began.'

'Bravo, young man,' gushed the viscount, 'when I heard, I just had to have him over. They are calling him the guest of honour at Tunbridge House.'

'Oh now,' said McAndrew bashfully while pointing at Roger Giles, 'this man here had more to do with it than me. I only plan things out. He does the bulk of the collecting, especially around Mostrim.'

'He means to say *Edgeworthstown*,' quipped Lord Colehill, 'and I thought we had him properly trained. But we'll let him away with a slip of the tongue this time.'

'Does he really,' asked the viscount, ignoring Lord Colehill's jibes. 'The last I heard of it, Giles was working for Randolph Routh. Now there is a turn up for the books.'

'I only guarded his food depots,' explained Giles. 'The *Vigilantes for Economy* gave me work when I was unemployed. It wasn't like I was changing parties.'

'No, more like changing horses… in mid-stream,' snapped the viscount. 'Or have you never heard the sentiment: *once a Tory, always a Tory*? I hope you lasted longer in your job than John Russell.'

Roger Giles stroked his grey beard in a huff as they wheeled right onto the great avenue of Tunbridge House and estate. The viscount looked out the carriage window again, only to see Hernandez making his way in the opposite direction towards Strawberry Hill Farm with a bag on his shoulder. He rang the bell immediately, bringing his driver to a halt, and pulled open the window.

'Hullo,' he bellowed.

Hernandez looked back, but then kept going.

'I say, Hernandez, come hither.'

Hernandez dropped the bag and came back to the carriage.

'I hope that's not a bag of eggs,' joked the viscount, and the only one who didn't laugh was Hernandez himself.

'Ola, senor, how may I help?'

'Would you give my man a hand with the luggage, Hernandez?'

'Si, senor.'

'Jolly good. You can follow us on up. Here's a little something for your trouble.'

The viscount tossed a shilling in the direction of Hernandez and closed out the window.

'Are you always so charitable towards your servants,' asked Lord Colehill.

'He is not my servant,' replied the viscount ruefully. 'Unfortunately, he belongs to the man who lives across from me.'

Lord Colehill adjusted his monocle for a better look at the

house the viscount was pointing at through the window.

'A fellow by the name of Shaun Burke,' continued Viscount de Bromley. 'Hernandez is his right-hand man. Despite offering Burke thrice the going rate, Colehill, he refuses to strike me a bargain. And who could blame him. If I got my hands on a man like Hernandez, I would not sell him either – not for all the tea in the Marquis of Salisbury's cellar.'

Lord Colehill blushed at the sound of Burke's name. But he had the good sense to remain silent, as the carriage turned into the forecourt where the viscountess and a procession of housemaids waited excitedly in a guard of honour either side of the entrance steps. The viscount was the first to alight, throwing his cane in the air and removing his stove-pipe for a theatrical bow. Tom McAndrew stepped down from the carriage in a somewhat more subdued manner. He turned and glared at the Burke residence as young Annie McKeon came into his mind. Then he returned his attention to the welcoming party. But to his sheer disappointment, his daughter was nowhere to be seen. So he just put on a smile and followed Roger Giles up the steps to the entrance, thanking the housemaids as they curtsied and kissing the viscountess's glove as he strolled by.

'My darling wife would like to invite you all to a champagne reception in the great room,' declared the viscount as he led the way, arm-in-arm with the viscountess.

As they passed under the grand stairwell, Tom McAndrew spotted his daughter at last – on the landing where the staircases came together. She seemed upset, but the moment she saw him she rushed down the steps and into his arms.

'Oh, Father,' she sobbed,' I've missed you so much.'

'I missed you too, child. What's the matter? I thought you'd be full of the joys of life, the first out to greet us.'

They remained in their embrace while the others continued on to the great room and Hernandez chugged by, weighed down with an assortment of luggage.

'I'm scared,' Sheila admitted.

'*Scared?* Whatever are you scared of, child?'

He broke from her hug to see her face, but she looked away guiltily.

'The police have been hounding me, Father. I don't know what to do.'

Tom McAndrew's face changed from an expression of mild concern to something a lot more serious.

'Is this to do with what that young McKeon girl has been saying?'

She nodded in the affirmative.

'Well then,' he continued, 'you don't need to be scared. All you need to do is tell the truth. It's very simple. Start right now with me. Tell me exactly what happened, beginning with Constance Ryan's alleged abduction. Tell me it all, and we'll figure the rest out together. I promise, my darling.'

As he stroked her neat ginger hair, the viscount reappeared from the great room. He looked even graver than Sheila.

'Excuse me,' stammered the viscount, 'they're expecting you in the hall, sir.'

'I'm having some time with my daughter,' Tom McAndrew replied curtly, 'whom I haven't seen since you moved her here a full year ago next week.'

'It's just that the Marquis has been asking after you,' continued the viscount.

'You go ahead,' answered Tom, 'tell him I'll be in when I'm ready.'

The viscount took a few tentative steps towards the great room and then turned on his heel.

'Miss McAndrew, the housemaids require your presence this

instant. There's an emergency of some sort in the kitchens.'

'*An emergency!*'

'Yes – and a sizable one too, by the way they were talking. Run along now. I'll see to your father until you get back.'

Sheila took to her heels in the direction of the kitchens while Viscount de Bromley ushered her father towards the great-room door.

'What sort of an emergency,' asked Tom.

'Who knows? Perhaps it's not even as big a deal as they're making out. You know how dramatic girls can be,' replied the viscount, as a wave of relief washed over him, 'sometimes they make a mountain from a mole hill.'

Twenty-two – The Bodysnatchers

They approached from the Benhall Mill Road direction and parked in the shade of an oak. Shaun Burke looked back at the long trailer and then across at the high walls and massive iron gates. The fog wasn't thick enough to call a proper friend.

'Are you sure he said eight o'clock,' Burke asked.

'*Around about eight*, those were his exact words,' replied Charles Langley, 'and he should know – he's the head janitor of King Charles the Martyr Church.'

'Well, there's still a light burning in there,' said Burke, pointing at the graveyard gates.

'Wait a minute, Mister Burke, that must be him. He's on the move now.'

Langley and Burke watched the lantern as it floated towards the gates. Then the caretaker's outline was close enough to see. He joined two ends of a heavy chain with a large padlock and, picking up the lantern again, headed off into the fog in the direction of Forest Road.

'Go and check the gear,' ordered Burke.

'What am I looking for,' asked Langley.

'The usual stuff. I thought you said you were a seasoned campaigner? Anyone would think you were on your first job.'

'You and all,' countered Langley. 'You're breathing very fast for a professional. Are you sure you're up to it?'

'Don't worry about me. You should be more concerned with getting on with business. Bring me the bolt cropper.'

Charles went back to the long trailer and uncovered the tools of his new trade. He noticed a couple of shovels, a pickaxe and a crowbar. He took the bolt cropper to the perch.

'And you're sure this place isn't manned,' asked Burke again.

'What do you think it is – Kensal Green? I told you before,' snapped Langley, 'only the very largest graveyards around London, like Highgate and Abney Park, are manned full-time nowadays. It seems like ours is a dying trade. Sack-'em-up men are no longer as feared as we once were.'

'And there won't be any town-crying about the fella we're about to lift?'

'No,' Langley asserted. 'We went over this already. He's an old widower called Wilson – William Wilson was his full name.'

'No children, brothers or sisters?'

'None at the funeral at any rate,' replied Langley. 'The vicar had to organise the pallbearers.'

'Right, I'll crack the lock and away you go,' instructed Burke. 'Remember what I said. If anyone comes along, get in behind the nearest yew tree – there's one directly across from that grave you'll be digging.'

'What do you mean, *you'll be digging*. I saw two shovels in the trailer – one for me and one for you.'

'No, one for you and the other for you – just in case you break a handle. I made it quite clear to Doctor Mortuland that I won't be doing any digging. If you don't like it, you can take it up with your employer. And, for heaven's sake, take off that stupid hat. Who ever heard of a graverobber going to work in a fedora?'

'I'll take it off if you agree to dig,' suggested Langley.

'Better hop to it,' said Burke, handing over the second shovel, 'extinguish your light when you reach the grave. I'll bring across the crowbar when you're down at the coffin. One other thing, Langley – if you get caught, you're on your own.'

Charles Langley went flat out. He faced the graveyard gates as he worked, stopping now and then to make sure there was nobody snooping around. When he wasn't digging, he was putting the pickaxe to use – breaking up ground and removing stubborn rocks. It wasn't an easy job despite the loose gravel of the freshly filled-in plot. But within the hour the nose of his shovel struck something with a hollow thud. He was there. It was time to give Burke the whistle. But as Charles was climbing out of the grave, he noticed a light coming in his direction. Lifting the substitute shovel, he ran behind the yew. He watched the white smoke of his breath as the outline got bigger and closer. He held the shovel aloft and waited to strike.

'Langley,' called a voice in the direction of the grave, 'where the fuck are you?'

It was only Burke bringing over the crowbar.

'I thought I said I'd give you a whistle,' said Charles angrily, stepping out again.

'I was testing you out,' quipped Burke. 'What's taking you so long? That hole was only filled in today.'

'I'm on my own here. You want it done faster – *you* dig.'

'Don't be such a baby, Langley. Here, open her up.'

Burke threw Charles the crowbar and he climbed down into the grave once more, snapped the lid off the coffin and handed it up to Burke.

'They don't make them like they used to,' Burke said, inspecting the twisted coffin hinges and running his hand along the wood.

Langley was face-to-face with William Wilson for a second time that day. Charles had seen him prior to the funeral service, before the vicar had the coffin closed. William looked so much at peace that Charles would have liked to leave him be.

'I thought you said he wouldn't smell,' Burke whispered into the hole.

'He doesn't,' replied Charles.

'It must be you then, Langley. Because someone reeks to high heaven.'

'Do you want me to leave him here,' snarled Charles. 'I don't mind, Mister Burke, I'll just walk away and tell Doctor Mortuland he can get someone else.'

'Keep your hat on, Langley. I was only trying to lighten things up.'

Charles made several attempts to take William Wilson out of what was supposed to be his final resting place. In the end he had to climb right into the coffin, swing the deceased's arms and torso across his own slender back, and use his skinny legs to drive them both upward.

'Grab him, quickly,' panted Charles, about to collapse under the weight, and Burke dragged the corpse the rest of the way to the surface.

'I'll take his legs,' said Burke, once Charles had climbed out of the grave and got his breath back.

They carried William Wilson's body from gravestone to gravestone. When they reached the long trailer, they hurriedly covered the deceased with bags of manure and headed for the Bayham Road. It was time to get back to Tunbridge estate as fast as the horses' legs could take them.

'I thought you said there would be no rigor mortis,' quipped Burke, as they wheeled away. 'He's as stiff as Benjamin Disraeli's upper lip.'

'Shut up,' snapped Charles Langley, 'and don't be annoying me. You try lifting a dead weight the like of him six feet out of a grave. I think my shoulder is out.'

'Ah, don't be always whining, Langley. It's a good feed you need – to put a bit of meat on those bony arms and legs.'

'I'm not whining, I'm injured for certain. And I'm not leaving your house until I'm back in the full of my health.'

'*My house,*' exclaimed Burke, not a bit happy at this new addition to the plan. 'Have you no home of your own to go to?'

'Yes, *your house,* or the next time you can go and fetch your own dead body.'

Twenty-three – By Invitation Only

Lady Ivens' heart soared to the clouds as she gazed upon the all-purpose room's amazing transformation. The scene had been beautifully set and everything was ready to go. Her mind returned to those halcyon days, when she and Lord Ivens were so blissfully in love. And the time – it was May 8, 1847 – when they had accompanied her uncle, Colonel de Bromley, to Covent Garden in London to see the premiere of *Maria di Rohan*. Lady Ivens could see him still, resplendent in his cutaway jacket, as she sat down in the front row and imagined how it would feel on her big night – the hum of the capacity crowd as they waited eagerly for the curtain call. She was right to insist on a new curtain. Replacing the tattered old red one gave the new stage an even bigger lift. Of course, her brother had fought her on this and every other issue since the troupe arrived. She felt the comfort of the new seating and thought back with satisfaction on her struggle to have it installed.

'Why not move your acting friends in on a permanent basis,' the viscount had suggested sarcastically, 'or, better still, sell the blighters the house. Because at the rate you are spending money on them, I will not be able to keep a roof over our heads much longer.'

'Oh Brother, do lighten up. They are only a few seats,' Lady Ivens had pointed out.

'Poppycock, only a few seats – *eighty* upholstered pads you say – when stools would have done the job. Before that, it was only a stage curtain – when the old curtain was just fine. Well, if you think I am spending any more hard-earned money on leather seating then you are very badly mistaken, Sister. Benches will have to do.'

'*Benches,*' Lady Ivens had exclaimed, 'how am I expected to look the Marquis of Salisbury or his elegant wife straight in the face while my less distinguished guests sit on benches too? I shall be the butt of every joke from here to Essex House.'

She felt relieved that she had stuck to her guns as Lady Ivens ran her fingers along one of the eighty, smooth, upholstered chairs. The only way to get the men in her life to loosen their purse strings was to shame them into it. It was the same with her estranged husband, before he scooted off with the half-his-age, hired-help, slut. Lady Ivens puffed harmoniously on a cigarette and suddenly realised she had left her drink in the drawing room.

On her way out, she got distracted by what Lady Ivens termed the *VIP area*. These were the special seats, raised on a makeshift platform and closest to the stage. They were the height of comfort, especially since the housemaids had embellished their upholstery with pillows and blankets. This was where the marquis and marchioness would perch themselves. The colonel, too, would be required to sit here – if only to keep an eye on him. Naturally, her brother and the viscountess were also catered for in the VIP area, as was Lord Colehill. But Lady Ivens made no provision for those two Irish fellows with him. She felt it would be somewhat distasteful if they were to be seen socialising on an even footing with the household. No, that would not do – at least not at one of Lady Ivens' soirees. Giles and McAndrew – or whatever their names – would just have to make do with the communal seating. There was nothing else for it.

She looked around the dimly-lit room. The sconces at full tilt would transform it, adding warmth and ambiance to the occasion. If only her brother had agreed to the installation of a chandelier – not even a new chandelier, but one borrowed from a back bedroom would have sufficed. It would have iced the cake for Lady Ivens.

'Your Ladyship, the caskets of wine you ordered for the reception have just arrived,' said one of the housemaids, taking her mistress out of a daydream, 'and Miss McAndrew is not around to sign.'

'That brother of mine will be the death of me, him and his emergency at Essex House.'

The housemaid stood with a blank look.

'I'm sorry, Your Ladyship, but the wine merchant will not accept a check-in from any of the rest of us. He insists on a signature from you or Miss McAndrew.'

Lady Ivens sighed loudly and plucked the cigarette from its holder.

'Am I to do everything about this place,' she grumbled. 'McAndrew is getting paid to be manageress. And yet my brother insists on taking her away to Essex for a whole week. Only for my guiding hand, this house would go to rack and ruin.'

The tired-looking housemaid stared back disbelievingly at her mistress.

'You sent off the invitations?'

'Yes, Your Ladyship,' answered the housemaid, 'pardon me, Your Ladyship, but you were one invite short.'

'Impossible,' said Lady Ivens. 'I had forty invitations sent back from the printing press on Pembury Road – forty invitations to match the forty names in my address book. Do not vex me, child, I counted them myself.'

'I'm sorry, Your Ladyship, but we had none for Madame Zukhov.'

'Are you calling me a liar, you little whelp?'

The housemaid curtsied and declared that she was by no

means calling her mistress a liar.

'Well then, run along and tell the wine merchant I shall be with him anon.'

The housemaid curtsied again and scurried away, while Lady Ivens took off her glove to search in her handbag. She was indeed a liar for she had not forty invitations sent back from the printing press, but forty-one. Now Lady Ivens would be forced to send Madame Zukhov, the decrepit old bitch, the invitation she was keeping as her souvenir. Taking it out, she put on her glasses to savour the words one last time:

Dear ....,

Viscount and Viscountess de Bromley, in conjunction with Lady Ivens, cordially invite you and a companion to the following performance:

MARIA DE ROHAN

AN OPERATIC PLAY BY THE TALBOT ACTING SOCIETY

ON FEBRUARY 14 AT 8 P.M.

IN TUNBRIDGE HOUSE

Followed by a champagne reception in the Great Hall

'Perhaps Madame's advancing age should be respected. She may be better off at home,' said Lady Ivens to an empty all-purpose room.

She folded the invitation and placed it in her bag once more. Suddenly it came to her. She would send Madame Zhukov a telegram instead. That way, Lady Ivens could hold on to her souvenir and still keep the old bitch sweet.

'It's like happy hou' around here tonight,' joked Breda, as she pulled on the pump once more.

'Every hour I spend in your company is a happy hour,' replied

Shaun Burke, 'give them all another drink. And make my friend's an Irish or Scotch. I wouldn't inflict English whiskey on my worst enemy,'

'But you've already gotten everyone a drink,' Breda pointed out.

'What are you, my financial advisor? Just do as you're told – like a good little girl.'

For a moment, Breda flashed a defiant green eye in Burke's direction. He was such an ill-mannered punk by times, she would have loved to fire the whiskey into his face. But then she remembered Constance, alone and afraid, and thought better of annoying him. She knew that she had to stay patient. After all, Burke was a hard one to break down. Not even an injured Charles Langley – his shoulder throbbing as he helped Burke stash a dead body in de Bromley's disused stable – was allowed inside the front door of the Burke residence.

'Go up to the big house,' Burke had suggested, when Langley pushed to gain admittance, 'they'll look after you. My wife and child are sleeping, and I don't want them roused.'

Despite the stern warnings from myself and the others at Cabbage Stalk Lane, Breda was still intent on succeeding where Charles Langley had failed. She would trick her new admirer – by seducing him – and gain access to his home. But she had to play her hand right. So, she smiled and filled the customers a second drink from Shaun Burke. Then she undid another button in her blouse and hiked up her skirt, before taking the iced water and Ballantine's finest down to the table where Burke sat with his close friend, Gerald the cravat-wearing Londoner.

'Good man, Burkey,' shouted someone from a stool at the counter, 'a decent fellow – no matter what they say about the Irish.'

Shaun Burke raised his glass and smiled in the direction of the shout. As Breda rested her tray and handed out the new drinks, she stooped deliberately low.

'How are the twins,' asked Burke cheekily.

'What twins,' she replied, still stooped and collecting empty tumblers from the table.

He was looking at her breasts under the low-buttoned blouse. It was only then she pretended to catch on to his meaning, faking embarrassment and covering up quickly.

'Well, I see that they're well nurtured at any rate. What do you think, Gerald?'

Gerald wasn't concentrating on the ripeness of Breda's breasts, he was tapping his folded gloves off the end of the table.

'I say, Gerald, what do you think ...'

'I heard you,' he snapped. 'Mmm.'

'Mmm? Is that all you can say,' rasped Burke. 'You that was ...'

'I think I'll leave you guys to it,' said Breda before fleeing back to the counter, empty glasses in one hand and her drinks tray in the other.

'Me that was what,' asked Gerald.

'You that was nearly wetting your trousers over her the last time you were here.'

'Well, that was the last time, wasn't it? I'm not wetting my trousers over her now.'

'What's wrong with you anyway? You're in awful funny humour tonight.'

'I wouldn't say that,' answered Gerald. 'I wouldn't say I'm any more humourous tonight than other nights.'

'You know what I mean – funny as in peculiar. For a start, you were all over Breda when you saw her first.'

'All over her?'

'Yes,' replied Burke, *'all over her*. You know exactly what I mean – in poontang terms. You seem to have gone off her, even before you've had a chance to get *on* her.'

Gerald pulled his reading glasses down his nose and rubbed his eyes.

'I don't know. There's something about her that just doesn't sit right,' he said. 'Do you notice the way she flirts with us, but not with the other customers?'

'Yeah,' quipped Burke, 'that's because she's gagging for a bit of Irish stewing meat. All barmaids are horny little jills. Why should she be any different?'

'I just don't know,' returned Gerald, lifting his whiskey to his lips. 'What's this?'

'A Scotch. That English whiskey you were drinking should be kept for sick cows.'

'I told you not to go spending all that money I gave you in one shop,' warned Gerald.

'Lighten up,' said Burke, 'it's a Scotch, not the Romerwein. Besides, everyone knows I'm a man of means. Nobody can suspect me of anything, no matter how much money I splash around the place.'

'Where's your mate,' asked Gerald. 'I thought he was supposed to be here by now.'

'Yeah, he will be, any minute. Why do you ask?'

'The doctor wants another job done,' said Gerald.

'Along the same lines as before?'

'No. A bit different – a cleaner job altogether.'

'I'm certain, whatever it is, we can fix it,' Burke assured him. 'Same price though – fifteen pounds.'

'Same price – fifteen pounds,' repeated Gerald, 'only don't say anything to Langley about it for now.'

Burke shot his business partner a confused look, then nodded his head in agreement.

'Speaking of money,' Burke added, looking towards the barmaid once more. 'Give me a moment.'

Gerald raised his eyes to the heavens as Burke raced back to the pub counter.

'I almost forgot your tip,' he said to Breda, placing something in her hand.

'This is *five shillings*,' she replied. 'I can't take this – it's too much.'

'You can and you will,' insisted Burke. 'Haven't you waited on us hand and foot. You deserve it and more besides.'

Breda attempted to return the money but Shaun Burke was having none of it.

'And what's more, I have another little present I want to give you.'

He searched in his coat pocket and pulled out a piece of paper.

'This is a much sought-after invitation to a very exclusive get-together,' he revealed, handing it across the counter for Breda to read. 'I got it especially for you.'

'Why especially fo' me,' she asked.

'Because we can look back on this as our first real date,' replied Burke, and he winked at Breda to underline his intentions.

'*First real date*,' she exclaimed, 'I hardly think so. Afte' all, ya hea' a lotta stuff tending ba', and I heard that you are a married man.'

Burke looked unsettled, but he soon regained his suave exterior.

'A married man I may be – but married only in name. My wife is a half-wit, worse still, an almost total idiot. It troubles me to say it, but I must finally face the truth. Her mind is not her own. We are only together for appearance sake. But I haven't the heart to divorce her. You see, I want her to remain at the marital home so

I can take care of her.'

'Such a pity,' said Breda sadly.

'Indeed,' added Burke, 'a young woman who should be in the prime of life.'

'It says here I can bring a companion,' chirped Breda. 'Oh goodie.'

'You're not attached,' asked Burke, failing to hide the alarm in his voice.

'Heavens no,' answered Breda, 'well, not in the same way you're attached. But we're all attached to somebody. My fathe' likes operatic plays, and I guess he hasn't seen *Maria de Rohan* since his last trip to Venice.'

'*Venice!* Is your father some sort of nobleman?'

Breda burst out laughing then.

'Of course. He's the Archduke of New York.'

She laughed again and Burke joined in.

'Would I be working in a tavern if my fathe' was a nobleman? But I'm not joking about taking him along, he loves a good stage production. He's been to every play I eve' acted in.'

'*Acted in? You,*' gushed Burke.

'Yes, *acted in*,' confirmed Breda. 'You're looking at one of the finest leading ladies who eve' threaded the boards of a New York theatre.'

'I don't believe you,' he continued. 'You're full of shite.'

'It's true,' said Breda. 'Regan, Desdemona, Ophelia, Juliet; I've played many of Shakespeare's leading ladies and a whole lot more besides.'

Burke was astounded to hear this. It only made him want her more.

'Perhaps I could send a carriage? Where do you live,' he probed.

'Neve' you mind. We'll take ou' own carriage, thank you all the same. My fathe' would be none too happy if a strange man was to interfere in his duty.'

'You still consider me a strange man then? And no wonder, we haven't yet been formally introduced,' Burke announced, bowing cordially, 'in fact, I don't even know your full name.'

'Indeed,' replied Breda, 'I'm well aware of that. And you won't know it eithe' – not until the night of the play.'

'Very well,' agreed Burke, taking her hand and kissing it tenderly, 'until the night of the play, or should I say, the night of Saint Valentine's – the most romantic night of the year.'

The squeaking sound put everything on hold. It was the first time in weeks that the letterbox of the salubrious *Loch Lomand* cottage on Ferndale Hill had been called into action. Then, after a lengthy suspense, the crossbar was swung back towards the fire and the tea-making process recommenced. In the hallway, a lone envelope awaited further inspection. The clipping sound of black, studded, riding boots was magnified on floor tiles. One set of pudgy little fingers reached down towards the floor, the other set combed through a head of black and grey hair. The envelope gave up its secret to the movement of large, purple, hanging jowls.

Dear Mister Pollach,

Viscount and Viscountess de Bromley, in conjunction with Lady Ivens, cordially invite you and a companion to the following performance:

MARIA DE ROHAN

AN OPERATIC PLAY BY THE TALBOT ACTING SOCIETY

ON FEBRUARY 14 AT 8 P.M.

IN TUNBRIDGE HOUSE

Followed by a champagne reception in the Great Room

'Well, well, well, Mister Burke. It looks like we're away to a party,' he whispered then, taking the new horsewhip from his belt and lashing it against the hall door.

'And am I going to be ever so glad to see you.'

Twenty-four – Eighteen

'He didn't send me any money for you, just the fifteen pounds for Mister Burke,' claimed Gerald.

Charles Langley shrugged his shoulders indifferently.

'I'll get paid when I go up to London,' was his riposte, 'did he at least thank me for my services?'

'No,' replied Gerald, 'not even a mention.'

'Good,' said Langley, 'least said, or in this case *written*, is soonest mended.'

Shaun Burke held up Gerald's whiskey glass along with two fingers and Breda reached for the bottle of Ballantine's single malt.

'You have to try out this new Scotch,' demanded Burke, 'our friend here says it's to die for.'

'I need to go 'round to your house again,' said Charles, 'I think I lost my watch and chain while we were stashing the ... merchandise.'

'I was in that stable since,' answered Burke defensively, 'no sign of any watch or chain.'

'Yeah, well, I've checked everywhere else. It's probably in the hay.'

'There's no need to come over,' returned Burke, clearly annoyed at Langley's persistence, 'I'll check the hay for you.'

Breda was back at their table, looking and smelling gorgeous.

'An iced wate' for you, Miste' Burke, and two shots of whiskey.'

Seizing his moment, and her beautiful fingers once more, Gerald went on the offensive and treated himself to a lingering kiss.

'Shall I compare thee to a summer's day.'

She laughed her beautiful laugh and remarked upon how cultured English gentlemen were compared to the wiseguys she had known while growing up on the hard-hitting streets of New York.

'Thou art more lovely and more temperate,' added Charles in an impromptu fashion. 'Rough winds do shake the darling buds of May; and summer's lease had all too short a date.'

Shaun Burke sprang to his feet in a fit of applause while Breda curtsied and pretended to catch her breath. Gerald sat quietly and sipped from his glass.

'You have to hand it to the Essex boy,' declared Shaun then, 'he upstaged you there, Gerald.'

'Indeed,' said Gerald. 'He knows his Shakespeare, I'll give him that.'

'Sonnet Eighteen,' Charles Langley pointed out, 'and you don't have to hand me anything. Because the truth of the matter is that I don't know my Shakespeare as well as I might pretend. It's actually just something someone used to say.'

'Oh, please, do tell,' insisted a much more interested Gerald. 'Who used to say it?'

'It doesn't matter,' replied Langley hurriedly, 'just some old schoolteacher I once knew – nobody important.'

'Well, I think it sounds lovely,' stated Breda, 'especially coming from you guys. I swea' I'll neve' tire of the gorgeous English accent. It's most stupendous.'

'I know you said you'd sort it, but I might come over myself and take a look tomorrow. That watch is very dear to me.'

Burke was getting annoyed again, his face beginning to redden at Langley's dogged pursuit of his jewellery.

'I told you before, I'll look after ...'

Suddenly, Burke received a kick from under the table.

'Let him come over and look,' interjected Gerald.

'But ...'

'No buts about it, Mister Burke. Langley is obviously anxious to find his timepiece, and I would be too. After all, a good pocket-watch and chain is worth its weight in gold. We head for Maidstone in the morning and ...'

'Maid...'

Burke received another kick on the shin.

'Yes, Maidstone,' confirmed Gerald, with the most subtle of winks, 'remember that delicate little matter you were on about earlier? Anyway, while we're away, Mister Langley could save you time and effort by searching the old stable himself.'

This was music to Charles Langley's ears. Not only had he now a valid excuse to return to Burke's house – where he was known to the protective agents – but Burke himself wouldn't even be there. This was the chance Charles had been waiting for.

'We'll have a briefing at some stage tomorrow,' continued Gerald, 'as Doctor Egon needs a corpse for early next week. So, Mister Langley, when you're finished searching in the stable, get the guard on duty to let you into the house. Is that okay with you, Mister Burke?'

Burke looked anything but okay with this suggestion.

'We should be back by dinnertime, Charles,' concluded Gerald, 'if you don't mind waiting inside for us, you know, away from prying eyes.'

Charles couldn't believe what he was hearing. He wanted to kiss Gerald's feet in gratitude and cheer to the rafters. The lucky break he had been seeking just kept getting better.

'And cuckold the Irishman while he's at it,' Burke barked at Gerald, 'over my dead body. He can wait for us outside.'

'I don't mind waiting at the stables,' Charles assured him. 'After all, I respect a man's home and his privacy.'

In the house or *at the stables* – it was all the same to Charles Langley. Because by dinnertime the next day, when they were due to have their briefing, he and Constance Ryan and her daughter Aoife would be a long way from the Burke family residence and the town of Tunbridge Wells and the beautiful garden county of Kent.

Twenty-five – Tootles to Trouble

The poll was split at two apiece. Charles would have the casting vote, if he ever showed up.

'He was in great humou' leaving the tavern last night,' stressed Breda, 'o' as you guys would say – *topping form*. A little tipsy maybe, but totally fine.'

'And you're sure Burke or this Gerald fella didn't overhear ye,' repeated Father Murtagh.

'He winked and said *everything is on course* – period.'

'And what about Burke and Gerald, did they see the wink,' continued the padre.

'No, Pops, they didn't. And even if they had done, it couldn't have aroused suspicion. Those guys were winking at me the whole night through.'

'You're sure that's all he said,' added Jim Gorman, trying his best to spark up a dudeen.

'That's it,' said Breda, 'he smiled and winked as he whispered it and then left without anothe' word.'

Father Murtagh had that *look* back on his face. It was the same look he wore the night he boarded the *Erin's Queen* in my place.

'Don't be getting carried away,' I told him. 'He's late, that's all.'

'Langley's never late,' Jim pointed out from behind a cloud of smoke.

'Will you go over to the fireplace,' snapped the padre, 'if you want to puff tobacco.'

'Well excuse me for breathing,' quipped Jim.

'Settle down, fellas,' I said. 'If he told Breda everything was on course, then I think it only fair to trust the gossan. After all, Charles is a very shrewd operator. If what I hear is true, a little ginger man had you two boys going about New York City chasing shadows.'

Both Jim and the padre shot a contrary look in Jeremiah Figg's direction.

'You wouldn't hold your piss,' said Jim.

'What,' replied Jeremiah, 'I didn't tell him.'

'Leave it to God now, lads, enough with the playacting,' I said, 'it's time for us to focus.'

The evening would be soon upon us and Breda would be going to work. So, I felt we had to press on without Charles for the time being. Breda had arrived home from the previous evening's shift with a very formal-looking invitation to a play and reception at Tunbridge House. That's what the vote had been over. Myself and Jeremiah wanted Breda to have nothing to do with it – Jeremiah making the valid point that Burke already held one girl against her will without adding a second. Father Murtagh and Jim Gorman were both in favour of Breda attending. Jim pointed out that we had come to Tunbridge Wells to rescue Constance, and refusing to take the opportunity this invitation now offered amounted to backing away from our responsibilities. The padre agreed, adding that as he would be escorting Breda for the duration of her stay at the estate, no harm could possibly come to her.

'After all,' he stated, as if concluding a sermon, 'there's an old Irish saying: *a bee was never caught in a shower*. And I'll be making sure our little bea is not caught up by that shower above in Tunbridge House.'

'Hold your horses, Father,' returned Jeremiah. 'Why should

you be the one who gets to escort her?'

'Because I'm the obvious choice,' replied the padre, and Breda's cheeks lit up. 'Besides, we have no other option.'

'Yes we do,' said Jeremiah, as jealousy flashed in his eyes, 'why can't I escort her and we'll tell Burke that her father couldn't make it?'

'No, Jeremiah, we won't do that. We've already discussed this,' continued the padre. 'Burke is obviously fixated on Breda. So, the last thing we want to do is send a youngster like yourself as her chaperone. That would serve no purpose except to incur Burke's wrath.'

'But you're a bit on the young side yourself,' argued Jeremiah, 'just because you're a *father* doesn't mean that you'd pass for *Breda's* father.'

'Jeremiah has a point there,' suggested Jim. 'You're too young for the job, Padre, plain and simple. I say Sugrue should pose as Breda's father.'

'How can I pose as her father, I used to work for Viscount de Bromley,' I said.

'So what,' muttered Jim, while intermittently puffing on his clay pipe, 'you only worked at his estate, the same as hundreds of other people. He wouldn't know you personally – and he would never recognise you. If we were talking about Roger Giles – or even Walter Pollach – then I'd agree, Sugrue, it couldn't be done. However, the viscount and you had no face-to-face dealings. But for a few badly-drawn *wanted* posters and a handful of newspaper articles – published almost five years ago, I might add – he wouldn't know you from the next man.'

'And by the time I'm finished fixing you' hai' and dolling you up,' added Breda, 'you' own mothe' would get it hard to be cognisant of you.'

'I should hope so,' joked the padre, 'she's in the Mostrim parish register-of-deaths a good many years by now.'

'I don't know,' I sighed. 'Burke can be a very tricky character. He's a danger at the best of times. I'd never forgive myself if I put young Breda in any kind of trouble – and this plan has the potential for serious trouble.'

I was thinking of my daughter-in-law, Ella May, and how I would react if she was in Breda's position.

'Tootles to trouble.'

The padre begged her pardon.

'I said *tootles to trouble*,' repeated Breda. 'You guys have all these Irish sayings but us New Yorkers have a few of ou' own. Need I remind you that we have an innocent young woman to save from the clutches of a dressed-up madman, so I'll say it again – tootles to trouble. I feel I'm pretty erudite to what this is gonna take. Because, many years ago, my own mothe' was forcibly removed from Ireland to be a breeding-stock bride in he' adopted country. I don't want this type of history repeating itself, so let's stand up to this wretched scoundrel and truncate his shambolic marriage once and fo' all.'

'What does that mean,' Jeremiah asked her, 'in layman's language?'

'It means it's time to get ou' asses ove' to Tunbridge House, gentlemen, and do whateve' it takes to set Constance Ryan free. I'm really looking forward to setting foot in Ireland fo' the first time, but I ain't setting foot in it without Constance by my side.'

Twenty-six – The Hunters and the Hunted (Part 1)

Twas early early all in the night, the yeomen cavalry gave me a fright;
The yeomen cavalry was my downfall, and taken was I by Lord Cornwall.

It was midday when Charles Langley walked the great avenue of Tunbridge estate. He could hear the chloroform sloshing around the bottle in his coat pocket. In the other pocket was his handkerchief and some lengths of cut rope. The justice of it all was not lost on Charles – poetic justice, as he called it. For if this Annie McKeon was to be believed – and there was no reason for her to be doubted – Constance Ryan had been drugged with a napkin drenched in chloroform before her unlawful removal from Cranley House.

The moment he entered the forecourt, Charles could see his victim-in-waiting – standing at the front entrance to the Burke residence, musket in hand and ready for use. Charles had it all planned out. He would ask the protective agent for his help in the stables. Then Charles would sneak up from behind and put him to sleep. But Charles didn't trust the chloroform to deaden a fully-grown man for long, so he brought along the ropes to be sure. Then Charles would relieve the protective agent of his bunch of keys and proceed to the house, taking those inside away to freedom. He smiled to himself as he imagined the look on our unsuspecting faces when he would unveil the elusive Constance Ryan and her daughter on the kitchen floor in Cabbage Stalk Lane.

'Are you the fellow for the stables,' asked the protective agent, resting the butt of his weapon against the door.

'I am indeed,' answered Charles, with as much naturality as he could muster.

'Mister Burke told me to tell you it could be teatime before they're back. He got a bit delayed this morning. He only left for Maidstone an hour ago.'

'No problem,' replied Charles.

'What did you lose anyway,' asked the protective agent.

'A pocket-watch and chain,' returned Charles, 'it's small enough. You wouldn't give me a hand look for it?'

The protective agent thought about it for a few moments.

'Ah, I might as well,' he uttered then. 'Sure, what else would I be doing. I'll tell you what, you go on ahead and I'll check in on the princess. I'll be along in a few minutes.'

Charles thanked him and walked around the gable towards the stable doors. This was working out a treat – like clockwork, thought Charles, and he smiled nervously at the pun. As soon as he disappeared into the unused stable, Charles crouched down inside the door. He pulled the handkerchief from his pocket and the lengths of rope went all over the straw floor. After uncorking the bottle of chloroform, Charles emptied a generous amount onto the handkerchief and adjusted his squat position. It was important that he be able to spring from his haunches. Looking around, he pulled an old trough to a position in front of him, allowing Charles to rest his elbows and take the pressure off his knees. There he stayed patiently, awaiting the arrival of the protective agent and his big chance.

Clunk!

'I bet that was a surprise,' said Gerald, wiping the horseshoe with a cloth before hanging it back on its nail above the door.

'It will be, when he comes around,' quipped Shaun Burke,

emerging from behind a haystack at the back of the stable.

'That's the thing about horseshoes,' added Gerald, adjusting the pin in his cravat, 'they're rather like the number seven – lucky for most people but not for everyone.'

Twenty-seven – The Hunters and the Hunted (Part 2)

Charles came around to the blurred image of Doctor Mortuland's man holding a bottle of ammonia under his nose.

'Wakey, wakey, arise and shaky,' quipped Gerald, 'this is no time to be lying down on the job. Especially when your timepiece is still missing. When you're finished there, Mister Burke, would you be a good sport and check that cock of hay beyond.'

Shaun Burke was finishing off the tying of Charles's legs. His arms were already secured to the wooden pillar in the middle of the stable.

'We should have cut the bastard's throat.'

'Hold your horses, Mister Burke,' said Gerald, 'don't do anything rash. Well, not until I've asked our *business partner* here a few easy questions.'

Gerald corked the ammonia bottle and put it in his trouser pocket. Charles could feel the blood tickling his neck and a throbbing pain somewhere over his right ear.

'Shall I compare thee to a summer's day. Thou art more lovely and more temperate. Please feel free to join in, Mister Langley. Don't go all shy now, we both know you have it off by heart.'

Removing his right glove with his teeth, Gerald slapped Charles across the face with it.

'Rough winds do shake the darling buds of May,' he continued, stopping the recital to grip his left glove between his teeth also, 'and summer's lease had all too short a date. Professor

Archibald would be most disappointed, Mister Langley, with your lack of enthusiasm.'

Charles returned a blank stare.

'Oh now, Mister Langley, stop this nonsense. I mention our dear old professor and you greet his name as if you've never heard of him. That's gratitude for you. I say, where is this country heading?'

Gerald gripped Charles by the lapels of his coat and dragged him forward until their noses were almost touching.

'You called him *just some old schoolteacher*, if memory serves me correctly. Imagine, the man who lectured you on conveyancing and tort law in the hallowed halls of Oxford University, and you haven't even the decency to address him by his proper title. The man who tutored you to a first-class honours degree in the laws of this land and you couldn't be bothered to give him his due acknowledgement. Well, *Mister Langley*, I am appalled. *Professor Archibald* – now say his name.'

Gerald slapped Charles across the face once more with his gloves.

'I said, *say his name.*'

'Professor Archibald,' said Charles. 'How did you find out?'

'It was easy. Who else in this world has ever recited Shakespeare's *Sonnet Eighteen* every moment he wasn't teaching? Who else taught it to every class he ever had? I called in to the Oxford University Law School just the other day – I'm an Oxon graduate too, my dear fellow, a lawman, just like you – and enquired about a Charles Langley. You should have used a different name when you tried to pull one over on me.'

'If you're a lawman too, what's this graverobbing business all about?'

'He's fingered us for sure, Gerald,' cried Burke, 'we're done for.'

'Will you relax,' said Gerald, turning right around to Burke. 'Charles has asked a simple question and I intend to pay him the courtesy of a full and frank disclosure.'

Then Gerald turned back again to Charles.

'By the way, I could ask you the same question – and I will in good time. As for me, I became interested in the work of resurrecting bodies to help out my old fraternity buddy and doctor of surgeries, Egon Mortuland. Did you know he's a member of the Oxford alumni, just like you and I? Of course you didn't, how could you. I know they're not as sought-after as they were at the turn of the century, but dead bodies are still a valuable commodity. Oh yes, you can make a killing from cadavers – provided you get your hands on enough of them. And at the price I'm paying your partner here – fifteen pounds per head – you'd want to be digging them up full time.'

'Who are you working with,' shouted Burke, taking his turn to grab Charles by the lapels.

'I won't tell you again,' said Gerald, 'settle down and stop shouting. Do you want the whole countryside in here on top of us?'

Burke let go and went silent again.

'We'll get around to all your queries, Mister Burke, with a civil tongue. But for now, it's my turn to ask the questions. What does a law graduate *like you* want with robbing dead bodies? It's obviously not the money.'

Charles nodded in agreement.

'Speak up,' growled Burke, 'or I'll break every bone in your body.'

'Mister Burke, I won't tell you again,' hissed Gerald. 'You're beginning to exhaust my patience. Let him go and stand back. Failing that, you can leave the stable.'

Once again, Burke was forced to check his temper and retire to his haystack at the back of the stable.

'If it's not the money, Mister Langley, then please enlighten us,' continued Gerald.

Burke groped around on the floor until he found a long, thick, horsehair rope. Gerald and Charles watched as he threw one end over the beam directly above the middle pillar.

'And I warn you,' added Gerald, pointing upwards at the dangling rope, 'do not make up lies, Mister Langley.'

'If I tell you will you let me go?'

'I may do,' answered Gerald.

'For the girl,' confessed Charles.

'The *girl*. What girl,' asked Gerald.

'It must be Breda he's on about,' said Burke. 'He does be whispering sweet nothings in her ear every time he gets our backs turned.'

'No, the girl in there.'

Burke looked over his shoulder at where Charles was nodding.

'I believe he's referring to your poontang,' quipped Gerald.

'I'm referring to Constance Ryan, his common-law wife,' explained Charles. 'Only everyone knows it's not a common-law marriage, but a complete sham.'

Burke, who had been winding the rope-end into a noose, was taken by a fit of rage and attempted to wrap the lasso around Charles Langley's neck. Gerald was forced to adjourn his line of questioning and hold Burke off with all his might.

'It was you who brought the coppers to my door,' roared Burke, and Gerald reiterated that there would be no more shouting in the stable.

'I don't know what you're on about,' replied Charles, 'but they will be around shortly. They know I'm coming over here. So, if I don't walk out of here unharmed, you boys are in big trouble.'

Burke looked worriedly at the noose he was redoing while Gerald took into a fit of wild laughter.

'The one small thing I requested and you couldn't even afford me that,' he said, when he had finished laughing. 'Did I not, Mister Langley, ask you for the simple truth?'

'It's nothing but the truth,' protested Charles. 'The police know the whole story, right from when Burke drugged and kidnapped the girl in the first place. If I don't leave here safe and sound, with Constance in tow, then you fellows are finished.'

'*Drugged and kidnapped*,' exclaimed Gerald.

Shaun Burke went to the door of the stable and took an anxious look around.

'Give it up, Shaun,' teased Gerald, 'I thought you had a bit more about you than all that. This bozo hasn't told the police a blessed thing. He hasn't been next nor near a barracks. Think about it – he walks in here alone, a bottle of chloroform in one pocket and some twine in the other. Use your brain, man. He's lying through his teeth to save his neck – literally.'

'Want to bet on that,' snarled Charles.

'Yes, actually, I do want to bet on it. There's no way you went to the police on this or any other matter.'

'How can you be so sure,' asked a concerned Shaun Burke.

'Because I have these things and these things.'

Gerald pointed to his eyes first and then his ears.

'And I heard this blockhead in the *Queen's Arms* referring to the police as *peelers*. That's an Irish term – and a derogatory one at that. There's no chance that anyone calling a policeman a *peeler* would look for his assistance.'

'So... pretending to be a graverobber for Mortuland was all about getting his hands on that bitch of a wife of mine? Is he soft in the head,' seethed Burke.

'I think he's to be commended. How very gallant. Charles obviously feels strongly about the young woman's plight, why else would he have come to save the day? Perhaps he knows some of her people. But a word to the wise, Mister Langley, women are very like dogs – it is imperative they have but one master and imperative they be contained on a short leash, lest they become spoilt and argumentative.'

It was then, while finishing off his hangman's collar, that Burke received his moment of clarity.

'You're with the guy who took Walter Pollach,' he exclaimed, pointing the new noose accusatively at Charles Langley's ginger head.

'I have no idea what you're going on about,' stuttered Charles.

'That makes two of us,' added Gerald.

'Constance's father, some mad Longford fucker, came looking for her a while back. When he got no satisfaction from the police, he decided to take a hostage for trading purposes – Walter Pollach, the former manager of Tunbridge estate. He sent me a couple of ransom notes before Christmas and I wiped my arse with them. But in his second note he mentioned an accomplice – obviously muggins here.'

Gerald sat up in the hay with a great big smile.

'Why would anybody feel the need to bring an acting troupe around this place,' he said with glee, 'with all the fun we're having – and just where is this Pollach fellow now?'

'Don't know – and I don't care.'

'You *don't know*. Is he alive at least?'

'I said I don't know, Gerald. Alive, maybe. Dead – hopefully. He's a surly auld Scottish cunt who won't be missed by many. Constance's father did us all a favour there. But enough about Pollach. We'd want to be thinking about this bucko and what we're going to do with him. No doubt he blabbed to some folk about the graverobbing. Who else knows, Langley? Tell us, before I string you up.'

Burke made another attempt to fit the noose on Charles before Gerald brought calm to the proceedings once more.

'I already told you, Mister Burke, that sort of behaviour is premature.'

'What do you mean, *premature*,' asked Charles, sensing a glimmer of hope.

'We'll give you every chance, Mister Langley. Tell us the whole truth – with a promise that you'll walk away from here and never look back – and your life may be spared. Tell us another fib, like the one about the police's imminent arrival, and you'll be the next body on Doctor Mortuland's slab at the Royal Hospital of Surgeons in London. Do you get my meaning?'

Charles nodded in agreement before Gerald pressed ahead.

'Who else knows about us – about the graverobbing?'

'Nobody,' replied Charles.

'Not even Breda?'

'*Breda?* As in Breda from the *Queen's Arms?* Why would I …'

'Just answer the fucking question,' growled Gerald.

'No,' said Charles.

Burke spun the noose ominously and it cut through the shafts of sunlight protruding from the cracks in the stable door.

'What about this Longford man, the mysterious Mister…'

'Ryan,' confirmed Shaun Burke.

'… mysterious Mister Ryan?'

'No,' repeated Charles, watching the knot twist in mid-air.

'Anybody else? Be very careful how you answer, Mister Langley.'

Charles looked Gerald in the eye, then shook his head from

side to side.

'And no police – you're clear on that?'

Again, Charles shook his head in the negative.

'Very well,' said Gerald, 'that will be all.'

He arose from the hay-covered floor and gave Burke the nod.

'Go ahead. I'll give you a hand with the rope.'

Without another word, Shaun Burke placed the noose around Charles Langley's thin neck.

'You were admiring my cravat, or so I was told, in the tavern the other night,' said Gerald, as Burke fixed the collar behind Charles' right ear. 'Well, now you have one of your own – a rope cravat. Goodbye, Mister Langley.'

Charles was hauled to his feet as Gerald cut him free from the pillar.

'I'm telling you the truth,' he protested, as Burke pulled on the rope. 'Let me go. I'm telling the truth.'

'I know you are,' replied Gerald, stepping behind Charles to give Burke a hand with the pulling.

'You said you'd…'

Then Charles Langley's feet left the ground, rising higher with each pull on the rope. His pleas were replaced with gasping and gurgling as he fought for every breath. The thinness of his body made the pulling an easy job. Gerald held the rope steady while Burke wrapped it around an old rusty anvil.

'No, I didn't say I *would*,' Gerald remarked calmly, as soon as the rope had been knotted into place, 'I said I *may* release you. Now, I know you've kept your side of the bargain by telling the truth, but I've decided not to release you.'

Charles' legs kicked out wildly, battling against fresh air. Yet the more he struggled, the worse his situation became.

'Not pleasant, I imagine,' said Gerald, as Burke looked on in silence. 'But don't worry, you're nearly done now.'

The struggling got weaker and the gurgling died down. Burke was first out of the old stable door. He stood in the sunlight and looked around. The protective agent was not at his post. He must have gone home, just as Burke had ordered. Then Gerald appeared.

'That's a handy fifteen pounds for you. I might get a few bob out of that one myself,' quipped Gerald. 'After all, it was my blow deadened him for you.'

Burke stood silently, as if he was dazed.

'Are you alright,' asked Gerald.

'You knew all the time,' replied Burke.

'Knew what?'

'You knew Langley was up to something, but you still had no problem letting him plunder a grave with me.'

'I had my doubts. But I didn't know for sure until I went to see the doctor,' explained Gerald.

'Why didn't you say something sooner?'

'Because, Mister Burke, there's no point in weaving the web until the fly is nearby. Would you not agree? One unsuspecting slip of the tongue – your tongue – below in the *Queen's Arms* and Mister Langley would have been over the fence and away in a jiffy.'

Burke thought hard about it and nodded his head.

'She's in on it too, you know.'

'Who,' asked Burke.

'Your little fancy tart from the *Queen's Arms*.'

'Breda?'

'Yes, Breda. Who did you think I meant, the busty bar wench from Margate?'

'No, she's not – not according to Langley anyway.'

'Wake up, Mister Burke. She's in on it alright. And I hope, for your sake, she hasn't the police in on it too.'

'She hasn't a shred of evidence,' Burke pointed out. 'So why would the police believe her?'

'Don't be so foolish. A constable would be a sight more accommodating towards an educated, sexy, American lass like young Breda than some bog-standard, shitty-arsed, mad Irish bastard like Mister Ryan – or should I say your father-in-law.'

Twenty-eight – Preparations Afoot

Sheila glanced around the corner and made a beeline for the grand stairwell. All she had to do was get past the dining room and she could be confident of safe passage the rest of the way to the colonel's bedroom. One of her staff had told her that the viscount was in a black mood since the previous night. She didn't want to run into him. Sheila was determined that nothing would spoil this day of days – when she would finally spend some catch-up time with her father.

'Yoo-hoo, Miss McAndrew,' shouted a voice from the other end of the hall.

Sheila turned right around to see Lady Ivens coming in her direction. She was both relieved and horrified.

'My dear girl, I am so glad of your return,' said the mistress of the house, to which Sheila curtsied and attempted to carry on. 'Whatever is so pressing, child?'

Sheila explained that she was on her way to Colonel de Bromley's private quarters and wanted to be on the dot – knowing the colonel's compulsion for rules and punctuality.

'Oh, never mind the old goat,' said Lady Ivens, 'he hardly knows what century he is in, never mind a few moments here and there.'

Sheila threw an anxious look towards the dining-room doors.

'Besides, he has been an intolerable thorn in my side since you departed for Essex. Those other girls leave a lot to be desired in a housemaid. I have never encountered such a crowd of babbling fools in all my time.'

Sheila made a movement towards the stairs but Lady Ivens took her by the wrist.

'Just yesterday morning, Harriet received the slightest nick of his bayonet while changing his bedsheets and she all but swooned at the sight of a trickle of blood.'

'Yes, I heard,' stammered Sheila, looking to break free, 'and with all due respect, my lady, it was enough to warrant a visit to the viscount's infirmary.'

'Nonsense talk,' said Lady Ivens, 'the infirmary, my eye. I often shed more blood from a pricked finger while tending my embroidery. By the way, Miss McAndrew, I trust you will not forget the colonel's red flannel underwear when you are leaving out his military uniform for tonight's performance. That young wench, Margaret, was having him dress in whites.'

'Don't say he had a breakout,' exclaimed Sheila.

'Oh, no,' replied Lady Ivens, 'but one cannot be too careful. I am only worried for his rheumatism. If it was not for me, nobody would worry about a solitary thing in this house.'

Sheila stifled a wry smile and attempted to gently free her wrist.

'I must push on,' she insisted, 'the colonel will be out on the landing if I wait any longer.'

'Tell me,' said Lady Ivens, taking possession of her wrist once more, 'how are they all at Essex House? I hope Lady Veronica is not drinking too much gin. She is partial to the liquor you know.'

'She's in great form,' Sheila assured her ladyship, 'never looked healthier. She's down to a bottle a day.'

Lady Ivens screwed up her nose at Sheila's joke and asked what the viscount was doing taking her away in the first place.

'Something to do with a staff shortage,' returned Sheila.

'A *staff shortage*,' repeated the mistress of the house, 'there are more girls at Essex than here. You do know that but for my intervention you would be there forever?'

This was news to Sheila.

'What do you mean,' she asked, forgetting all about her trapped wrist.

'It was my man and my carriage brought you back last night. It had nothing at all to do with my brother.'

Sheila could feel the anger rising within her. While dispatching her to Essex House, the viscount had promised she would be back in plenty of time to see her father. Sheila had been sure the horses and carriage of the previous evening had been the viscount's doing.

'Did you not know, my dear? I could hardly host this evening's entertainment without my best girl's help now, could I?'

Suddenly, it had all become clear to Sheila.

'Thank you, my lady,' she whispered, wresting her arm free and curtsying once more before making her way up the staircase towards Colonel de Bromley's quarters.

Lady Ivens continued on her way also, her head swimming with last-minute preparations. Entering the dining room, she noticed her brother reading the *London Times* amid a cluster of empty dishes.

'I take it you had an agreeable breakfast,' she said, sidling over towards his table.

He glanced sideways and shook his newspaper violently, before adjusting his chair to show her the full of his back.

'Oh please, Brother, desist from such childish impudence.'

He responded by rattling the pages again.

'I brought her back to help out tonight – to help *all of us out*. Our late mama was right; your pride is your downfall.'

'You leave mama out of this,' growled the viscount. 'It *is* true I am angry at you. But I am even more angry that I had to hear it from a snickering Shaun Burke. Why could you not have come and told me yourself. Everyone around here must surely be laughing at my lack of control in my own house.'

'Do not be nonsensical, Brother. Nobody is laughing at you. How could they – when you are the most wonderful head a household could wish for.'

'The most wonderful head who does not even know what is going on under his own roof,' added the viscount in a gruff manner.

Eleanor, one of the housemaids, arrived from the kitchens and asked Lady Ivens what she would like for breakfast. The viscount folded his newspaper and sat up intently.

'Miss Eleanor, when you have taken the good lady's order, would you be so kind as to summon the stable hands?'

Eleanor couldn't hide her surprise at such a request and neither could Lady Ivens.

'Have you gone mad entirely, Brother? Miss Eleanor is part of the breakfast crew, not a foreman from one of your farms.'

'Tell them to prepare the horses and hounds right away,' the viscount continued, doing his best to shut his sister out of the conversation.

'Horses and hounds? What on earth...,' stammered Lady Ivens. 'Are you bonkers?'

Miss Eleanor stood with her mouth open, some empty plates and a teacup in her hands, wondering was this some sort of joke.

'No, big sis, I am not bonkers. In fact, I was never as clear in my thinking. So much so that I have decided to do a spot of hunting. You know, to work off a hearty breakfast.'

He patted his weskit and smiled.

'Are you trying to sabotage this evening,' snapped Lady Ivens.

'This evening? Let me see now,' the viscount replied, pretending to be deep in thought.

'Oh my,' she sobbed, producing a napkin and forcing a tear from her eye, 'I have seen it all now. You are deliberately trying to ruin this evening's spectacle.'

'Only joking,' gushed the viscount, 'you were easily taken in, Sister. But I am going on a hunt – a mini hunt. It shan't take long. So, Miss Eleanor, rouse my Irish guests and send someone over to the Burke place. Come on now, chop, chop! It is riding jackets and boots all round.'

'But what about *my* guests,' asked Lady Ivens, 'they will be arriving to the sound of a pack of barking hounds and a host who is mucked from head to toe.'

The viscount shook with laughter, scattering his newspaper all over the table.

'Don't you worry,' he said eventually, 'by the time the first carriage rolls onto the forecourt this evening the hounds will be fed and watered and back in their kennels, and I will be standing like a new pin on the red-carpeted foyer. We are only going for a glorified trot in the countryside.'

'But why does it have to be today,' protested Lady Ivens.

'Now, Miss Eleanor,' continued the viscount, ignoring the mistress's pleas, 'leave your kitchen duties and fetch Lord Colehill, Mister Giles and Mister McAndrew at once. Tell them not to delay a single moment. And send someone over for Mister Burke.'

The viscount arose and kissed Lady Ivens' cheek.

'Dearest Sister, we shall be back before you know it.'

'He's preparing for a hunt,' exclaimed Shaun Burke, as the stable boy looked on and nodded, 'at eleven o'clock in the morning! Is this all part of the evening's performance?'

'Ne, senor.'

'Shut up, Pig, I was talking to the lad.'

'No, sir,' repeated the stable boy, 'he's very serious.'

'Is he now,' said Burke, 'well, who ever heard of a hunt starting at noon. Does he realise what day it is? We have the reception and performance in a matter of hours.'

'I'm only doing what I'm told,' replied the stable boy.

'Of course you are, and good on you,' said Burke, producing a farthing and handing it to the boy. 'Tell him I've a few things on, that I might follow him out the country.'

The stable boy nodded again and went off about his business. Hernandez made for the door as well.

'Where do you think you're going,' shouted Burke.

'Los estables,' answered Hernandez, 'dogs and horses. You go for hunt, no? After?'

'No, Pig. No. I'm going nowhere. Not now, or afterwards, or at any time. I just told the young fella that to get rid of him. I've too much to be doing today – with this evening's entertainment – to be going anywhere right now. And that fucking eejit, de Bromley, should know better than to be galivanting about the countryside today above all days. Keep going as far as the stables, Pig. Get the carriage ready and my two best horses.'

'El carruaje?'

'Just do it, Pig, and don't make a song and dance about it.'

Hernandez looked confused as he stood in the doorway.

'Oh, and by the way, load my Springfield. Put it in the perch, and make sure it's covered up.'

Hernandez bowed and set off again. Burke sat down by the piano and fingered the keys. This wasn't a day for hunting and he knew it. More to the point, the viscount knew it. Something wasn't right about it all. There was no way Burke was moving a muscle to go on any hunt, especially now that Doctor Mortuland's man, Gerald, had reneged on their latest meeting and had just completed – according to the receptionist at the Royal Victoria Hotel on Sandrock Road – the hastiest of checkouts from his penthouse suite. Shaun Burke was staying put, preparing for every eventuality – including a hasty check out of his own, if it came down to that.

Twenty-nine – The Return of the Prodigal Son

'M'lawd, m'lawd. M'loidy. Whit like. Whit like ye? How are you, m'loidy?'

Walter Pollach adjusted his wig and giggled into the mirror. It had always amused him how the English toffs pronounced their words. It was almost as weird and wonderful as the Welsh.

'The toffs. De toffs. De taffs. De toffs and de taffs had a tiff in Trafalgar.'

Walter had a swig from his glass. The sparkling pink champagne danced on his tongue. He had gone all out, right down to the pre-party refreshments. And why wouldn't he. This was no ordinary night. It was the night of his return – the night he had been anticipating for so long. Finally, it was here. And if he overspent on the wine, what harm. This night deserved to be marked in a very special way. Walter examined his drinking vessel – not a hair to be seen on the rim. The gum was dry at last.

'Oh no, m'lady, not a trace o' a Scottish twang,' he said into the mirror, comparing the wig to his unfinished beard.

It was a slightly darker grey – an identical match for the fake eyebrows – but who was going to notice. The viscount would be so busy pissing his pants over the Marquis of Salisbury and the viscountess fawning over her clutch of old dust-farting hens that Walter was confident he could have worn a clown's suit into the old stomping ground and those two wouldn't have passed a blind bit of notice. The young McAndrew one was a different matter. Walter knew he would have to be on his game for her.

'The rain in Spain falls mainly on the plain,' continued Walter, tucking his shirt into his straight black trousers.

He brushed some gum onto his replenished jowls and applied more fake hair. He buttoned his trousers and reached for his white waistcoat.

'Jolly good show. Oh my, please to mit you, mite you, meet you,' he said, taking the bottle of Veuve Clicquot and kissing it for a lady's hand.

He tugged gently at his hairy jowls. The gum had done its job. He picked up the eyebrows and almost put them on. Then he threw them back on the dresser. They might exaggerate the look. Besides, he would spend the whole evening worried about them staying in place. He went for the glasses instead.

'Respectables with spectacles,' he said, and smiled at himself in the mirror.

He was horrified all over again. The big gap-toothed smile. The gap that told a tale of his torture. The gap that used to remind him of his jailor, Finbar Ryan, but now only served to recall his debt to Shaun Burke. Walter spotted his whip in the reflection. It was coiled in the middle of the bed.

'Not tonight, my old reliable,' he whispered, unscrewing the box that held his dentures.

He was going to miss his whip tonight. He was going to miss using it on Burke. A bullet was too kind, too sudden for the fucker. Walter wanted some proper payback – a bloodbath of sorts. But what could he do – his old reliable was too hard to hide. And Lord Levington was hardly likely to attend an upmarket event with a whip hanging out of his belt.

'Tu-whit, Tu-who, a merry note; while greasy Joan doth keel the pot.'

Walter thought about what he had just said. It was the only thing he could remember from his schooldays in Glasgow. The lines sounded weird after all those years. The only thing he could remember, that was, with the exception of a bull-headed brute of a headmaster who beat his pupils to within an inch of their lives. He had another look at the whip. Oh to have that headmaster now, in that very room – him and Shaun Burke, and maybe Viscount de Bromley for good measure. Oh to wear their hides out with his trusty old whip. And stopping every now and then for a sip of champagne.

Walter fitted the plate inside his gum. The teeth filled the gaping hole perfectly. Better than that, they filled out his upper lip. He looked nothing like the old Walter Pollach as he sat down and reached for his footwear. The low-tie shoes were certainly a change, a challenge even. Walter could never remember a time in his adult life when he hadn't worn riding boots. He stamped his heels on the floor – no clicking sound. He stood up and walked around his bedroom like a drunken spider.

'Oh well, it's only for the one night,' he reasoned with the mirror, before seeking out his black tail-coat.

Walter pushed his tall stove-pipe into his curly wig and had one final look.

'I almost forgot,' he said to his image, finishing the glass of champagne.

He went to the open dresser drawer and took out the envelope. He examined the folded invitation. Not a trace of the ink anywhere. It was a good job – a great job even. The lithography had worked a treat. The Indian ink was flawless. Walter was so proud of his exploits that he just had to read it again:

Dear Lord Levington,

Viscount and Viscountess de Bromley, in conjunction with Lady Ivens, cordially invite you and a companion to the following performance:

MARIA DE ROHAN

AN OPERATIC PLAY BY THE TALBOT ACTING SOCIETY
ON FEBRUARY 14 AT 8 P.M.
IN TUNBRIDGE HOUSE

Followed by a champagne reception in the Great Hall

'Perhaps you could be my companion,' suggested Walter, looking to the corner of the bedroom where a weasel leapt up and down in its cage. 'You'd like that, wouldn't you?'

He checked the traps and then, when no dead mouse presented itself, Walter returned to the dresser for a lump of cheese.

'You wouldn't mind escorting Lord Levington, Fourth Earl of East Anglia, to the performance at Tunbridge House.'

He threw the cheese into the cage and the weasel devoured it.

'I could dress you up in a little top hat and tails and we'd look like a couple of regular gentlemen. What do you say, Captain Weasel? Want to tan on some toff's jugular at a fancy champagne reception?'

Walter lifted his glass in appreciation to his pet weasel.

'That's quite alright. I understand. Besides, Captain, we've got our own champagne. Nothing but the best for Lord Levington – eldest issue of Major Charles Levington, next in command to Lieutenant-Colonel Maximilian de Bromley at Jellalabad during the First Afghan War – and his right-hand man, Captain Weasel of the Second Cavalry Brigade.'

Walter refolded his invite and checked his Colt pocket pistol. Five silver bullets, lying snugly in their chambers, awaited their targets. He placed all in his pocket and buttoned his tail-coat. He could hear the horses' hooves on the cobbles. He checked his watch – his hansom cab was right on time.

'Don't worry, I'll see you later,' he said, looking through the bars of the weasel's cage. 'Be a good laddie and, listen to me now, daddy loves you.'

Thirty – Someone from a Previous Life

'Don't be so worried, Sugrue, nobody will know who you are. Sure, in those swanky togs, I barely recognise you myself.'

I knew Jim wasn't just saying it to make me feel better. But, as the horses jogged on towards Tunbridge House, I was going to worry anyway. I remember my dear departed mother telling that to visitors who would come to chat at our humble abode.

'That little gosur of mine,' she would say, 'if he didn't have anything to worry about, he'd make something up.'

But I wasn't the only one worried. I could tell by the long silences in the carriage. I caught Father Murtagh puffing his cheeks out when he thought no one was looking. He was nervous – so nervous he made everyone get down on their knees to say the Rosary before we left the house. Despite his attempts to humour me, Jim Gorman was the most nervous of us all. Up until the money was paid out for the renting of the horses and carriage, Jim – in a complete reversal from his original stance – had been eager to call the whole thing off.

'I have a bad feeling about this,' he had said earlier in the evening, 'almost four full days and not a word from Charles Langley. He hasn't been seen or heard from since leaving those two graverobbing bastards at the *Queen's Arms* on Tuesday night.'

'Language please,' said Father Murtagh.

'Yes, there's no need for obscenities,' I added, producing the hipflask from my coat pocket and handing it around.

There may have been no need for obscenities but I secretly

agreed with Jim Gorman. I looked across at Breda Nayle sitting on the carriage bench in her beautiful green ballroom gown, her black ringlets reaching for the woollen stole, and I prayed that I wasn't leading her into any further danger. Jeremiah was right in his observation – her dress brought out the colour of her lovely eyes. She shifted uneasily in her seat.

'I told you to bring a cushion,' I said across. 'These benches can be hard on the …'

'Ass,' she interjected, and Jim couldn't stop himself from blushing.

'I was going to say posterior,' I cracked, and Father Murtagh advised me that when you're in a hole, stop digging.

'Yeah, well, we call it *ass* in America.'

I looked out the window at the inky-blue clouds to stave off yet another bout of embarrassment and told myself everything was going to be okay. The padre asked if we should go over the plan again. I think he just wanted to pass the time.

'Florence,' cried Breda suddenly. 'His name isn't Sugrue, Pops, it's *Florence*. That's what I told Burke. If we don't start calling him by my father's name, we're gonna slip up.'

'Okay, Florence it is,' replied Father Murtagh apologetically. 'Now getting back to the plan, *Florence*, I want you to go over it one last time.'

'Jeremiah parks the carriage on the far side of the forecourt, as close to the Burke residence as possible,' I said. 'Breda and myself go into the opera. Jim and yourself, Father, remain hidden in the carriage while Jeremiah acts as footman. He is yere eyes and ears and he will tell ye when to proceed to the Burke house. Once the performance is in full flow, ye three spring into action, approaching the house from the stables – so as to remain hidden from the entrance of the big house. After the break in, ye move Constance and her baby out right away. When ye've transported them safely to Cabbage Stalk Lane, ye return to Tunbridge House to wait for Breda and myself, parking in the same place as before and remaining inside the carriage so as to avoid loitering in the forecourt and drawing attention to yourselves.'

'You're sure Constance won't be at the performance,' asked the padre.

'Yes,' answered Breda, 'I heard it from the horse's mouth in the tavern. Before pointing out to Burke that it was a father's duty to supply his unmarried daughter's transport, he told me his wife is an idiot – *not mentally capable* – and that they're only togethe' fo' appearance sake and because he hasn't the heart to divorce he'.'

'Ah, bless him,' said Jim Gorman.

'She's not in a position to partake in the festivities,' continued Breda, 'his prognosis being in his own words: *she will regrettably have to remain at home.*'

'Great! It's full steam ahead so. You won't have to worry about us,' gushed the padre, brandishing a crowbar, 'we'll be in and out of the Burke house in jig time.'

'What about the protective agents,' asked Jeremiah.

'God only help anyone, protective agent or not, who dares to stand in our way,' said Jim Gorman, securing a short stout truncheon in his belt, as Jeremiah steered the horses up the great avenue that led to Tunbridge House.

It was a long walk back from where Jeremiah parked our carriage to the grand entrance of Tunbridge House. As I pulled at the knot in my bow tie, I noticed some of the transport already parked on the forecourt. The carriages were breathtaking, the last word in modern-day travel comfort and design.

'You should have let me style you' hai',' whispered Breda, and I could tell by her voice that she too was barely holding it together.

'Leave it to God, Breda. My scar can't be seen, can it?'

She stopped me for a look and fixed my stove-pipe in a certain way.

'Now,' she said, as we stepped onto the red carpet of the entrance area, 'you're ready fo' action.'

There was a large crowd congregated around the entrance to Tunbridge House. Young women in matching pinafores and hair bands worked in tandem, checking invitations before escorting some of the more elderly guests into the house. One lady stood out in her sheepskin tippet – a drink in one hand and a cigarette suspended from a long holder in the other – as she conducted the young pinafore-wearing women's movements and referred to them as her *housemaids*. I moved closer and heard her talking with a bearded man, who gestured with his hands as he spoke.

'No, not at all, Lady Ivens,' the bearded man replied in a strange-sounding English accent. 'There's nothing to excuse. I'm the fourth earl.'

'Of East Anglia,' muttered this Lady Ivens, 'I cannot recall a ...'

'My father told me so much about the legendary Lieutenant-Colonel de Bromley. Your uncle is quite the hero in the town of Norwich. I can't wait to meet him in person.'

'Indeed. Your father's name again?'

Lady Ivens stared into space, racking her brain for all she was worth.

'Major Charles Levington,' said the bearded man, as if he was getting offended. 'Did the colonel not mention him?'

'I am sure he would have,' answered Lady Ivens. 'I just cannot recall.'

'They were together at Jellalabad during the first Afghan War. My father was the colonel's first-in-command. Your uncle used to call him his *lucky general*. And I shouldn't need to remind you what Colonel de Bromley's favourite line was back then – Napoleon's old chestnut – *I would rather a lucky general than a good* one.'

Lady Ivens took a sip from her glass and smiled.

'No, I cannot recall your family name. Must be the excitement of the evening,' she said dismissively and swivelled on her heel, leaving the bearded English gentleman to make his own way to the all-purpose room.

Breda took her invitation from her green pocket-purse and extended it to one of the housemaids at the door.

'I'll look after this,' said Shaun Burke, breaking through the line of servants and plucking the invitation from Breda's gloved fingers before taking her hand and kissing it tenderly.

Where he had come out of, God only knew. But he stood there on the top step, proud as a peacock. Not content with her hand, he boldly moved in and kissed the part of Breda's cheek closest to her lips – a manoeuvre that seemed to pique Lady Ivens' interest in yet another mysterious guest.

'This must be your father,' he declared, pumping my hand before Breda had time to answer. 'Well, am I honoured to meet you, sir.'

'Florence Nayle,' I said, 'pleased to …'

'Mister Burke, who is this most elegant young lady,' interjected Lady Ivens.

'Madam, this is my good friend and personal guest for the evening, Miss Breda Nayle, and her father …'

He looked at me for my name again. I knew he hadn't been listening.

'Florence,' I repeated.

'Indeed,' he said, a little embarrassed.

'As in the Italian city,' Lady Ivens probed.

'I suppose so,' replied Burke, 'I've never heard of it on a man. But that's not to say it isn't a fine name, Mister Nayle. Miss Breda is a thespian too, my lady.'

Lady Ivens remained silent, seemingly indifferent to this snippet of information.

'I take it you are not attached, Miss Nayle – when your papa is accompanying you in public,' she said at last. 'Are you attending university at the moment, my dear?'

'*University,*' exclaimed Breda.

'Yes, is that not where all aspiring young things, such as yourself, go to find a mate, er, I mean a suitor? Or have things changed that much since I was in girlhood?'

It was too late by the time my elbow tickled Breda's ribs.

'No,' she had already replied, 'I work at the *Queen's Arms* tavern in Mount Sion.'

'A *tavern,*' spat Lady Ivens, with the expression of a woman who had just drank a cup of hemlock.

'Yes, a tavern. And I really like my job,' added Breda.

'Hmm,' said the mistress of the house, before having a pull on her cigarette and taking Shaun Burke away to one side.

'Bringing a *prostitute* to my grandpapa's house,' she seethed, 'shame on you, Mister Burke. As if that earl from Norwich wasn't bad enough – I must have a word with whoever sent out the invitations – but a trollop from a public house!'

Lady Ivens walked off towards the reception area to have her glass replenished, leaving Breda and myself in the hospitable hands of Shaun Burke.

'Miss Eleanor will take your outer garments and show you to the all-purpose room and your seats,' he said, kissing Breda's gloved hand again. 'I must retreat for now, my lady, but you and your father may be assured of my prompt return.'

Then he bowed gracefully with one hand behind his back and said *Miss Nayle* and *Sir* to us before departing. Miss Eleanor took us from there to the cloakroom. The chandelier in the hallway was a magnificent sight. The splendour of the other rooms we passed through was lost on me due to the pounding of my panicked heart and the toing and froing of so many people. She led us into the all-purpose room and showed us to our seats. Then Miss Eleanor was gone again.

The all-purpose room was beautifully illuminated with large sconces burning at regular intervals in holders on the walls. A stage rose up before us, its beautiful red and white curtains shielding a world of last-minute activity and noise.

'Well, did he believe it,' I asked with bated breath.

'Oh yeah,' replied Breda, 'he bought it alright. A guy as arrogant as Shaun Burke wouldn't be kowtowing in front of you if he didn't think you were my dad. It's all part of his grand scheme to get me into bed, you know.'

Not for the first time that evening, I turned away with embarrassment while she laughed it up. Then, as Breda was explaining that she was only joking and how a laugh would do our nervous dispositions no harm at all, there was a tap on my shoulder. I turned around into the bearded Englishman who had been talking to Lady Ivens when we first arrived, the man whose father was Major Charles Levington – the first-in-command at some battle or war.

'How are you this evening,' he whispered.

'Very well, thank you,' I replied, 'and yourself?'

'I couldn't be better, *Mister Sugrue*. I almost didn't know you without your moustache.'

My whole world seemed to flip upside-down. I couldn't believe it. Panic seized my senses. I looked hard into the bearded man's face, then at his bushy grey curls. I had never seen him before in my life. Yet how did he know me.

'Who are you,' I stuttered.

'Nobody important, just someone from a previous life. I'm not here to annoy you, so enjoy the show,' he whispered, reading my worried face and moving away to the back-row seats.

'Who was that guy,' asked Breda.

I smiled as best I could to hide my alarm. There was no point in panicking Breda at this late stage. His words were still swimming in my brain. What could he mean: *someone from a previous life*.

'Because you look like you've just seen a ghost,' she added.

'Do you believe in reincarnation, Breda?'

She knitted her beautiful shapely eyebrows at my question.

'He's probably someone from a previous life,' I concluded, doing my best to pass it off.

Thirty-one – The One That Got Away

As I went walking up Wexford Street, my own first cousin I chanced to meet; My own first cousin did me betray, and for one bare guinea sold my life away.

I took out my hipflask and had a few nips to keep the nerves in check. Every now and then a housemaid would appear with an elderly gentleman or a glamourous old lady, plop them in a pew and be off again.

'Can I have a swig,' asked Breda.

I handed over the hipflask and told her how delighted I was that the room was filling so quickly.

'It allows us a better chance to hide in plain sight,' I added, remembering the tactic from my days in the Mostrim Ribbonmen. 'Take it easy with the hipflask, Breda, it's not what Victorian ladies would deem respectable.'

'Just as well I'm not a Victorian lady then, isn't it,' she quipped, tossing her head back and letting down a good deal of Richard Hennessy's finest brandy.

When the bulk of the guests were seated and the show about to commence you could sense the anticipation from the energy in the crowd. The red and white stage curtains shot open to reveal two trumpeters, who tested our eardrums to the full. A woman actor then came on stage and unfurled a long scroll.

'Welcome one and all,' she said, 'to the performance of the night, *Maria de Rohan*, courtesy of the Talbot Acting Troupe. Could you please be upstanding and show your appreciation for our generous hosts and their very special guests. Ladies and gentlemen, I give you Viscount de Bromley and his lovely viscountess.'

The stocky figure of the viscount swaggered into the room, saluting both sides as he went up the aisle. He still had his hair tied in a tail – and, amazingly, it was still as brown as ever. He looked ten years younger than his wife, who followed him through to the VIP area with a shy smile which she fanned occasionally. Both wore white clothes – the viscount in his evening suite and his wife in an elegant, sweeping, tulle dress.

'Lady Ivens, accompanied by Mister Shaun Burke, acting-manager of Tunbridge House and estate,' announced the speaker.

The *mistress of the house*, as she so controversially labelled herself, had a fresh cigarette in its holder and her customary glass of liquor in the other hand. Shaun Burke bowed with a hand behind his back, just as he had done when leaving us on the entrance steps, and waved a bit to the audience.

'Lieutenant-Colonel Maximilian de Bromley and Miss Sheila McAndrew, manageress of Tunbridge House and estate.'

Sheila escorted an old man up the aisle. She seemed to have aged significantly. But, then again, time waits for no one. As for her chaperone, he moved like the rattling of pots and pans. But he was a sight to behold. His head was adorned with a scarlet band, complete with the lion and crown cap badge. He wore grey pants and the shiniest knee-length boots I have ever seen. But his service dress-jacket was most impressive – the tailed-coatee in the mad-red of Britain boasted a star beneath a crown insignia. It held gold epaulettes and a white shoulder belt. There were seven or eight large ribboned medals attached at the left breast-pocket area and a long silver sword in its scabbard, chained where the shoulder belt met with the lieutenant-colonel's left trouser pocket. He neither waved nor smiled as he shunted along, his neat grey moustache and clear blue eyes a study of concentration.

'The Marquis of Salisbury and his enchanting marchioness,' declared the speaker.

Into the all-purpose room pranced another pony-tailed poser, with gold breeches to match his coat and bicorn hat, all complimented with white stockings and black, silver-buckled, shoes. The marchioness's hefty chest filled out her blue, jewel-encrusted, dress. She wore plumes in her hair, reminding me of some of the more elegant horses waiting in the forecourt. She fanned away as if her life depended on it, following her husband into the reserved seating.

'Lord Colehill of Shrule in the midlands of Ireland, chairman of the Foxhunters' Association there; Mister Roger Giles, a captain in the Irish yeomanry; Mister Thomas McAndrew, senior financial civil servant and chairman of the Tithe Proctors' Association of Ireland.'

After the initial shock of hearing their names, I felt sick to my stomach as I watched them make their way up the aisle. They saluted the acclaim of the crowd. Lord Colehill, a small round man, walked side-by-side with my erstwhile enemy, Roger Giles. This time his grey beard wouldn't hide his identity from me – even if he hadn't been introduced. Giles looked no different from the last time I had seen him – some three and a half years previously on Dun Leary pier. Behind them came my one-time best friend – the man I had spent much of my life fighting the British with – Tom McAndrew, escorted by his daughter Sheila, who was taking her second trip up the main aisle. He had lost some of his hair but looked trim and healthy nonetheless. It was strange to see him there – smiling and waving to the audience and savouring their applause. Sheila looked in our direction absentmindedly and I quickly raised a handkerchief to my face. They fitted snugly into the reserved seating with the other distinguished guests.

'*Maria di Rohan*. A three-act melodrama tragico by Gaetano

Donizetti. Act one, scene one,' proclaimed the woman actor, before rolling up her scroll and exiting the stage.

I can't say I took to the opera, at least not in the same way as Breda enjoyed it. Despite the circumstances surrounding Constance, the actress came out in the young American and she was soon engrossed. I was more concerned with the bearded gentleman – the man who knew my name – sitting in the back row. Each time I checked, he seemed to be revelling in the happenings of the stage. I remember thinking that maybe he got my name from Tom McAndrew – or, worse still, Roger Giles. No, that couldn't be the case. Neither McAndrew nor Giles knew I was there – yet. All I could do was keep one eye on my bearded friend in the back row and the other on my bearded enemy in the front row. The net was closing in, I could feel it.

Yet, despite the distractions, I had a fair idea of what was unfolding onstage. It was your classic love triangle scenario. Riccardo, Count of Chalais, falls in love with Maria, Countess of Rohan. The problem is that Maria has been forced to secretly marry Enrico, Duke of Chevreuse – a fella in big trouble as he has killed the nephew of the powerful Cardinal Richelieu. It ends up with an arranged duel between Chalais and Chevreuse. However, before the duel can take place, a shot can be heard in a secret passageway.

'Come out, you Ghilzai bastards,' shouted the old Colonel, standing up in the VIP area and drawing his sword. 'Show yourselves, you blighters.'

There was pandemonium in the reserved seating area. Sheila McAndrew, who sat next to Colonel de Bromley, locked his arm to prevent any further lunging and tried to wrestle the sword from his grasp. The viscount, with arms outstretched, shielded the marquis and marchioness from any harm. Viscountess de Bromley and her sister-in-law, Lady Ivens, moved away and plonked themselves on two ordinary, non-cushioned, chairs – the viscountess fanning her face for fear of swooning and the *mistress of the house* draining her glass for all she was worth. Shaun Burke sat back and laughed with all his might. Lord Colehill laughed too, thinking the colonel's actions were part of the performance. Roger Giles and Tom McAndrew looked at each other, not knowing what to do. Eventually, order was restored. The colonel's weapon was restored to its scabbard, he was restored to his chair, and the show restored to the stage.

Chevreuse appears with a smoking pistol and tells Maria that Chalais has turned the gun on himself. Then Maria begs her husband to turn the gun on her too.

'Life with infamy to you, faithless woman,' shouts Chevreuse, and the curtain falls.

We all got to our feet and gave a rousing applause, as the curtain reopened and the entire production team stood before us and bowed. I gave a glance to the rear but the bearded gentleman's seat was empty. Panic gripped my mind once more. I looked all around as the crowd gave another deafening cheer, but Major Levington's son, or whatever his name, was nowhere to be seen. He had somehow got away.

When the curtain dropped for the final time the audience proceeded to the reception area. The champagne was soon in full flow.

'You looked like you were enjoying the action,' I said.

'A wondrous production,' answered Breda, trying to pick up a square of cheese with a pointy wooden stick, 'the stage, the scenery, the singing, the acting, the whole freaking call sheet – down to the use of the props. It even sounded like a real gunshot.'

'It sure did, Breda. The poor auld colonel thought it was Napoleon back from the dead. He got fairly excited.'

'I thought he was gonna behead someone with that sword,' she added.

'Use your fingers,' I said eventually, as I watched her prodding the cheese, 'or that lump will be full of holes.'

'It's full of holes already,' Breda pointed out, throwing away her stick. 'But God made fingers first, I guess.'

'I'm going to have a look in the forecourt,' I whispered. 'You stay here, Breda. If our carriage is outside, we'll make a ...'

'There you are, you beautiful creature.'

When I turned around, Shaun Burke was coming towards us.

'I was looking for you everywhere,' he said, taking Breda's hand again for yet another kiss. 'Put that cheese down and follow me please.'

He took the drink out of Breda's other hand and attempted to drag her away.

'You're coming with me, young lady. I promised you a tour of the estate after the performance, and a tour of the estate you're going to get.'

Breda was taken unawares, stumbling forward into his waiting arms. It was time to put a stop to Burke's gallop.

'What's the meaning of this,' I snapped.

Gathering himself together, he smiled and then apologised.

'An oversight on my part, sir. I should have asked your permission first. May I, Mister Nayle, have the honour of taking your wonderful daughter on a grand tour of this humble palace. I promise to have her back to you in no more than half an hour.'

'No,' I said straight out. 'I'm afraid I must decline.'

'On what grounds,' he stammered, clearly offended.

'On the grounds that I don't know you well enough, Mister Burke. I'm not in the habit of leaving my daughter alone with strangers.'

'Oh, is that the way of it?'

'It is, Mister Burke, I'm sorry to say. And I would prefer if you read no more into it. I don't wish to insult you in any way.'

He smiled and shook my hand.

'No offence taken, Mister Nayle.'

'Maybe another time,' I suggested.

'Perhaps,' he whispered. 'Or perhaps I could save a little face, you know, in front of the other guests, and bring you along – as a chaperone. That way, we'll all be happy. I'll get to take your beautiful daughter on the tour I promised and prevent a deal of public embarrassment. And you won't be leaving her unaccompanied with a strange man. What do you say, Mister Nayle? Will you do me this favour?'

In the end, what *could* I say. The crafty Shaun Burke had me exactly where he wanted. So, I stalled him as long as possible while I drank my champagne. But before I could think something up, he led us out of the reception area – Breda looking wide-eyed with worry and I praying that the Burke residence would not be part of his grand tour of Tunbridge House.

Thirty-two – The Battle of Tunbridge House

Around the time that Colonel de Bromley was drawing his sword in anticipation of a Ghilzai onslaught, Jim Gorman, Father Murtagh and Jeremiah Figg were scaling the stable wall outside the Burke family home. The padre snapped the lock on the back door with a crowbar and they were in. They left the dark kitchen behind and proceeded towards the lit-up room at the end of the corridor.

'Be careful, the child could be awake,' whispered Jeremiah, taking a grip of Jim Gorman's shoulder to halt his progress. 'We'll scare the life out of her.'

'What are we supposed to do,' replied Jim.

'It'll be alright, Jeremiah,' said the padre, 'we're taking them away … to safety.'

They opened the door gently. The sitting room was illuminated with candles. The soft chair faced the fire. The padre approached it with caution.

'Miss Constance,' he said.

But the chair turned out to be empty.

'One false move and ye're dead,' a voice warned, as two protective agents with rifles aimed stepped out from behind the old piano.

'Tie the bastards up,' the voice ordered, 'and then fetch Mister Burke. Toss the crowbar. Careful, Stanley, that one's got a truncheon. If you happen to hear the sound of gunshots while you're away, Stanley, it'll be me blowing these scumbags to smithereens.'

The champagne reception was going a storm. Housemaids were being run ragged – refilling glasses and replacing food trays. The happy hum of conversation reverberated through the great room, the dining room and the study – the designated reception areas for the night – as the guests rehashed and replayed *Maria di Rohan* over and over again.

'You're fond of the biscuit, Miss McAndrew,' chuckled Lord Colehill, the pink catawba beginning to tell on his cheeks. 'You should try the gorgonzola.'

'Yuck, blue cheese never looked right,' said Roger Giles, 'the cheddar is nice.'

'As long as I finally get to spend some time with my daughter, I don't mind what she eats,' quipped Tom McAndrew. 'I tell you, between her being sent off to Essex and the viscount's hunting trips, we haven't had two words.'

'We'll change all that tonight,' Sheila promised, as she leaned in to her father's cheek and, a little to his embarrassment, kissed it.

'You're still daddy's girl,' teased Lord Colehill, and Roger Giles had a little chuckle at the senior civil servant's expense.

'That old colonel fella is as mad as a box of frogs,' declared Tom, trying to change the subject. 'Are you sure you're not putting yourself in danger, dear?'

'He's not that bad,' Sheila assured her father, 'his bark is much worse than his bite.'

'It's his sword I'd be weary of,' said Roger, 'not his false teeth.'

'Though one has to agree, he does look a stately chap in that uniform,' Lord Colehill pointed out, 'was he really at Waterloo?'

'He was for sure,' answered Sheila, 'it was one of his earliest campaigns.'

'I should say so,' continued Lord Colehill. 'And you look after him alone, Miss McAndrew?'

'Yes, my lord.'

'But not tonight,' interjected Tom, touching his glass off his daughter's and taking a sip. 'We have the whole night to ourselves.'

'Well, I thought the play was a marvellous achievement,' said Lord Colehill.

A great performance they all agreed, and this time they all touched glasses. Viscount de Bromley entered the study, saying quick hellos to the guests he encountered while looking around hurriedly.

'Miss McAndrew, there you are.'

The viscount paused and bowed at Sheila's company before continuing.

'Miss McAndrew, may I see you on the staircase a moment? Gentlemen.'

Sheila's smile disappeared as she set down her glass and followed the viscount to the grand stairwell.

'Miss McAndrew, I'm frightfully sorry,' he said, handing Sheila a door key, 'but I need you to …'

'Hold on there, Viscount,' snapped Tom McAndrew, who had followed them out of the study, 'I've just about had enough. I'm sick and tired of you interfering between myself and my daughter. Why are you deliberately spoiling our time together?'

'I assure you, sir, that's not the way of it.'

'Ever since I got here – almost a whole week ago – you've been keeping us apart,' growled Tom. 'Now I demand to know what your game is?'

'Sheila's my manageress, sir. She's in a pivotal role …'

The viscount turned his back on Sheila's father and whispered instructions for her to return to the room where *that other matter lies*, to lock the door and remain there.

'I understand all that, and I mean you no disrespect,' Tom continued, shuffling around to gain eye contact with the viscount once more, 'but you've already given her the night off. Can you not allow her one evening to enjoy with me on my holiday? We haven't talked properly in such a long time. Can't somebody else look after the colonel for a few hours?'

The viscount nodded and placed a hand on Tom McAndrew's shoulder. Sheila waited hopefully on the first step of the stairs.

'Mister McAndrew, this is not about my uncle's welfare,' he declared in a calm tone.

'Well, what's so bloody important then?'

'Okay, if you insist,' answered the viscount, 'we've a real emergency situation this time on our hands. A code red.'

'A *code red*,' exclaimed Sheila.

'Ssh, please, I don't want to cause panic among the other guests. Yes, a code red situation has arisen.'

'A code red indeed. Are you sure this is not just another ploy to take my daughter away from me? You've been very good at that since I've got here.'

The viscount shook his head and sighed.

'An emergency situation has arisen with regard to the Burke residence. I've been forced to send Stanley – one of my protective agents – for a constable.'

'A *constable*,' cried Sheila, while her father held a doubtful stare on the viscount.

'Okay, if that's the way you feel, come ahead. Follow me, Miss McAndrew, bring your papa too. He obviously still thinks I'm telling fibs.'

Tom remained by the grand stairwell, not knowing what to do.

'Come along, Mister McAndrew,' urged the viscount, 'take your friends with you.'

'Your Lordship, there's no need for ...'

'On the contrary, my dear fellow, there is every need. I fully understand how frustrating this must feel. So, please, allow me to show you. Colehill, Mister Giles, this way please.'

Lord Colehill cut a confused figure as the viscount beckoned him away from the study.

'Miss McAndrew, if you would attend to the *thing* in the bedroom. Yes, indeed, I shan't be but a few minutes,' concluded the viscount, before leading her father, Lord Colehill and Roger Giles across the red carpet of the foyer and towards the Burke family residence.

As we followed Shaun Burke across the forecourt, I noticed our carriage was back in the place where Jeremiah had parked it earlier in the evening. Therefore, I was supposing that Constance had already been safely transported to Cabbage Stalk Lane. Which was certain, of course, to cause a problem, considering Shaun Burke was bound to notice his wife missing from their own home. The padre, Jim and Jeremiah would be hidden away in that carriage, no doubt ready and waiting for Breda and me to depart the scene. But the chances of getting out of this predicament with Burke and stealing away were getting slimmer with each step we took towards his house. It was then, as I watched him unlock his front door, that I made up my mind – I would have to hit him over the head and make a run for it. At the earliest opportunity – with whatever I could lay my hands on – I would knock him out and dash away with Breda.

'At the back of that wall,' stated Burke, pointing beyond his gable end, 'are the stables, home to twenty carriage horses and a few good racers too. We don't have a farrier – never had a need for one with Strawberry Hill Farm beside us. There's a forge above, and a skilful little farrier to go with it.'

I bent down by the side of a flower bed and picked out a rock from its border. Breda took my other hand as we followed Burke inside. Her fingers were trembling.

'This is the hall. Down that corridor is the kitchen – every woman's favourite room,' joked Burke, continuing his guided tour. 'Wait until you see it. I got one of those fancy university ladies to deck it out from floor to ceiling – skirting boards and cornices, the whole lot. Those young ones leave no stone unturned. Solid-wood doors and all – teak.'

He took his hand away from the kitchen doorknob he was about to open and knocked on the wood instead, as if to demonstrate its durability.

'But, before I show you the kitchen, I want you to come into the sitting room. There's something very special I want you both to see.'

This was the point of no return. As he turned the knob on the sitting-room door, I got the rock ready and moved closer.

'Drop it and hold still,' said a voice, as the kitchen door swung open behind us.

I looked back to see a protective agent pointing a rifle. Burke turned around and laughed into my face.

'I'd do what he says if I was you,' he quipped, 'and you won't be needing this.'

He took the rock from my grasp and threw it towards the front door. I positioned myself between Breda and the rifle.

'How very gallant,' observed Burke, walking across to the guard with the rifle. 'You know, gallantry isn't what it used to be. Take these three fellas, for instance, look what they got for the gallant cause of trying to save some poor fucker's wife and set her free.'

I was horrified when Burke kicked the soft chair out of the way.

Slouched against the wall were Jeremiah, Jim and the padre – all gagged and bound.

'Ah well,' added Burke, testing out a length of rope, 'sure when it comes to gallantry, it's the thought that counts. Isn't that right, Mister Nayle – or should I say *Mister Sugrue*.'

'Why do you do it,' asked Constance, rubbing her stinging cheek with the eiderdown as she rocked the crying baby in her arms.

'Shut your face,' replied Sheila, half-dazed with worry, 'you may have a husband, but I'll always be your direct superior and don't you forget it.'

'Why do you still do the viscount's dirty work,' persisted Constance. 'As long as I have known you, you've been his little battering ram. I really hope the life of a sleeveen is worth the price he's paying.'

Sheila sat up in the dresser chair and, instead of turning around, showed Constance a key in the looking glass.

'Keep talking,' she urged, 'and I'll let you rot in this bedroom. Don't you realise I have the power to do as I please with you and your brat.'

'You're wrong,' answered Constance with a smile. 'You can slap my face as much as you want and you'll still be wrong. You have no power over me. The only power you think you have is what you're given by your master. You're not some pioneer for women's liberties. On the contrary, you're just a scared little girl who knows the end is near. And as for me, I'd much prefer to rot in this bed than live at the mercy of a lunatic like Shaun Burke. Isn't that right, Aoife, my beautiful little cailín.'

Constance waited for the customary response. But Sheila didn't seem to be listening. Instead, she stared at herself in the looking glass like some sort of half-wit.

'I'm right,' added Constance, 'the end *is* near. That's why Burke moved us out here in the first place. The end is coming and there's nothing you, the viscount, Shaun Burke or anybody else can do about it.'

Then something happened that shocked Constance. Sheila McAndrew bowed down where she sat and cried. She sobbed her heart out until it seemed like she had no tears left. When she turned to look at Constance, her tone was so soft it was almost inaudible.

'Ten of the best years of my life, and it has all been for nothing. You're right. There's nothing I can do about it now.'

'But there is,' said Constance. 'You can tell the truth.'

'The truth? What's that going to achieve at this late stage?'

'Everything, Sheila. Absolutely everything. The only way you can take back the power you so desperately crave is to tell the truth. That is the only way you can break this grip the viscount has over you.'

There were voices at the door. Viscount de Bromley was clearly distinguishable. But there were other men too – strange voices. Burke was worried, I could see it in his face. He – his knot half done – postponed the tying of my hands to go to the sitting-room door. I looked at Jim Gorman, who nodded his head as if trying to tell me something. He was tied with his back to the padre. Jeremiah was tied up alone.

'What are you doing here,' growled Burke, 'and where do you think you're parading those fellas?'

'I am taking these gentlemen to visit their old pal,' answered the viscount, 'Mister Patrick Sugrue.'

The viscount strolled into Burke's sitting room as calmly as if he was taking the country air, behind him Lord Colehill, Roger Giles and Tom McAndrew. I tried to look McAndrew in the eye, but he wouldn't return my stare. He looked disturbed – sick even. It was as if the blood had drained from his face. The viscount must have noticed this too, for he couldn't contain his joy at McAndrew's mortification at the very mention of my name.

'Are you not going to say hullo to your old friend, Tom?'

But McAndrew was in no fit state to exchange pleasantries with anyone. You could have knocked him over with a feather. Giles wasn't nearly as shocked and embarrassed to see me. In fact, he couldn't hide his smirk of delight.

'Surely, it is not the man who ran amok in Longford all those years ago,' cried Lord Colehill, 'the leader of that pack of thugs who called themselves the Sugrue Gang?'

'The one and only,' confirmed the viscount.

'How strange,' contended Lord Colehill. 'What on earth is he doing here?'

'Will you tell them or shall I,' the viscount said to Burke, whose silence encouraged the viscount's continuance. 'Sugrue's friends, those scoundrels who are tied up before you, broke into this house while we were distracted with the entertainment. Their aim was to kidnap and, no doubt, kill Shaun Burke's young wife and child.'

'Breaking and entry. Attempted abduction. Aforethought to murder. Villainous swine. If I had my trusty old cane,' roared Lord Colehill, 'I would beat the buggers to within an inch of their worthless lives.'

'Alas, Colehill, do not get frenzied,' declared the viscount, as Burke sorted out the rope for a second go at my binding, 'I have sent for a copper.'

'Why did you do such a foolish thing,' snapped Shaun Burke. 'I sent Stanley to get *you*, not the *police*. There's no need to involve the police. We can take care of this matter in our own way.'

'And I sent Stanley on to the barracks,' said the viscount. 'This is a very grave matter, Mister Burke, a lot graver than your attitude suggests.'

'*In our own way,*' repeated Lord Colehill, 'what, pray tell, does that mean?'

'It means this,' answered Burke, pointing to the rifle the protective agent had trained on me.

'There's no need to tie this one, Mister Burke,' said Roger Giles, producing a knife from inside his boot and gripping the lapel of my dinner jacket, 'I'll take charge of him.'

'And no need to tie this one either,' added Burke, putting his hands all over Breda while dragging her to where the protective agent stood. 'Just wait until I get you alone, poontang,' he whispered, before licking her face.

Jeremiah wriggled furiously on the ground until Burke threatened to open his skull with Jim's truncheon. I could feel the point of Giles's blade at my ribs as I kept my gaze on Tom McAndrew. It must have drove him to his wits' end. He wore the saddest of expressions. I could see his eyes shining in the candlelight. It was almost enough to make my eyes fill up as well. But I wanted Tom to feel that way. I didn't give a toss for Giles – or how he was feeling. I expected nothing more from him. But I really wanted my old friend – my dearest friend in the whole world – to feel bad. Because I felt bad as well.

'What's wrong, Burke,' I said, reading his worried face, 'are you afraid to involve the peelers, afraid they might get to know about the *real* abduction and the *real* murder?'

'Shut your mouth, Sugrue,' he snarled back, 'or I'll have you plugged here and now.'

'They'll find out all about it when their paddy wagon arrives – how de Bromley sold Consta...'

Burke drew on me then, almost lock-jawing me with a punch. But, despite the pain, I had to continue. I wanted Lord Colehill and the others to know just the kind of men Viscount de Bromley and Shaun Burke really were.

'Sold Constance,' I said, 'and then how you drugged and abducted the poor girl.'

'Come along, Colehill. You did not come all the way from Ireland to listen to such utter poppycock,' fumed the viscount. 'Mister McAndrew, shall we?'

Lord Colehill followed the viscount to the sitting-room door but Tom McAndrew didn't budge.

'Mister McAndrew, come along I say.'

'I'm going nowhere without Patrick Sugrue,' returned Tom.

'McAndrew, may I remind you of your position. It was my recommendation that secured your civic office in the first place.'

Tom McAndrew's eyes narrowed and he gritted his teeth.

'I told you already, Viscount, I'm not leaving Patrick's side.'

I couldn't help the pride I felt in Tom just then.

'I bet the viscount would like to know about the graverobbing, Burke,' I stated. 'I know the peelers will be interested too. Tell me, what did you do with Charles Langley?'

'*Graverobbing*,' exclaimed the viscount. 'Mister Burke, what's all this about?'

'I'm warning you, Sugrue,' Burke growled, 'for the very last time.'

But I didn't care for his warning. I had them where I wanted them – the viscount running for cover and Burke white in the face with contrariness.

'The graverobbing that Burke was involved in with a Doctor Mortuland of London – while using *your* stables to stash the bodies,' I pointed out.

It looked like the viscount was about to have a stroke.

'Goodbye now, Viscount. You run along with your little lapdog, Colehill. The peelers will know where to find you when

I'm finished giving them the lowdown on everything.'

Burke could take no more. He snapped the rifle from the protective agent's shaking hands and I closed my eyes. I could feel Giles shuffling nervously beside me and heard Breda shouting *no*. I was lucky. The bullet could only have missed me by inches. Then he cocked for a second go.

'Are you going to shut your mouth,' Burke shouted, 'next time it won't be a warning shot. Never mind him, my lord, he's a dirty lying bastard.'

'Who is shooting whom,' a voice called out from the hall.

There appeared in the doorway the bearded Englishman, Major Charles Levington's son, with a small silver gun in his hand.

'Who the fuck is that,' exclaimed Roger Giles, the point of his blade finding my ribcage once more.

'He must be from the local constabulary,' said the viscount, 'one of these new plain-clothes men. We have apprehended the villains and performed a citizen's arrest. They are all yours, Detective.'

'He's no plain-clothes man,' countered Burke, fearing the worst, 'look at the cut of his jacket. I saw him at the play tonight. Who are you, and what's your business in my house?'

'Who am I,' replied the bearded Englishman, 'let me see. Actually, that is a very valid question.'

He took an envelope from his pocket.

'Well, *to whom it may concern,* I'm not the man on this invitation,' he confessed, ripping the envelope in two. 'So, *who* am I – or is it, *whom* am I? Maybe Mister Burke can fill us in? After all, he did receive two ransom letters with regard to my name. He kept them well hidden from you, my lord, and everyone else at Tunbridge House. Didn't you, Mister Burke?'

He pulled at his beard and it came away from his face. Then he took his hat and wig and flung them on the ground, transforming into Walter Pollach before our startled eyes.

'Now do you know who I am,' he asked, any trace of an English accent swallowed up in his familiar, thistly, tone.

Before anyone could say another word, Pollach let rip with his handgun. Through the cloud of smoke that followed, bodies milled in all directions. The viscount and Lord Colehill retreated from where Pollach stood in the doorway. The protective agent broke a window with his sleeve. Burke clutched his shoulder with one hand, while groping for the rifle he had dropped with the other. I toppled the soft chair, trying to give Jim, the padre and Jeremiah some sort of cover behind it.

A second shot struck the protective agent in the leg, putting an end to his ambition of escaping through the window. Amid all the chaos, Giles had me in a choke-hold – his knife still scratching at my side. Breda huddled behind the soft chair, keeping out of the firing line while pulling at Jeremiah's binds.

A third shot sent the rifle that Shaun Burke had just retrieved bouncing across the floor. The viscount cowered behind the old piano with Lord Colehill for company. Tom McAndrew struck Roger Giles a blow in an attempt to force my release. It was then it happened. As Giles was turning his attention on Tom, I could feel the point of his knife puncturing the skin above my left hip. I thought nothing of it, especially at the time, and Giles couldn't have known much about it. I went to my knees and watched as McAndrew and Giles grappled for the knife. They had a right old tussle and then McAndrew fell to the floor, pressing his hands to his stomach.

'Pollach, you nincompoop, the police will be arriving anon. Go while you still can,' shouted the viscount as he eyed the pendulum clock for better cover.

Pollach smiled back in the direction of his old master's voice and squeezed the trigger again. The bullet played a note on the piano and Burke made a dart for the broken window.

I was crawling on my hands and knees when Giles stomped on my back. He lifted me by the scruff of the neck.

'We have to get out,' I said.

'You're not getting away this time,' he grunted, pushing his bushy beard into my face, 'except on the end of a rope.'

He wiped the blade on the sleeve of his coat, glaring down as saliva whitened his lips. He looked in my eyes and began his plunge. For a second time in as many minutes I thought I was finished. Suddenly, there was another crack and Giles's eyes widened. His body stiffened. When he fell backwards there was Breda, kneeling behind the soft chair and the protective agent's rifle smoking in her hands.

Burke broke out the edges of the jagged window pane as Pollach advanced from the doorway. He got a leg outside.

'Don't do it,' warned Pollach, just as Burke was about to swing his other leg through.

He thought better of it as Pollach stood in front of him, lifted his handgun and took aim. Burke was a sitting duck. Another shot rang out. Pollach stumbled forward, trying to stay upright. Behind him, a policeman repeated his warning. The gun spilled from Pollach's hand as he searched for the wall. He fell in a heap of broken glass. Burke ignored the policeman's order to freeze. He climbed the rest of the way out through the window and ran for the carriage prepared by Hernandez.

'Outside,' shouted a policeman, 'he's heading around the back.'

Sheila McAndrew ordered Constance to *shut that baby up* and locked the door behind her.

'What's all the commotion,' she asked one of the housemaids who was racing along the landing. 'Was that a gunshot?'

'No,' replied Eleanor, 'it was a firecracker.'

'*A firecracker,*' exclaimed Sheila, 'how do you know?'

'The viscountess,' explained Eleanor. 'The guests were becoming uneasy until the viscountess explained that they were just letting off a firework down at Strawberry Hill Farm. The guests thought it was gunfire too.'

'Eleanor, listen to me. I want you to find Colonel de Bromley and take him to his room. All this uproar is enough to send him ...'

'*Colonel de Bromley*. I'm sorry, Miss McAndrew, but Lady Ivens has banned me from going near the colonel. She said he's your responsibility now that you're back.'

Another gunshot pierced the air.

'Eleanor, are you paying attention? This is ser...'

But Eleanor was already bounding down the stairs. Sheila unlocked the door and went back in to Constance. Firecracker indeed. Sheila had a bad feeling that this was more to do with the viscount's *code red emergency* than a fireworks' display.

'There it goes again,' said Constance.

'They're only firecrackers from above at Strawberry Hill Farm,' Sheila pointed out.

'That's no firecracker, Sheila, and well you know it. And it's not coming from Strawberry Hill Farm. It's the sound of shooting and it's from across the way at our house.'

A fourth shot rang out and Sheila could hold back no longer.

'I'm going to check it out,' she declared, 'I'll give you the key. If I'm not back in fifteen minutes, unlock the door and make a run for it.'

Sheila removed the room key from the big bunch on her belt and threw it on the bed.

'Thank you,' whispered Constance, 'and be careful.'

The sound of another shot whistled through the night air.

'Father,' cried Sheila, and bolted for the stairs.

Tunbridge House had descended into chaos. Guests were running in all directions – some looking for personal escorts, others their footmen. Housemaids had long since given up trying to pacify them. Tables of the best wines were overturned and food was scattered all over the dining room and study.

Sheila met the colonel at the bottom of the grand stairwell. He was cock-a-hoop with all the madness and didn't seem to recognise her.

'Colonel, it's not safe here. I need you to go to your room,' she insisted. 'I want you to find one of the housemaids and go with her.'

'Housemaids, Captain? Are you suffering from shellshock? I demand a rapier and a couple of firearms.'

'Colonel, you don't understand. It's not safe he...'

'On the contrary, Captain. I understand only too well. The enemy has advanced and, as with any worthwhile offensive, they have caught us unawares.'

'Colonel de Bromley, I need you to listen to me very carefully. I have no time to explain this fully right now, but ...'

'But nothing. *You* need to listen to *me*. I want my rapier and my flintlocks on the double. That is a direct order, Captain, do not make me call a court martial.'

He went to draw the sword that had been taken from him after the performance, finding only its empty scabbard. Sheila realised there was nothing she could do with him. So she left the colonel at the butt of the stairs – babbling away about formations and attacking strategies – and fought her way through the panic-stricken patrons until she found herself in the foyer. Her heart beat like mad as she raced through the forecourt, dodging the departing horses and carriages on her way to the besieged Burke residence.

Waiting in the stable yard were Burke's two loyal Suffolk Punch stallions, the carriage at their backs, just as he had ordered. He threw the gate open, raced up the carriage steps and seized the reins.

'Gee up,' Burke shouted, and the horses walked out through the gap with straps and buckle loops dangling loose, leaving the untied straight traces and the rest of the carriage standing in the yard.

'Stay right where you are,' warned another policeman, pointing his musket nervously.

'Don't shoot,' said Burke, as he dropped the reins and held up his hands.

There was a rustling from one of the stable doors and then Hernandez appeared in the yard.

'Thank heavens you're here, Constable,' said Burke, 'that's your man over there. He's the one who escaped through the window. I was afraid he was going to kill me.'

Burke made an attempt to climb down from the carriage but the policeman told both him and Hernandez to freeze and, failing this, their next move would be their last. While he was standing with his hands in the air, Burke noticed the police cart in the forecourt. It was empty. There were only the two constables. If there was some way of getting to the police cart first, he would be out the avenue in a shot – never to be seen again. Then he remembered his Springfield. He scanned the perch and there it was – just where Hernandez had been ordered to put it – with its handle sticking out from under a blanket.

'Climb down from the carriage now, nice and easy,' instructed the policeman. 'Keep those hands where I can see them.'

'Yes, Constable,' replied Burke. 'May I take the lantern, for safety sake.'

Burke took the carriage lamp and flung it at the policeman's head. He bent down and snatched his rifle, aimed it and pulled the trigger. Clack – nothing but the sound of the trigger drum.

'Herna...'

The policeman fired his musket. Horses neighed and dogs yelped. Shaun Burke fell from the perch. The policeman kept his musket aimed as he walked towards him.

'Come over here beside me,' he said to Hernandez, 'and don't move another muscle.'

Hernandez did what the constable commanded and walked over to where Burke lay sprawled on the cobbles of the stable yard. He held out a fist and dropped a half dozen bullets on his dying master's chest.

'Hernandez, you treacherous dog,' sighed Burke.

Hernandez looked down and smiled.

'Que va, senor, treacherous pig,' replied Hernandez, 'al igual que mi maestro.'

Shaun Burke coughed out some blood and closed his eyes for the last time.

I passed out at some stage. When I came to, Breda was rubbing my forehead. Jeremiah was with her, free of his binds. Father Murtagh was kneeling with Tom McAndrew, who was pale and still. Sheila McAndrew came storming into the room, the policeman unable to hold her in the hall any longer. She ran to her father's side, wailing like a banshee. Jim Gorman attempted to comfort her, but there was no point. The padre took her by the wrists and held her until she stopped hitting out. Tom McAndrew had lost a lot of blood, but he seemed at peace.

'Sheila, where are you,' he said, and she kissed his cheek.

'I'm here, Daddy,' she returned, and took into another fit of crying.

'Sheila, listen to me darling. I have something very important for you now. Always tell the truth. Promise me you'll do that.'

'I promise, I promise,' she declared. 'Don't talk now. Don't talk. The ambulance is on its way. Hold on, Daddy. Hold on.'

He stared into space, clearly unaware of his surroundings, as the padre took a stole from his pocket.

'Come here,' he whispered, and Sheila was forced to bend down even closer. 'Tell Patrick that I'm sor… Patri.. Sugrue that I'm so …'

He died right there on Burke's sitting-room floor – from the stab of a knife which was meant for me. The padre finished his Last Rites ceremony, kissing the stole and folding it away. Sheila went into a fit of hysteria. Jeremiah hugged and kissed Breda.

When I got my bearings, I hobbled across the floor. Something else had caught my eye. Roger Giles was alive, but only hanging on. I pulled open his coat. His shirt was soaked. There was a hole in his weskit where the bullet went through. There was nothing could be done. So, I took out my old beaten-up hipflask – or should I say, Roger's powder flask – and uncorked it one last time.

'Here,' I said, 'drink some of this brandy.'

His face was shuddering with the pain. I placed the powder flask to his lips. But he moved his head away.

'Go on,' I insisted, 'have it.'

Again, he moved his lips away from the rim of the flask. He was trying to say something. I bent down beside his ear.

'Why did it come to this, Roger,' I whispered. 'All those years we spent fighting, sworn enemies, and for what?'

Then he said something which astounded me. He gripped my collar with trembling hands and tried to raise his head from the floor.

'No quarter asked for,' he wheezed, and died in my arms.

'And none given,' I answered, replacing his head gently on the floorboards.

I recorked the powder flask and placed it in his inside pocket. Then I closed his coat and buttoned it. I did a quick sum in my head. For the first time in over fifty-two years – since the day I took it from him on a battlefield in Ballinamuck – Roger Giles had his old powder flask back in his possession. Better late than never, I suppose.

Thirty-three – Epilogue

Charles Langley's body turned up eventually. We filled out a report with the Tunbridge peelers, who traced it to a medical laboratory in the Royal Hospital of Surgeons, London. He was found with broken lines drawn on his shaven head and a piece missing from his ear. Nonetheless, Lord Teale claimed Charles as his servant and we gave him a fitting Christian send off. The Mostrim Ribbonmen could not pay their respects and appreciation, it being a Protestant funeral and all that, but Reverend George Charmers did the necessary with loving care and attention. It was my first time at a service in Saint John's, and I have to admit their boundary wall is just as comfortable as our Catholic equivalent. Unfortunately, nobody was ever brought to book over Charles's murder. The mysterious Doctor Egon Mortuland was taken in for questioning, only to be let out after an hour or two. Gerald, the doctor's cravat-wearing dogsbody, and his associate, Mister Prenderville, were never heard of again.

Viscount de Bromley was not so lucky. Outraged at having been summoned to court in the first place, his powerhouse London legal team did a wonderful job of blaming Constance's ordeal solely on Shaun Burke. They persuaded the judge that the viscount was a victim of sorts in the whole affair who had only acted so out-of-character due to the duress Burke inflicted on him. Dropping the charges, the trial judge urged the viscount to purge the guilt of his limited involvement by making a handsome donation to the court poor box. However, Mister Thornton – Lord

Teale's barrister-at-law – pushed for a review of the case on the grounds that he had the star witnesses to the facts. Sheila McAndrew, who could have used the original court finding to her own advantage, waived her chance to go free by rubbishing the claims that Burke was the main controlling influence. She looked her old master in the eye and never flinched while testifying that the viscount was just as culpable in the drugging, kidnap, sale and forced marriage. Constance, this time under the guidance and support of Mister Thornton and his legal bench, backed up Sheila's claim and was finally believed. The appeal caused quite the little scandal – with Viscount de Bromley receiving a five-year incarceration at Her Majesty's prison, Dartmoor.

The only downside to Sheila McAndrew's testimony against her former employer was that in doing so she was throwing herself to the wolves. She also received a five-year stretch, reduced to twenty-four months due to her assistance to the prosecution and the genuine contrition she expressed from the dock. She has the distinction of being one of the first prisoners sent to Holloway women's prison, and therefore the authorities allowed her a companion for the journey. Annie McKeon, in her pretty pink bonnet, escorted Sheila from the court to the jailhouse in the back of the police wagon. Lady Jane Teale, who had sailed across with Annie, followed close behind. They will renew acquaintances when Sheila is released – as she will be coming home to work at Lacken House for Lord and Lady Teale.

The bodies of Tom McAndrew and Roger Giles were shipped back to Ireland. Tom was buried in Aughafin – our old flag of the golden harp on a field of green draping his casket – to the sound of a lone bugler from the Mostrim Ribbonmen. Pius Mooney spoke at his funeral, about freedom fighting and decency and sacrifice and all the things in life we can have and lose and find again. I don't know why but I attended Roger's funeral too. I got to sit on Saint John's presbytery wall a second time. I won't pretend that it reconciled me, but maybe it helped me come to terms in some small way with Roger's point of view. I wonder did they bury his powder flask with him. I hope they did.

Walter Pollach's remains was supposedly sent back to Scotland and buried in the family plot on the Isle of Jura, where his elderly mother still lived. I don't know what happened to his pet weasel – or should I say Captain Weasel of the Second Cavalry Brigade.

We returned to Ireland with some degree of fame – or infamy, depending on your point of view. On the way across I decided to crop my hair, leaving it in the Irish Sea as a tribute to Finbar Ryan and also to the men I fought with at Ballinamuck all those years ago. Everyone in Mostrim had heard about the Battle of Tunbridge House – despite the fact that it had taken place outside of Tunbridge House. But the *Kentish Gazette* had referred to it as thus and the name stuck. Then the *London Times* picked up the story, following the viscount's court appearances and the aftermath. It was inevitable that the *Freeman's Journal* would get in on the act on the other side of the pond. Locals, who once took our presence for granted, looked at us with a new kind of wonder and awe. Jeremiah loved the attention of it all and, to tell you the truth, I probably would have liked it also if I was his age.

Not long after returning, I hobbled my way across to the clachan in Lacken. Lord Teale had kindly offered a carriage, but I respectfully declined. It was a most dreadful thing I had to do, and I felt I had to do it alone. Constance opened her grandmother's door, her daughter toddling at her skirt. I took off my hat and stepped inside. This was the moment that had haunted me, but I promised myself I would make a full and honest disclosure of everything I knew. I thought she was going to hit me with the tongs. In fact, I was hoping she would. Instead, old Missus Ryan smiled back with such happiness and pride. Then – in a move that shocked the life out of me – she got up from her stool, walked over and kissed my cheek.

'Did you not hear what I just said,' I asked. 'I left his body where it lay, his quarterstaff yanked from his skull.'

'He was dead by then,' replied the old woman, straightening the scarf on her bald head, 'there was nothing more you could do. You have to let it go now. I'm proud of Finbar. And I'm proud of you as well.'

'But what about his send off, Missus Ryan?'

'Don't worry about such things. The Lord Jesus Christ will see my Finbar right. We'll light a candle and say a little prayer.'

She looked around at her granddaughter.

'You brought Constance back to me, and her little girl, when I thought I had lost her forever. And for that, Patrick Sugrue, I will be eternally grateful. God bless you and save you, a stor.'

I was almost at the half-door when I thought of it. I rummaged in my coat pocket as I walked back to old Missus Ryan, taking her hand unannounced.

'Remember this,' I said, pressing the cold steel into the palm of her hand.

She let out a gasp of excitement.

'Finbar's roadbowling ball,' she whispered, and I left her then, gazing at the metal orb through tear-stained eyes.

The wedding – or should I say *weddings* – day will be talked about for many a long year. It was a much-anticipated affair – as looked forward to by those at Lacken House as any summer holiday at Loch Owel. To be fair to them, Lord and Lady Teale pulled out all the stops. It ended up being a double-wedding, with Breda Nayle joining Constance Ryan in her walk up the aisle. They looked a picture of beauty – Constance's suntanned smiley face and Breda's flowing black curls tumbling to her shoulders. As the warm Mayday sun shone beneath the lintels, the glint of gold caught my eye. It was Constance's Saint Anthony's medal, worn proudly outside her wedding dress for everyone to see. Missus Ryan sat beside me in the front pew in a brightly-coloured linen headscarf, nursing Aoife on her knee. She looked so happy as she watched her granddaughter step it out to Lady Jane Teale's *Here Comes the Bride* on the church piano. Seeing the old lady's sheer delight made the pain in my side all the more worth it. I couldn't help but think of Finbar in that moment. I whispered a prayer for him.

'I like the scarf, Missus Ryan, it brightens up the place.'

'A little present,' she replied, 'Shay brought it back from a fair day in Longford in the year of forty-five.'

Father Murtagh was back in harness at the altar of Saint Mary's and it was all Lord Teale's doing. It was he who brokered a fragile peace between the former curate of Mostrim and his one-time parish priest, Canon Reidy. The canon wouldn't hear tell of it when asked if the padre could marry the couples. He was even threatening to revisit the peelers over his former understudy's taking of the canon's precious chalice. But Lord Teale settled the matter with sensible dialogue – after, of course, buying a new chalice fit for a king and presenting it to Canon Reidy. Resting on the padre's shoulders, and occasionally walking on his head, was a strange-looking monkey, who he gave to Jim Gorman for safekeeping while he performed the marital rites.

Waiting for their beautiful brides alongside the padre were Jeremiah Figg and Shay Gorman. They looked magnificent in their wedding suits, their youthful features belying the trials and tribulations of the previous years. Maggie Gorman – Jim's daughter – and Annie McKeon were the matrons of honour. Terence Barry stood at the altar too, groomsman to Shay. He read a paragraph from Scripture. Missus Ryan confided in me that it was awful hard to make out the Cork accent. As the boys declared their *I do's*, I looked across at Jim Gorman. He beamed with pride as he held his wife Mairead, Father Murtagh's monkey searching his breast pocket while tears of joy dropped to the church's wooden floor. Along with the wedding ring, Terence handed Shay a white handkerchief to give to Constance. It was instantly recognisable – with its red and green embroidered, Celtic Cross design.

The padre showed us a telegram delivered earlier that day from Jabber Farrell, his wife Melanie, and their *four* children – Constance, Bartholomew Shay, Milly and Patrick – in San Diego, California. They sent their congratulations and wished they could have been there. We wished they could have been there too. As if that wasn't enough, a letter from America was brought to the altar with the procession of gifts. The padre told us it had come all the way from the parish of Saint James on the Lower East Side of Manhattan, New York. Breda averted her eyes as her mother's words were read out to the congregation. Missus Bridget Nayle conveyed the pride she felt in her daughter and how happy she was with her son-in-law, Jeremiah. Her final word was kept for Constance and Shay, saying how glad she was that it had all worked out in the end.

Father Murtagh also spoke about some people from the past, people that meant so much to us who knew them. He prayed for Turk O'Nuallain – who Lord Teale had a headstone commissioned for and placed over his final resting place, Peter Hogan, Micheal Mooney, Milly Farrell, Finbar Ryan and Tom McAndrew. I could hear a croak in the padre's voice and see the trace of a tear in his eye. Then he prayed for the soul of Missus Davern, Anthony's mother, who would be waked the next day in the clachan.

Later in the evening, with the reception in full flow, Lord Teale had Carruthers detain a nervous-looking Terence Barry for a second time at Lacken House – but not to eject him from the premises or await the arrival of a constable. This time, instead of a choke-hold, he had his rather burly man-servant present Terence with a glass of Middleton Rare to join in a toast with Jim Gorman, Father Murtagh, and yours truly.

We all walked Shay and Constance to their new cabin – the cabin that Lord Teale had prepared for them in the clachan of Lacken and the place I once called home. With a big orange summer sky behind us, we toasted Jeremiah and Breda Figg and the new Mister and Missus Gorman. And that's where my luck ran out. As I drank my mug of beer the pain worsened in my side and I collapsed on the spot. A doctor was called, cellulitis was diagnosed, and bed rest was prescribed. Missus Langan was nominated as my jailor – sorry, my nurse – and that is why I regale you with my story from the comfort of one of her big broad feather beds.

I blamed my cellulitis on wet Kentish weather, too much sea air and Lord Teale's exotic wines. Even when he asked me about the cut on my side, I told the doctor it was just an old wound that had resurfaced. He shook his head and smiled, then told me to call into him when I was back on my feet. Never once was the pointy end of Roger Giles's knife mentioned. That's the way I prefer it. Ours was not a family used to cribbing and crying. I think I might be about to do a Milly Farrell on it – slip off, nice and gentle, in the same bed at Missus Langan's house. When your time is up, it's up – that's the way of the world. I can feel it slowly ebbing away.

'It's in Dungannon where this young man died; And in Dungannon where his body lies.
So all good people who do pass by, do drop a tear for the croppy boy.'

My eyes are tired; my breath is weak. But I'm a happy man.

'Now I lay me down to sleep, I pray the Lord my soul to.... keep. If I should die.... before I.... wake, I pray to God my.... soul to take. If I.... should live for.... other days, I.... pray.... the Lord to.... guide.... my.... ways. A man.... Amen.'

Acknowledgements

I would like to thank all my family. Particular thanks to Glen and Daniel, who have helped me out with technology issues and mapping.

I would like to once again thank Eamonn Morgan and Daniel Cassidy for their time and thorough proofreading.

I would also like to thank all at Strokestown Famine Museum, Strokestown House, Co. Roscommon, for their hospitality and experience.

A big thank you to Mr. Martin Morris and all at Longford County Library for their dedicated assistance and help.

Thanks to all at EPIC: The Irish Emigration Museum, Custom House Quay, North Dock, Dublin 1.

Thank you also to Pure Cork: Spike Island Harbour Tours at Kennedy Pier, Cobh, Co. Cork.

To Mary Fleming, for your wonderful cover design and attention to detail.

Finally, to Deirdre Devine and Michelle Bradley at Choice Publishing, Drogheda, County Louth, without whom this project wouldn't be possible.

Is mise le meas, Marc O Caiside.

References

Castle Rackrent, Maria Edgeworth, Oxford University Press, 2008.

Early Irish Myths and Sagas, Betty Radice (ed.), Penguin Books, 1981.

Edgeworthstown, Myths and Memories: Seo is Siud, Mostrim Heritage and Historical Society, self-published, 2007.

Edgeworthstown, Parish of Mostrim: O Theach Go Teach, Mostrim Heritage and Historical Society, self-published, 2003.

Local Red Book: Tunbridge Wells, Tonbridge, Crowborough, Paddock, Estate Publications, 2004.

Longford, History and Society, Martin Morris and Fergus O'Ferrall (eds.), Geography Publications, 2010.

Maria di Rohan, opera by Gaetano Donizetti, premiered at the Karntnertortheater, Vienna, on 5 June 1843.

Murder, Mutiny and Mayhem: The Blackest-Hearted Villains from Irish History, Joe O'Shea, The O'Brien Press, 2012.

Philip's Post-Primary School Atlas, Folen's Publishers, 2004.

The Croppy Boy, song by Carroll Malone, lyrics first appeared in *The Nation* newspaper on 4 January 1845.

The Elements of Style, William Strunk jr. and E.B. White, Pearson Longman, 2009.

500 Words You Should Know, Caroline Taggart, Michael O'Mara Books Ltd., 2014.